INFILTRATED

Concealed in Shadows

RUBY SMOKE

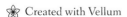 Created with Vellum

For all of those who almost lost the will to live, to keep going, and are still here.
To those who found that reading was their life's pulse.
&
Finally, to those who realized that the power of ink on a page can literally become the air in your lungs.

Keep going. *The fight may hurt, you may feel lost, but we are still here. As a survivor who struggles everyday, **I am here with you.***

INFILTRATED

CONCEALED IN SHADOWS BOOK ONE

What's Hidden in the Shadows, Will be Brought to Light

Insanely Hot Reads

World of Smoke and Shadows

BOOKS BY RUBY

Concealed in Myths

Veiled (Snag Here)
Verdant Kiss (Pre-Order Here)
Crowned

Concealed in Shadows

Infiltrated
Insurrection
Decimation
Resurgence

Concealed in Blood

Book 1
Book 2
Book 3

READING ORDER FOR
MAXIMUM ENJOYMENT

Veiled; Concealed in Myths
Infiltrated; Concealed in Shadows
Verdant Kiss; Concealed in Myths
Insurrection; Concealed in Shadows
Crowned; Concealed in Myths
Book 1; Concealed in Blood
Decimation; Concealed in Shadows
Book 2; Concealed in Blood
Book 3; Concealed in Blood

AUTHOR NOTE

Author Note

I realized when writing Verdant Kiss that there were some things that were going to be brought to light that just wouldn't make sense without you all reading Infiltrated first. I would be doing a disservice to Verdant Kiss, if I didn't ask you to read this book first.

Now, Infiltrated CAN be read as a standalone series, BUT at least when you read the Concealed in Myths Series, you'll have a leg up. Maybe. Now, there may be some confusion, but trust me, I wouldn't lead you astray. Enjoy Charlie and her mates, because shit is about to get real.

This is the start of several smaller-sized, but not really novels surrounding Concealed in Shadows. Something about this crew screams that I need to let their story develop beyond a trilogy and I'm going to follow my heart and the voices in my head.

Reverse Harem, a shit-ton of cursing, f/f scenes

FOREWORD

For hundreds of years, we have had people who delved in magic around us; whether that magic was elemental in nature, or centered around the unnatural, blood magic. There are those that understood that magic was a gift, not a right. There are those who honed that magic with practice, who helped others, and in time Magical Communities rose. These communities used their knowledge of magic and physical training to make their people strong against those who would wish to do the community harm. These communities were a pillar of strength and hope. Despite a few political squabbles, these users thrived; they sent their children to Magick Universities and their population served for the overall progression of the populace. *Time moved on, generations forgot about other communities that existed that didn't follow the same methods of magickal use.*

However, there were those who saw the power as a chance for them to go stronger but leave others—the weaker—behind. They, too, built Magickal Communities, although they were reclusive. Their people were divided by class, power, and abilities. In truth, everyone had the same opportunity to gain strength but when surrounded by oppression, no one saw any other way. After generations, their origin became lost and the old ways became the only ways. These communities held Councils who held themselves above the people, and instead of helping, they twisted magick for their own personal gain. They continued to seek more magick through unnatural means. *These unnatural means served the purpose of one Entity. One who's entire purpose was to touch and destroy something that was never hers. These communities, due to the action of their Councils, were in more danger than they could ever imagine.*

Readers, please understand. Unnatural use of magick will only have one result. Death. Whether it be from the possession of an unnatural entity or from the corrosion of one's soul from the use of dark magick—you will meet only one end. For when the addiction of dark magic starts to unravel the mind, there is no way back. No tears will help anyone see reason. If you oppose, you are an obstacle. You will meet a painful death. These minds cannot see reason.

For those of you who have twisted magic and have invited the presence of an Entity beyond your understanding, I pity you. Magick is pure, in that, it has no obstacles. Despite the words on the contrary, your soul is now forfeit. Soon, it will be as if you never existed.

Nici, Imposter Queen

I SAT in my war-darken chambers, consoled by the sounds of the screams coming from the dungeons behind me. The dark gray walls, the worn brown table, lack of windows, and the opium wafting from the corner of the room, adding to the overall ambiance. *It's good to be a twisted bitch.* After all this time, people still chose to rebel against my rule, still chose to believe the silly little prophecy that would give someone else back the power to the Seelie. *Not if I can help it.* I scoffed, staring at the chess board in front of me, trying to make better sense of my next move.

My gaze flicked up to the historian at the right of my table. "Tell me, how divided are these Magickal Communities, again?" I didn't really need to ask twice. I knew there were two very separate worlds of magick users; two factions, if you will, separated by their levels of thirst for power. It was a fair assessment that one of these factions was ruled by intelligence, and the other by sheer stupidity. That stupidity, I might as well use to my advantage.

"Very. It's as if they no longer have any knowledge of each other. However, we know the individual councils per community are aware of one another, but the people, for the most part, are kept unaware. Factions are completely apart and warded accordingly." My historian remarks, his fierce blue eyes pulling me in, his voice captivating me. I bit back a smirk and ignored the jolt of pleasure from having him here. *I loved the sounds of take-overs, in the morning.*

"Well then," I started, coming to my final decision. "What better way to gain allies against this...threat." I rolled my eyes at that. The idea that this prophecy was any more than a joke, but I didn't get this far from underestimating possibilities. I accounted for everything and moved my pieces accordingly.

"How do you mean?" I looked over to my left, my war advisor, Ren, sitting up intrigued. If there is anyone as bloodthirsty as I, it was him.

"The faction that seeks power wants something I can provide, and they have something to provide me." I paused, leaning back against my chair and propping my bloody feet up on the table. No one at the table flinched.

At this point, from the dungeon and back to planning, what was the point of keeping the blood off my body until the end of the night.

"ANOTHER ARMY," I added, looking away from my chess board. Humans can be quite droll, but this game was an excellent way to calm the mind. So was murder, but I was fresh out of desire to do that, and was filled with the fury to destroy the chances of this prophecy, coming to fruition as we get closer to the end of my timeline.

"SO, WHAT DO YOU PROPOSE?" Ren inquired.

I LOOKED AT HIM CLOSELY, a slow smile stretching my face. "Make contact with the Council that represents the ones who are the most divided—who thirsts for power. We will start there and work our way in." I smiled, the bloodthirsty smiles in the room bringing me a sick pleasure. *These are my people.* The Fae were so steeped in tradition that it led to the ultimate lack of awareness; those who have deserted and are in hiding would hardly find the merit in looking for outside sources for allies in the upcoming war. Me? I will use everything at my disposal to make sure the enemy is destroyed; I will sow the seeds of discord. Failure wasn't an option. Time was ticking, *forty years left.*

MY ATTENTION SNAPPED to my historian as he looked down at his list. "I'll make contact with the Darnika

Council immediately." He nodded and made his way to leave my planning chambers, striding out with a gleeful look of determination.

I SAT BACK and looked at Ren. "Any news on the Seelie's new location?"

HE LOOKED AT ME, slightly irritated. "They are warded well, and we haven't been able to pin down the secret keepers from Scail," he said scathingly. "The Seelie rebels are proving hard to find and right when we think we are close... they disappear." He stood up angrily, approaching my chair. I breathed in, trying to control the spike of anger that flowed through me. This *Scail* was proving to be problematic for several years now. He had a network of spies that was downright impossible to penetrate, and I hated being taken for a fool.

I SIGHED as Ren stood behind me and started to unbutton my dress, his hands skimming my neck, the smell of dried blood from his hands an aphrodisiac. "Any news from the infiltrator?" I asked, moaning softly as his hand wandered right to where I was now aching.

HE PRESSED an openmouthed kiss to my neck, his sharpened teeth drawing a piercing, satisfying, pain. "Mmm, yes, he will be back later, and will be the best fae to carry out this new plan of yours," he answered.

· · ·

A SLIVER of doubt ran rampant, but I bit back the possibility that this infiltrator may actually be against me, but he has proven his loyalty too many times. Although I had to wonder... *never mind*, I thought, shaking my head. *I had a contingency plan.*

I SMILED as Ren picked me up and set me on the table. "We can discuss this later, for now, please your Queen."

HE SMIRKED WICKEDLY. "AS YOU WISH."

＄ I ぞ

"When life hits you hard, get up and say you hit like a
bitch," - **Unknown**
"Assuming that bitch lands the first punch. Right? Right?"-
Charlie

C harlie

I WIPED the blood from my favorite blade. *Sigh.* Nothing
better than serving justice to some sick motherfucker who
thinks he can get away with whatever he wants. Granted,
in this case, I was killing three birds with one stone, is that
even a thing? Never mind. I looked down at the serial
killer/gargoyle shifter—a shady, stupid motherfucker—
and waved my hand over his body, summoning my fire,
burning the body, before using air manipulation to scatter
the ashes into the water, surrounding the abandoned
boating dock. I found him feasting on one of the gifted

kids who had been reported missing. I am just pissed it took three dead children for me in order to finally pick up his trail. I have no idea why he had been fascinated with killing the children, and to be honest, I didn't give a flying fuck; he needed to die, I had an itch to kill something, and everything worked out. At least, I was able to fortify my blade with the blood of a gargoyle.

Using magick had its perks, one of them being that every creature I killed imbued my blade with their particular powers or quirks, and transferred some of that power to me, whatever power I don't already have, anyway; which is to say, barely any. Nonetheless, this blade has become an extension of my arm if I am out on patrol, like tonight. I paid a lot of money, a few years ago, before I learned how to spell properly or this shit to be spelled by some hidden witch in West bumble-fuck Pajila, another magickal community, but larger, north of Darnika, which was my home, in a sense. We were a decent-sized community made up of three castes: low, middle, and high; and yes you guessed it, the castes were named and placed for the level of power of the people in those communities. Same applies for the socio-economic status of those castes as well. I hated it, and my plan was to get everyone on the same playing field instead of the division instilled by the Council of Magick over the past few years. I did my research, albeit illegally, but not all communities were set up the way ours was. But for now, Darnica was my responsibility to fix.

We also had a decent outer-lying communities made of shifters, vampires, demons, and a few otherworldly creatures, although they weren't policed by us unless they attacked us outright; then all bets were off. No, they pretty much handled themselves, just stayed within the ward to avoid human interaction. Not that that always controlled the Vampires who had their ways to make it into the human world undetected. But I had an understanding with that community. Stay the fuck out of my way and live. Simple.

But first I had to protect and serve, and more importantly take out murderous sons of bitches. Gargoyles are hard to kill. Although, rogue shifters in general, are. But gargoyles? They are just some big assholes and it took a lot more than just magick to take care of them. You had to be quick and efficient enough to strike right under the wing where they are the most vulnerable. It didn't take any chance of turning human but as I went out of my way to find this shifter and to kill this slimy-child-thieving murderer, the look of shock on its face when I won, was particularly delicious. My blade is stronger, a serial killer is dead, and my blood lust is satisfied—for now.

I looked around as I tucked my blade into my holster. Slightly glowing, it sent a delicious shiver up my spine and I took a brief second to acclimate to the powers transferred to me. Grinning wickedly, I gave another brief look around as I tested my new powers. I have never killed a gargoyle so I didn't know what to expect. In truth, they were strong, they could fly, had a tendency to have harder hides, and were heavy as fuck, so being pinned by one was surely death. My philosophy? Never be fucking pinned by someone bigger than you. My back started to itch through my new leather jacket and I felt it rip as wings sprouted on my back.

I groaned. *Fuck me. My new riding jacket. I just got this shit.* Looks like the perk for this particular murder was wings! I may have lost my jacket, but fuck it.

I wonder if I could fly? I put the idea in the back of

9

my head to try later as I heard a small sound coming from my right. I ignored all the thoughts that flitted through my head as I headed over to the child, now cowering on the floor. The child. *It had to be a rough time for her as it is, especially now that she saw me go all murder and mayhem.* Well, that doesn't exactly set the stage for trust.

"Hey honey, my name is Charlie, you can call me Ellie. What's your name and how old are you?" I attempted to ask in my best motherly tone. Which means my voice probably came out as more of a husky growl, and judging by her flinch, I was right. She wasn't convinced by my attempted motherly nature. Well, I wouldn't blame her. I don't really have one, but still I tried.

"Hi, Ellie, I...I'm Ambrosia, thank you for kil...helping me." I smirked at her attempt to cover up what I did, but the truth was, I did kill him, so I shrugged.

"Don't mention it," I said as softly as I could. I took a casual once over and realized her leg was at an odd angle and she was bleeding from her neck, where the gargoyle was trying to hold her down. A fury rose deep within me and I'm sure my eyes were glowing red, a nifty trick I got for killing a murderous vampire, a year ago. Ambrosia looked at my face and whimpered, for sure trying to figure out what I was at this point. *You and me both, kid.* I shoved the anger down after a few seconds of breathing and tried to focus. I killed him, she's safe, and I will make sure she stays safe.

"I see you have some nasty injuries there, but guess what? I have pretty strong healing powers to help you but since your leg seems to be broken, this may hurt." Who was I kidding, it was going to hurt like a bitch but the child seemed to be a little bit more comfortable as I spoke quietly, so I didn't want to freak her out.

"S-sure, it hurts so much."

Without waiting or any prior warning, I put my hands over her body and pulled on my healing powers from deep within the recesses of my soul. Sounds strange, but that is where anyone's power comes from. Their soul. People forget that the soul is a constant energy that cannot be easily destroyed.

When my power finally peaked, I put my hands over Ambrosia and let my power work slowly, trying to at least alleviate some of the pain. When healing, a typical healer needs to focus and touch their patient, for me, I didn't have to touch, but it was always good practice to make myself look as inconspicuous as possible in this world. So overtime, I mentally developed what I would call a power condom; it didn't feel good but I had to fuck with the constrictions of it.

Ambrosia took a deep breath and made a small sound in the back of her throat but continued keeping a brave face. Impressive. Most people would flip their shit. I wanted to wrap her up in a hug, but that was more Pixie's thing, not mine.

While my power worked, Ambrosia seemed determined to keep the pain from her voice, and said, "I'm eleven by the way," answering my previous question.

I cursed under my breath. Eleven years old, kidnapped, hurt, and having to deal with a Gargoyle and whatever the fuck I am (again, later.)

Ambrosia looked at me. "You curse a lot. My foster mother never lets me curse. She believes it is beneath me." She looks at me speculatively. "But you curse a lot and you're saving my life, so it can't be a good way to judge someone's character." She takes a deep breath as her leg adjusts. I let out a surprised laugh. I admit she is a strong kid if she can take that level of pain. I have had to reset my legs quite a bit over the past six years since I have been on my own and it was not pleasant.

"There, all done. Would you like me to take you home now?" I cursed inwardly as I realized I brought my beautiful cherry-red and black motor cycle, and it was no place for a child. *Sigh*. As much I hated giving away all my secrets, there was no way I could take a kid back home on a bike, when every magickal law enforcement was out looking for this particular child, *that I have already saved, useless fuckers.*

"Please, I know my mom must be worried and I just want to be home," Ambrosia said softly, looking exhausted. Being healed, especially after such injuries, takes a toll.

"Ambrosia, I need you to keep what you saw me do tonight a secret, can you do that for me?" Something about this girl told me she would, but I don't trust anyone. Not anymore. Not after...no, I ignore that memory trying to rise, and focus on the little girl in front of me. She nodded gently.

"Thank you. I will take you home now. What does your home look like, picture it in your mind." I picked her up gently and surprisingly, she was lighter than I expected, but again, thanks to my badass abilities, I am stronger than your average magick user. She gave me a tired smile, and projected a quick picture of her home. I picked up the image of her home from her head, right before she passed out in my arms. Thank goodness, I was able to ask her before she fell asleep. I needed it to create the portal, and while I could have taken it while she was sleeping, without consent, she would have had a heck of a headache, not to mention I don't do anything without consent. Period.

I quickly threw an illusion, hiding my beautiful bike, Beast. I wasn't Belle, but we could share; he looks like a motherfucker with some serious stamina.

I opened a portal, then quickly and quietly stepped through, sighing in relief as I looked down and saw that Ambrosia was still sleeping. Portals tend to make you feel as if someone is stretching you to make you into a human Laffy Taffy. Not fun. I don't let people know the extent of my powers. Hell, I don't even know the full extent of my powers. I keep learning more every day. *Being this badass was a process.* Anyway, what I did know is that with every kill of a depraved Druko, I was stronger and took on a little of their powers, rather perks, as well. For example, I couldn't kill an elemental with fire and take their power because I already had elemental fire. Also, killing a shifter doesn't give me power to go through a full shift, but I can still create an impenetrable illusion of that person, that even mimicked certain personality traits. Learning. Process.

Unlike the other children who have to go through the Surge—our magickal awakening that gave us our powers— I was born with it. It had never happened before as far as I knew, or at least it was never documented, I should know, I have done the research. My parents kept my unusual birth a secret, and kept me hidden, so even despite their resources and connections, they couldn't make waves to alert anyone on the Magick Council—the Council that controlled the magick population for our community pocket anyway. Sigh. When I was born, I let out a burst of fire magick and damaged my mother from being able to carry children in the future. Although, according to my parents, they had intervention to have me, and chances are I was a one-off without more help.

Regardless, they always loved me and never made me feel bad about it. My parents were strong elementals and well-known; while my mom could control water better than anyone, my dad could control fire and heat. So opposite, but for magick, it wasn't about what power you had, it was more so about how your magick called to one another. Once that bond tugged, you blended into one another. Some call it the bond, others referred to it as the Call. Their love for each other was just perfect and well-balanced, it made me who I am, and I will always be grateful to them.

I smiled sadly, I missed them. I missed their smiles when I manipulated my bath water to make water balls when I was two, I even missed their anger when I set the backyard on fire when I was practicing my fire magick when I was four. I missed their shocked faces when I did something extraordinary like regrowing the grass, trees, and my mother's flowers, shortly after the fire without breaking a sweat. I have always been different, my power was vast, and unlike most Magicks I did not seem to have a refractory period. I scoffed, like men who need thirty minutes just to get it up for two minutes of grunting. I liked being different. But often times, different meant lonely and I had always been lonely, my parents couldn't allow me to be around other children to avoid anyone learning of my power. I was tutored at home and my parents did everything they could to make me laugh and happy. Still I was alone. I wanted to go out, I wanted to play, hell, I just wanted to be normal.

Lost in my thoughts, I blinked as I suddenly found myself in front of a gorgeous southern style home with a wraparound porch and swings right in front of the door. Magickal Law Enforcement, I scowl, also known as a pain in my sweet round ass, must have left earlier after asking their questions. Useless if you ask me. I heard the alert on the app I illegally had installed into my phone, *don't judge me*, as I was patrolling the city from the shadows and was able to find her pretty quickly. Granted, it took me three days to figure out the gargoyle's patterns, three children who will never see their friends and families again, who will constantly be mourned. I may not have been able to save those other children, but I was able to save one and any future victims by killing the filthy, fucking, murdering garbage.

I quickly created an illusion—another perk of my powers—of a stout officer with a heavy mustache. I made sure the green and yellow uniform that I had worn, indicating I was from the MLE, was perfect and crisp. Yuck, definitely not my colors, and quite frankly if they were going to suck at their jobs, at least they could dress better and try to look badass. Anyways, I knocked on the door, and a frantic woman in her bathrobe opened the door, and screamed and started sobbing. *Ouch. Why do women scream?!* I hid my wince. I held in the urge to shuffle my feet as she quickly grabbed Ambrosia and called out for her husband.

"Chad...Chad, she's home!" she yelled.

A blond man, with permanent laugh wrinkles in his eyes, came to the door, and sighed in relief. He was wearing a college jersey and sweats, and looked just as rough and emotional as his wife.

"Hello ma'am, we were able to find your daughter near the docks before any harm was done, and we caught the Druko responsible." I schooled my features into a look of relief and happiness, which to be honest wasn't hard to do because I was feeling both.

Even though I do not do well with emotions, I smiled. In the Magickal Communities, foster parents were a lot different than those in the human world, on the other side of the magical border. We valued our children and did not tolerate abuse of any kind. These kids were fortunate enough to be able to be loved and taken care of by another magickal family who understood their coming powers. I'm not sure how Ambrosia lost her parents, but I'm not one to pry.

I sighed, a lot of these foster parents have lost a child of their own when those children came into their power; it's a grueling process and can take a toll on the body because some kids just don't survive the Surge. Most kids came into their power when they turn twelve. I didn't sense any power on Ambrosia, so she has yet to go through the transition. I hope she survives. I can feel that she has a fortitude in her that reminds me of myself when I was younger.

Ambrosia's parents thanked me for saving their child, and finally I made my way from their porch and further down the road before I was able to use my hacked phone, to send an encrypted message that the missing child was found and to call off the search. The MLE wouldn't be able to tell who sent the message but knowing them, they wouldn't even give a fuck.

The MLE was just a front, the real people who protected the city, protected in shadows. Hell, they were called the Shadows, pretentious fuckers. They were primarily made up of men, and as my dad once eloquently put, they were little bitches of the Magick Council. Ten users that helped contain and use paranormal beings who have special abilities for whatever the Council needed them for. My mother and father were on the Council for years, being the strongest elementals with their perspective power, and being one of the five founding families, they were voices of reason on that corrupt ass-fucking board. For hundreds of years, the Elimentis were known to be very affluent, strong, and level-headed. *Our surname turned heads, used to anyway,* I thought sadly. Then suddenly on my thirteenth birthday, they didn't come home. My parents never missed a birthday and they always came home every night. After two days, I put forth our emergency plan, but I knew they were gone. Not just gone, but murdered, because my parents would never leave me. Not willingly.

I didn't mourn, logically, there was no time. I opened my heart, said goodbye, cleared my mind and focused on finding the truth. I had no proof...yet. I used that time to continue my magickal training and abilities through the vast amounts of information in my childhood home.

I made illusions to go over the border into the human world and underwent intense training in all forms of martial arts to hone my body and mind even further. Why the human side? Because the council fuckers didn't believe in their people learning to defend themselves, if we had the Shadows. What was the purpose, right? Fuck that. So for six years, I trained. After about a year, I felt the pull of my magick to a beautiful girl marred in bruises in one of my classes. I smiled at the thought of Pixie. She was perfect.

At the time I was confused why there was another magick in the same place, but like I said, the process is like a pull. A pull so young was rare, but when have I ever been normal. Pixie had been in the human realm with her dick-head human foster parents, and had wanted to learn how to fight. She snuck out, and the gym gave her free lessons once they picked up on her injuries. Why they didn't help her was beyond me, regardless she was tenacious then, and even more so now.

She didn't know about Darnika, hell, she didn't even know about her powers, and that I felt some of the strongest mental abilities emanating from her, other than me. I was cocky as fuck, but truth was truth. After a few weeks and sessions, the bruises started getting worse. I asked her if she would want to come home with me to my world instead. She wasn't the most trusting individual, from what I had observed, over the weeks. Always looking around, keeping to herself, unless it was time to train. She always gravitated toward me, even with seemingly no knowledge of Magick; she couldn't help the pull of the bond. The night I asked, she left the human realm and never looked back. We continued to train, our bodies becoming weapons and our magick becoming one. While we felt the pull young, we never crossed the line to fully bond until we were much older. We focused on hard work and knowledge.

We took it a step further, and learned every form of hacking and data encryption, there was to learn, and used that knowledge to hack into the Council's database, waiting for a slip-up on information via email, files, or chats. I was a ghost, a hungry one. After several years of searching, nothing popped up about my parents, just very small details about the new Council members that replaced them. Two weak elementals. I scoffed as the thought crossed my mind. No one on that Council was weak, they couldn't afford to be because they needed to maintain power. No. Someone is hiding something and

I'm going to fucking find it. And I had the perfect plan. I needed to get closer. Pixie and I are going to infiltrate the motherfucking Shadows. Not just the Shadows, but we were going to get into their Elite Squad, closer to the Council, closer to the truth.

※ 2 ※

"I don't need a weapon, I'm one." - **Unknown**
"I mean, really. This is just scarily accurate." - **Charlie**

Charlie

TAKING A DEEP BREATH, I focused on my surroundings
and didn't sense anyone nearby. I dropped my gross-ass
illusion while creating a portal to get back to my bike. My
darling, my Beast. If I could pole dance for that bike, I
would. Since I stripped off the illusion, I looked down at
my black leather pants, black combat boots, and my long-
sleeved sweater, that showed my ripped stomach off. I
looked it up, there are no rules about looking like a
grandma when killing the fuck outta people and plus, I
also like black. I let out a sigh as I took in my ripped
jacket. *All of my fucking powers, and I cannot make
clothes.*

That would have been bloody fucking useful on days like this. I set the jacket on fire as I fake cried, then chuckled as the smell of burned leather filled the air when the jacket disappeared, and I blew the ashes into the wind. There. No evidence. I need a fucking drink. Maybe some entertainment as well, of the naked variety. The night was young but I still needed to patrol, I would have to wait for naked entertainment later. At that moment, as if I was calling her, my phone rang. I hated this shit, always buzzing. It didn't matter that we could connect mind-to-mind anywhere we were, we needed to keep up appearances.

I picked up the phone via coms in my ears, and heard the thumping of sensual music in the background. Pixie was set up in the only Elite strip clubs near the capital instead of patrolling with me. As much as I hated it, it was the perfect way for her to pick up rumors of Shadow recruitments and capital gossip. It helped to be a mind reader. "Hey, my little tinker bell, learn anything interesting?" I snickered at the nickname because she loathed it with a passion. But I took joy in these little things.

"I'll cut you bitch," she retorted.

"Well, that is just hot. So you've accomplished nothing but gotten me excited to come home." I laughed, looking around and making my way to my bike. At least the dock was quiet.

"Listen up, Exousia," she started, using my nickname, known to the lower castes when I patrolled, unknown, "I picked up some information from the minds of these pervs, apparently they will be sending some Shadows Elites to find out about the Vigilantes taking care of the violence in the lower castes, and perhaps solving tonight's kidnapping case?" she finished softly.

Her use of my alias expressed the importance of this information. I just solved that case, how the fuck did they know? *Ooo, this was like Carmen Santiago.*

"Yeah, uh about that, I just solved that case like ten minutes ago, so how the fuck do they even know that? As for the Shadows coming, I'm already tired of waiting for these stupid fucks to make a move. Eventually, we knew their fragile egos couldn't take the slight of having their precious world actually taken care of," I replied.

"Well, it turns out that there was an MLE in the club tonight, which is weird but not uncommon really, and he got the alert that it was solved; he was already drunk and started cursing about the 'goddamn vigilante always butting in where it didn't belong and how they would have solved it eventually.'"

I scoffed at that. "Yeah, sure. Back to the Elites, when you say sending—"

"Yeah, they are already here, apparently patrolling the lower castes, so keep a clear head and remember the end game," Pixie cut me off.

"Thanks, baby. Make them interested but not murderous, got it. Should be easy, although it would have been better with you here, but I will make my usual runs and then head home. I'll pick you up at 3." I hang up the phone and sigh.

Well, all of this means that I needed to make these runs faster and check on the families that may need some extra cash or help. Since I've been patrolling, crime in the area is pretty much gone, but there were always a few fuckers that had to push me. Well, I'm blood-thirsty again, and I'm going to drink my fill tonight.

....

I swung my legs over my bike, and it purred under

me. I had it spelled for speed and balance, and I also created a shield for it that prevents it from getting any type of damage. I made sure to shield myself in case of an accident, safety first and all that, and turned up the music on the bike and got myself mentally ready to head downtown for patrol. As "Back That Azz Up" by Juvenile pumps though my speakers, I let myself twerk a little bit, *okay...a lot,* as I pull up to a red light. My bike was spelled to make my music audible even if wind whipped through my hair. Lost in the music and still dancing but not dumb enough to let my guard down, I notice a sleek truck pull up next to me with its windows rolled down. The fuckers had some type of classical music playing in their truck. Offended, I turned my music up and continued to dance.

I was being petty, but it was just that type of night. I felt eyes on me, and I looked over into the truck with a perfectly arched eyebrow, and locked my gaze, with quite honestly, the most fucking gorgeous guy I have ever seen. Shit, make that four incredibly gorgeous guys. My pussy jumped. *Calm down, you meat pocket,* I thought to myself. Openly staring now, I looked inside the car. The driver had a set of green eyes that looked like they were piercing my soul, scruffed face, and a beautiful kissable mouth that was turned up into a scowl. *Can angels even scowl?* Shit, he looked like a Liam Hemsworth's double, and suddenly my vagina was auditioning for Hunger Games. Keeping the lust off my face, I scowled right back. As the light turned green, I lowered my volume and said loudly, "Your music fucking sucks," and threw up my middle finger as I peeled off. Mr. Green Eye Fucker opened his eyes wide, his scowl now more pronounced as I took off, putting distance between us. Not before I was able to hear the peals of laughter from the rest of the men.

I drove faster, allowing my thoughts to take me to muse about the men in the car. Not before changing my song to "How Many Licks" by Lil Kim. No reason. No reason whatsoever. Just a song. Yup. While the other men were sitting further in the truck, I still saw them clear as day. My vision was sharp and I could pierce the darkness, also one of my perks.

They were gorgeous; Mr. Blue Eyes sat next to green eyes and had a perfectly shaven face with a sharp model-like features, picture Dean Winchester.

In the back, I noticed Mr. Scary as he looked like he enjoyed killing more than breathing, but I can get down with that. Mr. Scary reminded me a lot of Damon from Vampire Diaries—all grown up with bigger muscles.

Last but certainly not the least was Mr. What The Fuck, as in WTF—he was certainly created in the water—because he looked like a walking wet dream. They were all hot but he felt like he dripped sex. I wonder if he was part sex. Is that even a power? Shit, I want to find out. I may just change his name to Mr. Spanish Wet Dream. He certainly had Latin features, with hazel eyes, and looked like he belonged in a Novella. Being part Latin myself, that is one flavor I can totally get behind. Yum. Like a fucking adobo commercial.

Unfortunately, that car oozed power, so these guys are strong as fuck. Which means one thing, four Shadows, also referred to as an Elite team. A team who saw me and definitely couldn't pick up on what I was. I didn't even know what I was. But them seeing me meant curiosity. I don't need that shit tonight. I needed that shit as much as I need nails in my fucking eyeballs. Fuck me.

. . .

Luca

DESPITE THE SCOWL on my face, I was completely taken aback by the beauty on the bike. Never mind the insult to my music, I can ignore that. What I couldn't ignore was that I couldn't pick up her powers. Who was she? I pulled over to the side of the road as she flew off into the night on her bike. I had to adjust myself as I couldn't help but picture her bouncing on my dick instead of the bike.

There was no time for that unfortunately, because we were here to find this murdering vigilante and had limited time to do so. This person was a fucking ghost we had nothing to go off except the papers given to us before we left for the mission. We arrived and started asking questions in the lower castes a few hours ago. This vigilante had no description, no photo, no video footage. Absolutely fucking nothing other than a cryptic old lady telling us to fuck off because Exousia helps the lower castes, and not the Shadows, before she spat at our feet and slammed the door. I scoffed at that as we turned away and piled back into the car. Shadows have been patrolling for years, and the ones on shift have never seen her, in fact, all they keep saying is that their job has been easier than usual, and that the communities have been undergoing renovations.

We thought that would be a break, I mean workers were bound to notice something, but the company doing the renovations just employs the workers and they have no idea who their boss was, nor who was patrolling the area while they worked. Even their deposits were untraceable as if it magickally appeared. I rubbed my head, this is a fucking puzzle. I don't care about the renovations, but something tells me if we find this Exousia, then we may find an underground network and figure out who is giving money to these communities. There has to be a connection. Two things the capital cannot control happening at once? Not a chance.

"Fuck, who the hell was that? They don't have women like that in the capital. Her curves are ridiculous and fucking yummy..." Dante was rambling in the background. I couldn't help but agree about his assessment but something felt, off.

"Dante, shut the fuck up. I couldn't trace powers from her," I said.

Etienne perked up next to me. "What do you mean? Like you couldn't figure it out or you didn't pick up anything at all?"

"No, more like I picked up the strength of her soul, but couldn't grasp her powers," I mused.

"Okay, so you picked up her soul, that's good. What was the limit then? Maybe that can give us an idea of what powers she has and how strong she is."

"There was no limit that I could pick up," I admitted, confused. Every Magick user had a limit, a point where their magick ran out before they needed to recuperate. The deeper the limit, the stronger the person. I realized the boys had gone silent.

"Well then, it looks like we found our first clue," Dimitri spoke up from the back with a wicked smile on his face.

"Fuck it, back to the lower castes we go. We can scope out the bars and see if we pick up anything that might be easier than just questioning people," I admitted. I pulled off the curb and followed her bike into the night. I hope it was a clue, but if it wasn't, then maybe we can make time for the purple-haired beauty. I would love to feel her curves pressed up against me.

Charlie

I PULLED into the lower magick caste area, hopped off my Beast, and stretched. I set up an illusion so my bike looked like an abandoned broken down car. I quickly did my rounds and took mental notes about which homes will need renovations. I made sure to cloud myself in the shadows as I went door-to-door, and provided money for families struggling, and asked if they were okay and safe or needed any help. They all gave me deets about Shadows asking around for Exousia. I knocked on the last door, and an old lady opened the door.

"Mary, may I come in?" I said, with a smile, that she couldn't see yet.

"Of course, Exousia, come in quickly. There were people asking for you," she warned.

I removed the clouds and gave her a hug. She was one of the few who knew what I looked like as the Exousia. A lot of others suspected who I was but never asked, there was no need, they understood their safety was my top priority and we didn't snitch here. We had enough heat with the council.

"So, people are asking for me?" I questioned as I reached to eat some of her cookies she always had ready just for me and Pixie.

"Four large, sexy men and they all had to be over six

feet. I will project the image to you," she said, and moved around the kitchen to bring me some milk to drink with the cookies. I thanked her while laughing at her brazenness. I took note of the picture she projected and groaned.

"Yeah, I saw them earlier. I told one of them that their music sucked and drove off. They are definitely as gorgeous as I remember from the car though. Thanks, Mary, I'll keep a lookout. They didn't give you any trouble, right?"

She chuckled. "Me? No, I would have put them over my knee, spit at their feet, and told them Exousia protects us, not the Shadows," she said, and I broke out in laughter.

"Charlie," she said, suddenly seriously, "I wanted to let you know that Amy's husband—they live down the road—is still beating her, and I have it on good authority that he will be at the bar downtown. Go beat his ass for me?" Mary asked. I assured her he would have his ass kicked as I gave her another hug, and stepped out.

I stripped my shadows down the road and walked to the bar. Plenty of people were out and they all smiled at me as I walked. Everyone here knew me, not as the Exousia as she only visited in the shadows, but as the no nonsense, but fun member of their crowd. It allowed me to learn everything I needed to know about the community I was helping to rebuild. I loved these people, they were just given a bad hand, and their magick wasn't as strong, but that doesn't make them any less valuable or loveable. Not to mention, they could be stronger if they all practiced, but one step at a time. I sighed. I stepped into one of my favorite bars on the road, nothing like pool, darts, and good music. I could actually shake my ass here as it played more hip hop than anything. I noticed Amy's husband, Richard, at the end of the bar, wrapped around a random redhead.

I frowned. Amy didn't mention anything. I hate when women feel helpless. I made a mental note to offer to train her so she wouldn't feel like that again. The entire community has a cellphone with an SOS button, they can reach Exousia for emergencies. I wonder why she didn't send me one.

I looked at my watch, I still had another two hours before I had to pick up Pixie. So I could relax a bit before I kicked some ass. I made my way to the bathroom, peed, washed my hands and the road wind off my face, and took a look in the mirror. Feeling cleaner, I admired my hazel eyes that changed color, depending on my mood and took in my lips, which were a natural deep pouty pink. My Latin features, long purple hair and curves, were a wet dream, but only for Pixie. A deep yearning in my chest broke out as I reached for our mental connection. Being bonded, we could never be without at least brushing our minds together.

Hey baby, at a bar downtown, getting a drink, beating a woman-beater, and missing you. I whispered to her. *I miss you too, can't wait to see you*, she replied mentally, and sent me a mental picture of exactly why. God, I needed to get home. I kept our minds brushing against one another and stepped out of the bathroom.

I kept my eye on Richard as I ordered a couple of shots and a beer; alcohol doesn't really affect me much as my magick burned through it all. But a few minutes of a buzz wouldn't be remiss. I smiled at Burns, the bartender and owner of the bar, and thanked him.

"You cannot smile at me like that Ellie, you're a

bonded woman, and might give this old man a heart attack," he teased me, and I threw my head back and laughed.

"Puhleaze, Burns, you're far from old, and you know Pixie will cut you. I cannot control that woman outside the bedroom," I threw back at him.

"Okay, here, take your liquor. I need those images out of my head, you two are going to be the death of me." He paused before adding, "You know some men were in the community, asking around for the vigilante earlier." He glanced at me while polishing a cup.

I leaned against the bar and sipped my beer and looked around. "Hmm, really sounds like they will be searching for a long time. I hear Exousia is untraceable. I heard something about Elite Shadows in the area, I wonder if it is all connected?" I mused. He took a long look at me, and sighed.

"Just be careful, Charlie," he said softly.

"I don't know what you mean, Burns, I'm always a good girl," I joked. At that, he laughed loudly and sent me on my way but not before yelling, "Don't kick someone's ass tonight, Ellie. I don't have energy tonight for the extra cleaning!" I laughed and made my way to the dartboard. He knows I always pay for the cleaning, but that was his way of letting everyone know that I was here and not to fuck with me. He ruins all my fun.

☙ 3 ❧

*"I'm different, f**k your opinion."- **Unknown***
*"It's like you truly know me."- **Charlie***

L uca

WE STEPPED INTO THE BAR, and people turned to look at us but then quickly looked away. Couldn't deny we made an imposing show of force. Four Shadows in a world that apparently hated us. New territory. We made our way into the packed place, full of worn down tables and scuffed floors. Approaching the bar, I noticed pictures of the purple bombshell on the wall with a gorgeous short-haired woman and random patrons. It looked like everyone here truly was a little family. That gave me a sense of peace and then confusion. We sat back at the bar, covered in graffiti and knife cuts, and ordered beers. The bartender gave us a hard look but served us before making his way to laugh with the other patrons at the bar as well.

"You guys notice how everyone here for the most part seems pretty tight nit?" I gestured at the wall, and the guys peered at it a bit closer.

"At least, they don't seem to need Shadows when they rely on each other. Especially with someone out there serving their own form of justice." Dante leaned back and continued assessing the room with his eyes.

"Interesting though, isn't it? If anything, they should be up in arms with the information we have," muttered Etienne, his French accent thick when deep in thought.

I glanced at Dimitri, who seemed murderously contemplative. If those words even went together. I had already noticed her immediately, even with a bar this full, she was hard to miss. She was dancing to the music blasting from the speakers, while playing a game of darts with a group of guys. I growled. I didn't like that at all.

"She's in the corner playing darts with some people." I let the boys know quietly.

"No need to tell us, as if we can miss her dancing like that," Dante spit out. Looked like he didn't like the group she was with either. I smirked.

Her curves were unreal and her abs were on perfect display with that scrap of a sweater she had on. I found myself just fantasizing about wrapping my hands around her waist and pulling her plump ass against my dick. I cleared my throat. "Well, let's go play a game."

We made our way through the people dancing and settled around the dart area. She made the target each time without fail, her body flexing as she turned and shifted. Everyone groaned around her as she laughed and winked at the crowd. "Alright, alright, I won't make you pay up this time, it wouldn't be fair. You're all drunk anyway," she said as she threw back her head and laughed. Fuck, that laugh went straight to my dick. *Stupid fucking cock.*

I took a look around, none of the people she was playing with were remotely drunk, interesting. Either she didn't know or she didn't want to take money from anyone in the lower castes. I'm betting it's the former.

"Ellie, we could be magickal fucking unicorns and we still wouldn't beat you, you got an arm on you girl. If I wasn't bonded, I would snatch you right up," joked an older guy, next to her. I growled internally.

I paused, taking a breath. I don't know what was wrong with me. I don't know this girl worth a damn and I definitely shouldn't be upset about her laughing with what seemed to be her peers. Ellie, hmm...Her name didn't feel quite right for a person in leather, combat boots, tattoos, and a motorcycle. But when she laughed and lit up the room, it fit. In fact, it was perfect. I liked to see her laugh. It was sexy as fuck.

From the corner of my eye, I felt Dimitri shift and start to walk over to her. "Anyone can hit a target if they are facing it head on, they probably just don't want to hurt your feelings, little girl." Everyone fell silent, even with the music playing it seemed as if everyone's attention was on Ellie. As if in a room with four Shadows, she was still the one to fear. *She gets more interesting every second.*

I hid my smirk as she turned around slowly, faced him, looked him up and down, and immediately dismissed him. Dimitri bristled, he tends to be the most controlled in the group, a stone cold killer, not many went toe-to-toe with him if they cared about their lives, so this reaction was...not ideal.

"Little girl...that's interesting, Vampire, because from what I see when I wake up in the morning is a fat ass, toned abs, and thick thighs. I'm hardly a little girl." She sighed dramatically. "No, it looks like you want a challenge. Which is fine, just ask for one like a man instead of insulting me like a pussy. So be ready to get fucked... over." Her challenge hung in the air. Everyone backed up and gave them a wide berth while continuing their fun. However, they all watched with rapt fascination.

Dimitri growled, "Pussy? Is that a challenge?" He strode into her space and got real close to her, at six-foot-five, he was an imposing figure. But she looked up at him and scoffed. Actually scoffed. Dimitri looked stuck like he just didn't know what to make of her. I had to stop myself from bursting out laughing. Dante had no such qualms.

She stepped around him, and said, "Well, it definitely isn't an invitation to mine, and calm the fuck down. This isn't Beauty and the Beast, vampire. I'll even let you go first." By this point, Dante was having trouble breathing, he was laughing so hard.

"How about we all play?" I spoke up. I needed to get closer to get a read on her. I could not put my finger on it, and it made me uneasy.

"Your funeral, fuckers," she said as she grabbed more darts and lined herself up. She turned around, her back facing the target and took a swig of her beer. She seemed to be looking for someone, I wonder who.

The thought was forgotten as she threw six darts in rapid succession and hit the bull's eye each time. I couldn't even finish blinking. She then took a step to the side and angled her darts and spun around while she threw the darts and hit the bull's eye again. She was, incredible, to say the least.

Dante walked to Dimitri and clapped him on the back, laughing. "Well, you're fucked, and not in a good way."

She turned around. "So, you still want to do this?"

Dimitri walked up to the board, took all the darts out, and held them in his palm. "Good job, little girl, but can you hit a moving target? Etienne, if you will do the honors." Etienne, who had just been observing this entire time, lets out a deep sigh, and used his power of air manipulation to make the target move around Dimitri and Ellie like a mini dart tornado.

Dimitri centered himself, took a deep breath, and spun while shooting the darts. When he was done, Etienne stopped the target and held it up. Dimitri got all 12 on the target but two were off-centered. He was pissed. I was loving this.

"Well, well, well, seems like two of these were off mark. Care to place a wager then? I win and you guys leave me the fuck alone and walk out that door. I got someplace to be. Cool? Fucking Shadows," Ellie spit out, and we all frowned. Looks like she was ready to get rid of us. We had a job to do, so why did that make me feel like shit?

"You. Mr. Blue Eyes, go ahead and start the spinning, but this time, spin faster." She smirked. The men and I looked at each other. There was no way she can hit the target if it spins any faster, so what was she playing at? She threw her hair up into a bun and stretched, her sweater rising to show off a peek of her purple lace bra. I bit my lip, she noticed the action, and threw me a wink. Little minx.

Etienne started the spinning and she focused on herself, blew out a deep breath, stared straight ahead, and instead of spinning like Dimitri, she stood in one place while she threw the darts. When she was done, Etienne stopped the board. All. Dead. Center. She shook out her hair and sauntered away. "Bye, pussies." My dick was hard as fuck.

Dimitri

I WANT HER.

Charlie

FUCK, I had to go pick up Pixie but I had just enough time to beat Richard senseless for fucking with his wife. Fucking sexy Shadows wasting my time. I don't back down from a fucking challenge and I'm the strongest magickal person they will ever come across. So fuck that machismo bullshit.

I noticed Richard duck out the back with the redhead. I followed for about a block before I clouded myself, and spoke, "Richard, Richard, Richard...I hear you've been attacking people in my city?" It was very Arrow-esque but Oliver Queen was sexy, so fuck it.

He jumped up and tried to run, forgetting the redhead that was with him. I grabbed him, punched him in the face and swept his legs out from under him. I laughed as the redhead ran down the street without looking back. I stood over him, and hissed, "Get the fuck away from Amy, if I see you in these streets again, you will be dead. Understand?"

"Stupid bitch, I'll kill you both!" he screamed. Wrong answer. I laughed darkly. I took a second to reach into his mind and saw that he had been hitting Amy and started in on his children recently. Yeah, fuck that. Split decision, I snapped his neck and dragged his body into the alley nearest me. I set his body on fire and distributed the ashes into the wind.

Murder doesn't bother me. You know what bothers me? Men beating on women. People do bad shit, people get away with it, and I fucking hate it. Especially here, these people have suffered enough due to the negligence of the council. Not anymore. Fuck that.

What is unfortunate is the consistent narrative of women being weak. Women aren't weak, if properly trained, they can go head to head with any male; it's not about strength, it's about technique. As I made my way to the other side of the alley, I removed the cloud of darkness that hid me and made a mental note to open a free self-defense gym in the castes. I walked back into the bar, and waved goodbye to Burns.

I quickly transferred some money in Amy's account, now that Richard has made a sudden tragic disappearance. I scoffed.

I paused and smiled as I reached where my bike was covered with the illusion. I removed it and threw my leg over to straddle it. I love my Beast.

As I started my bike, I addressed the four men who have been following me since I left the bar from the front entrance, "Gentlemen, you know that following a lady is considered rude and creepy, right?" I revved my bike up as they slinked out of the Shadows. "Very smooth, guys. Quite sexy to slide out of the shadows, but you know what is even sexier? Not following someone." I cocked my head to the side. "Go ahead and add staring to that list too." I rolled my eyes. "What do you want?"

Mr. Green Eyed Fucker started, "I can't get a read on you, what are your powers?"

"None of your fucking business, anything else?" I replied.

"That is where you are wrong, everything is Shadow business, little girl," Vampire spoke up. God, he was hot. Stupid, but hot.

I laughed in his face. Hilarious. This guy should do some fucking stand-up comedy. "Yeah, okay Vampire, I'm sure if you ask around, you'll find out that this area hasn't been Shadow-anything for quite a bit. Thanks for the laugh though." I winked at them and licked my lips dramatically, showing off my tongue rings.

"Bye boys! Good luck finding out shit about me." I said loudly. As I pulled away, the Green Eyed Fucker reached out as if to grab me. I sped away to pick up Pixie, opening my mental link to fill her in, ignoring that as he reached out to grab me, purple sparks jumped from each of the men and toward me. *Nope. Not Possible.*

❊ 4 ❊

"There's just some magic in truth and honesty and openness." - **Frank Ocean**

"Sure, if I use my magick to peer into that openness. You call it intrusion, I call it mindreading." - **Charlie**

C harlie
One Week Later

I PULLED into the Elite Strip Club, where only the top members of the society were allowed, parked my bike in the VIP spot and swung my leg over my bike and stretched. I loved riding. It really helped me think and process. Sometimes after "working," I would just ride for hours with no end in sight, simply to empty my head to later fill it up with more endless information and studies. As I sauntered to the entrance I drew many hungry gazes, and some jealous ones. I had on a low halter top and black jeans that cupped my ass and sat low on my hips, combat boots completed my outfit because heels don't help anyone kick ass. My outfit showed off the tattoo that covered my entire back, a watercolor tinker-bell, sprinkling pixie dust surrounded by purple streaks. I got it after me and Pixie completed the bond. I ignored the stares, at five foot two, hazel eyes, with long purple hair that hit my lower back, an ass that can rival Kim Kardashian except mine was real, toned legs and abs, C bordering D cups, I was pretty much a rap video come to life. I didn't have to create an illusion to look good, I just had good genetics. I worked hard to tone my body, and fuck, if I was going to tamper down my looks for anyone. I didn't resemble my parents except for my eyes and hair, I had my mother's eyes. Except she wasn't Lily Potter and she didn't dye her hair, when I just couldn't bear to see the long dark tresses anymore, the image and memory was too painful, I dyed it the same color of the streaks on my back. A deep purple. I didn't have time for pain, I needed focus, strength, and a clear mind.

I took notice of the line, walked straight to the door, nodded at the huge, muscular bouncer Twinkie. No, seriously, his nickname was Twinkie and if you ask him about it he would punch you right in the face. I gave him a fist bump and walked right in. I was well known. It was for a reason. My powers were tampered down, and everyone thought I was simply a badass. My reputation was ruthless but again I needed to make sure it was, they didn't need to know who I was. Whispers and rumors travel just as fast as truths. My whispers gave me my badass reputation, well that, and the fact that I would probably break your face before you have a chance to insult me twice. I was typically given a wide berth, oh well. Bright side is, while everyone has a specific dress code due to the "elite" status of this strip club, I wore whatever the fuck I wanted. I walked up to the bar where Pixie was working tonight. Pixie danced part time and worked the bar, and if I thought I loved her when we were younger, it was nothing compared to our bond now. She was gorgeous. Curvy, with a short layered brunette bob that framed her face but looked wind swept, toned legs from the pole dancing and training, and striking eyes; one blue, one green. Her lips were nothing short of a wet dream, people pay for those type of lips. I, of course, got them for free, from Pixie. Our bond tugged and she looked at me and made eye contact. I felt the air leave my lungs. She is the only person I trusted and the only one who knew everything about my life. That type of bond, not solely magick, but true friendship, cannot be replaced.

I smiled at her, nodded toward an empty booth in front of the stage so I can watch her dance in a few. She took this job in order to be close to the elite members in society. Pixie had the power of mind reading and manipulation, however she can break down any barrier and completely destroy your walls without causing any pain and turning the person into mush. That type of control, if anyone knew, would be highly coveted. We were counting on it. We needed her position here in order to pick up any information about the Shadow world and the Council. The only other person with that amount of power and control was me, and I helped train and hone her skill over the years. She was perfect. In every way.

The pole dancing was a perk we came up with when we set her up in this club. Truth was, you want to break into a mind? You do it when the only thing on a mind was sex. Easy. So we started to include that in our training and gained a new respect for all pole dancers everywhere. We flared up muscles we didn't know we had. It was brutal. I sat down and a few moments later, Pixie brought me a line of ten rainbow shots and set them on fire, and gave me kiss garnering the eyes of every patron. I smacked her ass as she sauntered away. Yeah, I was the only one who got to do that, this was a look-don't-touch-type of establishment and the owner, Pixie's friend, James, who wasn't happy about his "baby sister" dancing, was actually a mean motherfucker who had no problem breaking a few bones to make that clear. He loves me, he has no choice as I was, by association, his second annoying little sister who was in love with his sister. Besides, I shrugged internally, even if he didn't like me, Pixie can be a scary bitch when provoked, and well, there aren't that many people who can take me.

"Are you sure you can handle all that liquor, sexy lady," some sleazeball greasy looking motherfucker, with an expensive suit, said as he tried to slide into my private booth. He must be new or stupid. Probably both. I mean my booth was technically for eight, and no one but me ever sat here, and everyone knew it.

"Buttons" by the PussyCat Dolls started blasting from the radio, and this motherfucker was not going to intrude on my post-work time.

"I can handle several things," I purred menacingly. Still not getting the hint, desire lit his eyes as he tried to get his belly into the booth.

"I'm sure you can, sweetheart. Why don't we grab a private room? I have quite a bit of money for a lonely girl like you," he wheezed out.

I took out the blade from my boot and twirled it around my fingers, sighing and settling back.

"Want to make a wager that the only lonely thing

here will be one of your balls once I slice off the other?" I gave him a glare, and he yelped, scampering away.

I laughed as he wheezed about crazy bitches and went to reach for my first shot when a prickle of awareness hit my internal, *fuck this shit,* sensors. I looked back toward the door, and yup, just my luck the fucking Shadows from the other night we here. I rubbed my temples as I told myself that we needed information and the Elite were the perfect opportunity. Didn't mean I had to love the idea of it all. But other than the vigilante talk, there had been nothing about recruitment. At least these fuckers would be a cesspool of information. I smirked, and my inner bitch did a dance.

They noticed me at the exact same time and moved as a unit toward the bar. Shots temporarily forgotten, I studied them and I wasn't shy about it either, I looked... they looked back. They called to me in a deep way, my heart started to race and I groaned. I was not in the mood for any type of pull with any Shadowy motherfuckers. I opened my mental link with Pixie so she could see, hear, and feel what was happening.

Did you feel that by any chance? When they walked up to the bar? I whispered in her mind.

I felt something alright, another complication. We will figure it out, she answered.

They seemed to communicate with their eyes and they started to walk toward me. Very militant, these guys can use a little stress reliever. *Yeah, me,* Pixie whispered in my head. I laughed and I had to tell my inner hussy to calm the fuck down. Mr. Spanish Wet Dream WTF sauntered up to my booth and started speaking. Yeah, I have no idea what the fuck he said because I was too busy having ear sex with his voice.

"Yeah, sorry repeat that, the music is kinda loud," I said.

"Hmmm, I asked if you'd mind if me and my brothers sit with you, you have the best booth here." He smiled knowingly and winked.

"Well yeah, because it's my booth," I said plainly.

Dimitri chose that time to speak up and his dark voice sent shivers of trepidation down my spine, *fuck yes I can be tied up and fucked with that voice.* "Your booth?"

I laughed huskily and leaned forward, showing off my cleavage, and tossed my purple hair back. "Yes, my booth." I rolled my eyes.

He let out a surprised laugh while the others were fighting a smirk.

"May we sit with you?" Ever the gentleman. My inner bitch doesn't like gentle but was willing to train him.

I nodded toward the seats, I had no real reason to say no since I needed information. "Sure, sit down." To be honest, they would have sat down anyway but I appreciated the show of respect.

As they settled in and spread out in the large booth, they were so damn large that Dante and Luca's thighs momentarily pressed against mine. It immediately caused a bolt of electricity to hit between us. They looked at me, and I pretended it never happened. Yup, I can play that game.

I felt a zing, I said to Pixie, mentally.

Baby, this isn't Hotel Transylvania, she replied with a voice full of humor, even in my head. I sent her a mental scowl.

As they got comfortable, I signaled to Pixie who put

on a convincing confused and slightly jealous face; very sexy look on her, I might add.

"Pixie, baby, can you light my shots up again, they went out." I made an exaggerated pout. She looked around the table and raised her eyebrow.

I told you they were fucking hot, I said in her head.

Yeah, but fuck, she replied.

"Hello. Ellie never lets anyone sit in her booth, you must all be pretty special." Pixie grinned, reaching out to shake their hands but quickly took her hand back when she also felt that electric charge. The men looked at each other and stared at both of us curiously. She cleared her throat. "Umm, I'm Pixie, Ellie's equal opportunity girlfriend." She threw a saucy wink. Their eyebrows shot up, and I laughed.

"Honey, you know it's only equal opportunity if we are both on the menu," I added huskily, unable to keep the image of me and her being ravished by these four men from my head. I projected the image to her, and she blushed. I went as far as to project the image very lightly to the men, just to get them to let their guards down and think they thought about it all on their own. I continued, and ignored how the temperature shot up around us, "Pixie is actually my bonded."

The men raised their eyebrows, but now looked a bit confused. Join the club, fucking fuckers. Bonded already, so why do we like you. *Right, Focus.* I cleared my throat. "Pix, let me introduce you. That one at the end is Mr. Scary Vampire aka Dimitri—he sucks really bad at darts; the one next to him is Mr. Green Eyed Fucker aka Luca— he has terrible taste in music; on my other side we have Mr. WTF— also known as Mr. Spanish Wet Dream aka Dante; and at the other end we have Mr. Blue Eyes aka

Etienne—he spins shit," I finished off with a flare. I winked at Pixie.

"You would name them all, ha, I wonder what other names we can give them though. I'm partial to Ay Papi." She fake-moaned and looked around appraisingly, interest in her gaze.

Their eyes bugged out of their heads. Best way to glean information? Make a man horny. You can get past any defense then.

I opened a mental link between me and Pixie, and gave her a mental high-five.

"Well, it was nice to meet you all. I'll be back shortly, I have to get ready." She sends them a saucy wink.

We paused to admire her ass jiggle in her work shorts, which were more like boy shorts. God, I love her. Anyways, I snapped my fingers at the boys.

"So, this is sure to be quite a fascinating night. Elite team, right?" I smirked.

Etienne spoke up first, "How did you know?"

"It could have been the all black, the sense of superiority, the sexy brooding. Or the more obvious fact that you're all ridiculously built, over six feet, and still move with the silence and fluidity of the wind! Maybe it's the fact that each of you have knives strapped to your legs but most importantly, you all have the Shadow standard, concealed body sword on your right pant leg which explains the utility belt with no weapons on it. You hide them inside. Am I wrong" I resisted the under to show my confusion on my face for that.., the standard body sword, I never understood the need to carry it inside the pant leg, but I guess that's a secret for the Academy to share. As it was, it felt like the start of a possible Magick Mike moment.

I kept going before they responded, drumming my hands on the table. "But you're not regular Shadows because you reek of dominance, you're traveling in a team of four instead of patrolling in a team of two as is standard. Which means you all bring a certain level of game changing powers to the table and are strong as fuck. Which also means that the four of you together are nigh-impossible to beat."

They stilled and the intensity of their gaze all focused on me. Dante shook it off first going for his natural charisma, but with a mental push to see how I tick, which pissed me the fuck off. Fucker. Normal magicks wouldn't have noticed, but I wasn't normal. It also wasn't in me to let it slide.

"Well, damn sexy, observant, smart, and you beat Dimitri's ass. I wonder what else you have hidden," he said.

I leaned in close to him, ran my hand up his leg and brushed his dick, ignoring the shock of electricity, and said loud enough for everyone to hear, "A tight pussy and the ability to kick your ass if you try to use your powers on me again." I smirked.

Dante cleared his throat. "Well, umm, errr, I'm sorry about the powers." He looked choked up and turned on. *Good, now that makes both of us.*

"I have to ask," he drawled, "I am pretty skilled. How did you know I was trying to get into your mind?" He had a confident voice, not one that indicated that he was cocky in any way. I could appreciate that.

They seemed to sit up a bit straighter to hear my answer. I looked around the club, taking my sweet time to answer. I took in the personal booths, full of societies' highest and the girls taking a few of the members into the back rooms. I laughed a bit, they will probably just take five minutes in there. Sex starved men by their prude high caste wives. Poor them. I looked at Dante. "Well, the answer is simple. I'm stronger." I smirked and took a swig of his beer before he put it to his mouth.

Luca chose that moment to speak up, "Impossible." That's it. One word.

"Wow, man of many words! Well, it's not only possible, but it's the truth. Truth Hurts. And in the words of Lizzo, 'Why men great till they gotta be great.' You were great, until you met me. Step up your game, boys. You're going to find I'm full of surprises. I mean, I'm assuming that's why you followed me, right? Although not very well, it did take you a week, unless you're actually not too fascinated by me, and are looking for something else?"

He cleared his throat, looking a bit uncomfortable. Then our thighs touched again and the electricity spiked down my leg this time. Sigh, *fuck a flying donkey and make dragon babies, this attraction was definitely not a fluke, then.* "Let me introduce everyone," he continued. "I'm Luca, the one you call Blue Eyes is Etienne, next to me is Dimitri, and the, um, wet dream is Dante," he finished, albeit a bit uncomfortably, at saying Dante's nickname.

"Well gentlemen, despite the stalking me into a strip club portion of our night, it's a pleasure to meet you. I'm Charlie, also known as Ellie," I said, not unkindly.

"We know," said Dimitri. "People seem to speak highly of you in the surrounding area; a fighter who takes care of others. You've made a pretty impression on almost everyone we have met. That, or they are terrified of you. There is no in between."

I shrugged. "Hmm, sounds about right, what do you

think about me?" I asked, genuinely curious despite myself.

"I think you're cocky as fuck and have a mouth you probably can't back up..." he trailed off.

I laughed. "We'll see. I'll bet on that, Dimitri."

I turned to my right, blowing off Dimitri entirely, to observe Etienne a bit more since he wouldn't stop staring at me.

"Etienne, that is a very sexy name, means Crown in French. Very royal. I guess that is why you observe more than you speak. Staring is rude, by the way, but I'm going to go ahead and assume you pick up on body language and tells, which makes you LEDD's walking lie detector. That's pretty cool," I finished, looking casual as this was something anyone can guess after ten minutes.

I keep looking around taking note of everyone around, and I let out a deep sigh. "You are all staring again, it is getting kind of intense, is this where the porn music starts?" I laugh because I'm fucking hilarious. They cracked a smirk.

Before Etienne could respond, Dante questioned, "LEDD?"

"Oh"—I waved my hand—"I like acronyms, you all are now LEDD. You're welcome."

Before he could respond, Etienne continued with his French accent thick in the air, "Not a lot of people, hell barely anyone, can tell what my powers are. The fact that you do is very...intriguing to say the least." Wow, that was incredibly sexy. My mouth was dry and I cleared my throat to try to focus.

I didn't miss his emphasis on the word intriguing. It can either mean he is genuinely intrigued or he has marked me as a potential enemy, or bed mate. Only time will tell.

"Well, you used air manipulation last time we met, and usually everyone who is Elite has two powers." Then I threw in for the heck of it. "Your French accent completely threw me for a loop, but I must say I really like it," I said with a smile.

"Why is that, Chérie?" Etienne smirked with mirth in his eyes.

"Well, because I'm thinking about being your buttered croissant." I shrug, and turn my head as he chokes on what's left of his beer.

I look back toward Dimitri now. "Why are the angry ones always named Dimitri or Dracula?" I said purpose-fully, trying to get on his nerves. He just looks so work-up able, is that even a word? It was sexy in an infuriating, punching-you-in-the-dick kind of way.

Dimitri, on the other end growled, "I'm not angry, I'm a realist, and I'm not a damn vampire. Why do you keep calling me that?"

I lowly whispered, "Because. You. Look. Like. A. Fucking. Blood-sucking. Demon. From. Hell. But if that bothers you, let's pick another word! Sullen, perturbed, grumpy, although you only have three other dwarves and not the other six, so maybe not grumpy." The others started to complain about being called dwarves, but I held up my hand. I wanted to see his reaction to my insults, if he's as intense as he shows himself to be.

He opened his mouth in indignation, but was cut off by Pixie walking up and giving them their new beers, and me a lighter for my shots. Even as she passed them out, I was transfixed. She had changed into her dance outfit while she was gone. Gone was the simple makeup and bar outfit, and now she glowed with dark eye shadow, blue lipstick, and gold glitter across her cheeks, she looked like a fairy brought to life. Since she was set to hit the stage, she was covered up in a light green robe that will soon be gone, revealing her amazing curves. It was tied off at the waist hiding her from me, and my inner whore didn't like that. She blushed from head to toe when she caught my gaze and caught the thoughts of what I wanted to do to her, the extra color just adding to her allure. I chuckled, she can dance for all these people but one look from me has her blushing. Being bonded was like being next to a magnet at all times, the urge to be together was downright impossible to ignore.

As such, forgetting the men around me, I stood up slowly, maintaining eye contact with her, and stepped around the booth. When I reached her, I pulled her off to the side, and started roaming my hands under her robe, my actions hidden by the dark room, and gripped her perfectly round hips. I grabbed her ass, sat her on a small table to the right of the booth, and stepped between her legs. Her outfit, just from what I felt, was going to blow everyone away. But right this second, she was mine. Period. My full focus was on her and as the room faded away, I pressed my lips against her neck and licked a trail to the front of the robe. She moaned softly and closed her eyes; I hummed against her neck. God, I loved her little sounds. I kissed her lips softly then lost myself as we deepened the kiss, pulling a deep moan from both of us. I slid my fingers into her panties and played with her clit softly. She moaned loudly but it was captured by my mouth. I rubbed her clit in small circles with my thumb, inserting two fingers inside of her and after a few moments, she came apart and I caught her screams as I continued to kiss her. As she came down, we noticed purple streaks fly across the table toward the men, luckily they were too distracted, talking to each other to notice. We heard the sound to signal the next dancer, and I drew my hand out of her now-soaking panties, used my clean hand to grip her hair, and whispered, "Make sure that show is just for me," as I slowly licked my fingers clean.

She walked away in a little bit of a daze and as she cleared her head, she strutted up to the stage.

Thanks for the extra incentive, baby, she whispered in my head.

As I turned to sit, I licked my fingers again, savoring her taste, moisture dripping to my panties. I had to brush against Etienne on my way back to the center of the table and another shot of electricity shot up my core. Was it even possible to feel a connection with so many at once?

I ignored his stare and lit my shots before she started. I always needed liquor to stop myself from beating the shit out of anyone looking at her but we have a purpose, a plan, and we will make sure it stays that way.

I noticed Etienne, Dimitri, Dante and Luca's heated stares as I sat down. I also noticed them adjusting themselves, swallowing to clear their throat. I smirked. Their reactions gave me shivers down my spine. We haven't been particularly interested in men, but these four, Jesus they are just sexy as fuck. I can even get past the grumpy vampire. I lit my ten rainbow shots, and Dante whispered in my ear, "That, princess, was fucking sexy." I raised my eyebrow. "I'm no princess," I retorted. I slammed one shot after the next and in less than thirty seconds, they were gone. The men took turns looking awed, shocked, or in Dante's case, enamored.

"I think I met my soulmate." He stared at me with fake adoration.

I chuckled.

"I love to hear you laugh," Luca said. I was shocked, shit, he even looked shocked while the rest of the group looked taken aback.

He cleared his throat to save his face. "You know, princess," he started. I narrowed my eyes at that. "You never did try to tell me what my power was, care to guess?"

You can tell the rest of the table zoomed in to listen. "Easy, you're a tracker. The way you hold yourself, the way you flare your nose and seemingly pick up scents of everyone around you." I paused. "Which by the way, you're welcome. Pixie smells like candy. Anyways, you're the one that can detect paranormals." I shrugged. "You're also an elemental as you have scars on your hands that indicate that you were learning about your fire. That's pretty rare, an elemental and a tracker combination." I let out a low whistle.

Everyone looks impressed instead of confused this time, I guess they don't doubt me anymore. I didn't miss the fact that Dimitri didn't ask me to name his power, but it didn't mean I didn't already pick up on it.

Luca leaned down to whisper in my ear, "There is something strange about you, little one, and I'm going to figure it out. In fact, let's make it a game. One I plan to win." He took a nip and lick of my ear lobe. I had to bite back a moan, as the electricity seemed to be closing in on us.

I looked dead at him but before I could respond, the stage darkened and "Wetter" by Twista, started to play. Pixie was in the middle of the stage and it was impossible for anyone else to look elsewhere. She slid off her robe and threw it into my booth. I squirmed in my seat and the men chuckled. Luca took a deep breath, and gave me a heated glance. He can scent my arousal, well, that's going to make shit harder for him. Focusing back on Pixie, she wore a green and blue shimmery set that complimented her eyes. She grabbed the pole behind her and slowly slid into a split. Her curves were out of this world, something women get surgery to achieve. She pulled herself up, turned around and bent over, showing her covered pussy in her shimmery boy shorts but the wet spot I put there was noticeable. I groaned softly at my claim. The men around me chuckled. She reached up and took herself to the top of the pole, and hung upside down and did a little spin while opening her legs and still hanging on by her hands. She made it look effortless.

Dimitri chose that moment to break my trance. "How can you watch your bonded dance for other people?" He sounded upset, confused, and turned on. Interesting.

"I wouldn't stop her from doing something she likes. It's a bond, not bondage, although we like that too." The men chuckled lightly. "Besides, we took the same classes. She does it for fun, and I do it for fitness. Maybe one day we will let you watch us." I gave a little wink and their eyes widened, picking up the double meaning. God, my inner whore was on fire today.

I focused my eyes back to the stage right as she stopped, dropped, and then gripped the pole with her thighs, her head barely an inch off the ground, and everyone around gasped. She looked at me and winked. I knew the signal, everyone would be thoroughly engrossed. I started to open up my mental walls to everyone but these four fuckers next to me, leaving them for last, as their walls would be better built. I couldn't have them knowing about me... yet.

We had a goal, we needed to find out when the Shadow fuckers were going to have their next recruitment so that Pixie and I can join their ranks. After years of searching for information about my parents' murders, we were at an impasse. As good as I am, I cannot hack into what doesn't exist if it isn't computerized. We were hoping to get close enough to find whatever paper copies they may have filed away. It wouldn't be easy, and only an idiot would be overconfident enough to leave such incriminating evidence, but I have a strong feeling that the Council feels quite all powerful. We would get into their ranks, didn't matter if it was all men, we are the best, we just needed an in. I had a feeling these fuckers next to me wouldn't answer questions. I knew what drove them here tonight was that they couldn't get a read on me, and they never would. However, now I figured we were going to be drawn to each other, no matter what. This fucking zing was annoying, and while Pixie and I would try to ignore as much as possible, the power of a potential bonding made shit like a fucking sit-com. This is Darnika, damnit, not fucking One Tree Hill.

As I opened my mind to the whispers in the minds of those around us, I started to read the room. I ignored the lust, and the drunken spouses cheating, and tried to pick up a hint of anything related to the Shadows. After several moments, I picked up nothing useful and just felt icky. Ugh. I mentally projected my emotions to Pixie, and she got the signal to continue with her charade.

Pixie continued the spin as the song ended, and nodded imperceptibly. She signaled the DJ for another song. The lights changed as the pole was pulled up into the ceiling, and despite her stopping, the crowd remained transfixed. Someone brought a heavy steel chair onto the stage and made sure it was secured in the chair holders, to prevent the chair from tipping over as the heady beat of "Red Light Special" by TLC started to thump from the surrounding sound system. Pixie stepped off the stage, with a light sheen of sweat on her skin, and grabbed my hand. As I stepped around the two men on my side, I heard one of them whisper "Oh fuck" but I was too stuck on Pixie, walking me onto the stage, to really give a fuck. The lights turned red and centered on the chair as she sat me down and straddled as the first verse started. She grabbed my hair in her fist and brought my head down to her ample chest. Then she tossed my head back, kicked one leg over and bent over in front of me. She walked over to stand in front of me, her back to my front and slowly brought her ass onto my lap while grabbing my hands and using them to spread her. She brought my hand close to her pussy and the crowd groaned collectively as I drew my finger on the outside of her panties and brought my fingers to my mouth and sucked on her dripping juices, until my fingers were clean. I made a real show of it too while she moved off my lap and dropped to the floor into a split. I took that opportunity to look at the men in my booth directly in front of us. The heat in their gazes and their barely restrained postures told me it was time to start digging.

Seemingly distracted by Pixie, now on her knees in front of me, licking me between my legs through my jean shorts, I moaned while reaching out with my mental feelers and went into the minds of the four men in front of me. Without a doubt, I am the strongest person in the room, hell, in our world as far as I knew, but I needed to make sure they didn't know I was in their heads. I sent out my mental feelers in their direction, pictured smoky tendrils looking for any openings and slowly penetrating the mind. Even though they were completely transfixed by our little show, I still had to put in some more effort to get through their defenses undetected. Going beyond the lust, I was able to pick up that they were on the search of a vigilante working in the castes going by Exousia. That would be me, which means they knew my alter ego by name. I found what I was looking for in Dante's head, the next Shadow Recruitment was in two months and it was invitation only, those who wanted to compete would have the chance only if brought in by Shadow. Cool, so I had to figure out how to get these guys to invite me and Pixie. That should be easy enough.

Got the information. I sent to Pixie.

She looked at me, and ended the song with a smirk on her lips and my nipples in her hands. I had to stop myself from laughing; as I was digging in their heads, this bitch rolled up my top and took my tits out of my bra, at least she kept them covered. The stage darkened and she stepped off the stage to the back to get dressed and I went back to our, I *mean my* booth.

But when I arrived, LEDD had disappeared.

5

"I declare to you that woman must not depend upon the protection of man, but must be taught to protect herself, and there I take my stand."
—Susan B. Anthony
"Take my stand. I like that, but can I add "and give my first punch" to that?"- Charlie

Luca

WE DIDN'T REALIZE she would be here tonight until we saw her bike fly by us on the road. It's the first time we have seen her since last week. But I have a feeling that unless she wanted to be found, she wouldn't be. We walked into the club and noticed her immediately. Shit, she was hard to miss even with the lights low to protect identities. The light banter at her booth just allowed me to study her features a bit more. Dimitri, for all his bluster and stand-offish attitude, couldn't stop talking about her this entire week, and I was ready to throat-punch him. Seeing her tonight will be a blessing and a curse for us.

When we sat down, we saw a riveting woman walk toward us, and when Ellie introduced her as her bonded, I felt deflated. I don't think we imagined the sparks but stranger things have happened. But when she went to introduce herself to us, electricity sparked then too, before she snatched her hands back. I looked at her curiously. She was beautiful, her hair tossed in a just fucked type of look. She was a little lighter in coloring compared to Ellie, but had the same curves. What was most striking about her was her eyes, two different colors but not only that, they were filled with a brightness, she must be the more easy going of the two but something told me she would be more fiery when provoked, because you wouldn't see her coming. When the electricity between us hit, I groaned inwardly...things just became a lot harder.

Etienne

ELLIE'S ABILITY TO pick up on my powers put me on edge. There was something more about her but I couldn't put my finger on it. I continued to observe her, feeling like if I stared hard enough I would be able to figure out what made her tick. She was hiding something, I was sure of it, but I just couldn't figure it out. Despite her comments about my staring, I just couldn't stop. It wasn't in my nature, it was my job. I picked up on body language and scents of lies, but no matter what, I couldn't figure her out. It was frustrating.

I was disrupted from my thoughts as Pixie came back to the table to give us new beers. She was captivating in her green robe and some glittery shit on her face. The club was dark, our booth was no exception but from what I could see, she was magnificent. I found myself excited to see her dance. Not much interests me these days, and I'm not sure I liked the feeling.

I noticed Ellie coming around the booth and what she was wearing barely registered. It was like it was painted on her. How do these two women possibly throw me off and captivate me at the same time? All thoughts ceased as Ellie picked up Pixie and set her on the edge of the table to devour her mouth, making her claim clear. The small moans from their kissing went straight to my dick, and I don't think I had ever been harder.

Dante

FUCK, Ellie slipped her hands into Pixie's panties and was working her over in the dark. We couldn't see much but from my position, I knew Ellie's hand was gone, and Pixie was moaning a lot harder into her mouth. All I wanted to do was take her place, and put my face between her thighs to taste her. When she came, Ellie caught her screams and helped her off the table to the side. She then whispered in her ear and made a show of licking her fingers clean. Now, I just wanted Ellie's fucking pouty lips on my dick.

Ellie came back around and started to light her shots and I just couldn't help myself, I had to lean in to catch the scent of arousal around her.

"That, princess, was fucking sexy," I said hoarsely. She raised an eyebrow and replied, "I am not a princess." Then took all ten shots back to back. *Fuck me sideways.*

"I think I met my soulmate," I said with a smile. I wasn't kidding though. We have noticed the bonding sparks between us and the four of us have been putting off the conversation. I'm just not sure how much longer we were going to be able to do that. I didn't want to wait. People in the Magick Community married for power, for connections, and often times, they never truly find their bonded. My parents were like that. Hell, all of our parents were like that. Luca's parents, even more so. But I didn't want that. I wanted love, to be wanted, and to be trusted beyond the trust I have with my brothers. I yearned for it. We will have to talk about this soon, because we cannot deny it any longer. I won't let them.

I heard Luca whisper in Ellie's ear right before Pixie started dancing. "There is something strange about you, little one, and I'm going to figure it out. In fact, let's make it a game. One I plan to win." I looked at him but he wouldn't meet my gaze. What the fuck was that about.

Dimitri

I HAD no idea how she could sit there and watch Pixie dance, and I said as much. I understood your bonded wasn't your property per se, but I just don't think I could ever let mine dance for a room, full of horny high class society fuckers. As I looked at Pixie dance, I was completely taken with her, it was hard not to be. However, when she took Ellie to the stage for a lap dance, it was over for me. The control I had over my anger was quickly fading. I could not bear to see either of them in front of this crowd. I had to leave before the dance was done, before I dragged them off the stage and hid them from everyone's gaze. I was done. I got up quickly and my brothers followed behind me, the darkness hiding our exit.

Luca

As we stepped outside following Dimitri, he held up a finger and we headed to the parking lot in the back of the club.

"I couldn't take it anymore, I could not see them dance for those sons of bitches," Dimitri growled.

He was calm to a certain point but he always had a current of anger flowing though him, it's what made him the most lethal in our group.

"Yeah, I see what you mean, but I'm not sure why it bothers you that much, not like they are ours," I reply, at least not yet, but I keep that to myself.

"Cut the bullshit, you all saw the sparks happen more than once. We could have pretended the first time was a fluke but it's been happening all night. They are meant to be ours. I'm not even sure how it works. I have never seen a bonded pair bond to someone else, but I don't give a flying fuck. Luca, you studied the same shit we studied, you know what purple sparks mean. This is far from normal, and we just can't walk away from that," Dante said as he paced back and forth, running his hands through his hair.

"The purple streaks were considered a myth, "Etienne snapped. "Something is up with those two. Something more," he continued, waving his hands in the air. "We have a mission to complete and then recruitment for the incoming Shadows. We don't have time to sit around and figure this shit out."

As Etienne spoke, we listened. He rarely ever lost control and he looked very put off. I know he doesn't like unsolved mysteries and these women were exactly that, not to mention the stress and pressure from the Council to find the fucking vigilante. This entire week, we kept getting the same run around, the castes wouldn't help, they protected this person, hell, they revered them. All the cameras pulled were clean, no proof. It's like the vigilante was a ghost. There was no trail, no slip up.

"Okay, so what do you suggest? You're saying there is something more about them, in what way?" I said, genuinely intrigued.

"Well, for one"—he started to tick the numbers on his fingers—"in the bars, she is loved, but she's a well-known fighter too. Two, people warn to avoid getting on her bad side. That alone makes me wonder how she gained those skills. No one gains that reputation through rumors alone, no, she had to have been seen by quite a few people for that. Three, remember that her aim and skill with the darts was incredible, we have never seen anything like that before. Not to mention, Luca, you still can't pick up on her powers, and I'll bet you couldn't pick up on Pixie's either as they are bonded," he finished.

"So what? We draw them out? Fight them to gauge their skill? Dude, this isn't a fucking movie where we can hurt them. Dammit guys, they are meant to be ours now. We are going to beat the shit out of them to test their powers? Are you kidding me?" Dante yelled in frustration.

"I see the merit in the plan, we also don't have to do much, just go in at twenty percent and see what they can do. I agree that something is a little off. Hell, as well-known as Ellie is, she may even have information we can use to find this vigilante, and I have a feeling she just won't talk to us openly. We go in soft just to test them out and use what we know as leverage?" I asked. Something about that doesn't sit right with me, I also have a feeling Ellie seems the type to say fuck leverage and put sugar in our gas tank as a giant fuck you.

Dante laughed. "You clearly haven't been talking to or observing the same woman. Ellie wouldn't just think of it as leverage, she would feel betrayed. Then, where will we be?"

"It is the only plan we have, logically speaking, we do not have time to stay here forever and get information," Dimitri jumped in.

"So, three out of four. Majority rules, we wait back here until they leave to go home." I gestured to her bike. "They will definitely come this way, so let's wait," I said.

We leaned back into the Shadows to wait.

Charlie

INWARDLY, I growled in frustration. Outwardly, I sat back in my booth, sipped on a few beers and waited for my bonded to come off shift. A few of the other men tried to come into my personal space, I guess they thought that because LEDD was able to, they would be too. After a few twisted arms and a couple broken fingers, a few crazy bitch comments that ended in a broken jaw, or two, okay five, but that is no way to talk to a fucking lady, they got the general idea. After around 3 am, Pixie was done closing up the bar, and we walked into the cool air to go home.

I stretched and was looking forward to going home. We owned a beautiful penthouse in a new high rise with high security and well trained guards. I would know, I trained them and they were loyal to a fault. Truth is I gained a lot of friends over the past few years from hanging around the bars. Some people from the lower magick castes came to me for training and a job on my team to help their families. Knowing from always patrolling and helping the community as Exousia, that life wasn't as easy for others as it was for me growing up in a loving home, albeit only for thirteen years, I never said no.

How did I afford the penthouse, the building, and these salaries? Simple. My powers not only grew in strength, but my mind did too. I was not kidding when I said I was smart as fuck. I may had been only thirteen when my parents died, but I wasn't fucking stupid. Two days after my parents didn't return, I knew they were dead. I just knew it. The Elimentis family always had a place on the Council of Magicks from inception, and we had amassed quite an estate over the years. I was not going to let their money be taken by the greedy mother-fucking Council. So, I made sure I emptied out all our accounts. I had logged into our accounts and trusts, emptied out the funds.

My only problem was I was hidden away so I had to make it seem as if the money was being put into a trust of a child who they had been considering fostering but weren't able to. My parents were always very generous and altruistic so it wouldn't raise any eyebrows. They instilled those same values in me. The trust was going to be available to that person at 18. AKA Me, a new foster that was suddenly in the system and inherited about 490 billion dollars. I had taken that other 10 billion and put it in an untraceable account. No one could hack my encryptions or security, my money was safe and so was my parents' legacy. It was a tall order, but they didn't call people child geniuses for nothing.

I took that money and when I came of age, I invested it in various different companies and products. So my net worth, on the down low? Well, it's obscene. Kinda like me. It wasn't that I valued the money, no, more like I considered it as a way to honor my parents. They would be proud that I was using my powers and money to protect people, help others with their businesses, and be an all-around good person. Yeah, I killed shit, but I killed bad shit; yeah, I also hurt shit but they fucking deserved it first. I mentally stuck out my tongue.

I took a deep breath of the air and stiffened. Something felt off. I opened my link to Pixie, leaned down to pretend to whisper in her ear and she immediately threw me a thought, *Yeah, I feel it too. I knew something was strange when you said the Shadows left so quickly. You think they were able to pick up your mental probe?* She pretended to whisper back to me, while talking mentally, and I threw my head back and laughed. I was a pretty good actress.

They, in no way, picked up my abilities. More like they were freaked out that I was able to get a read on them so quickly, and took off. I'm actually going to go ahead and say that they are here. Luca is a tracker, he can find and throw off scents. Let's just keep walking toward the bike but I have a feeling they will come in hard and strong and expect us to be weak enough to beat but strong enough to fight back.

I hugged Pixie close to me and nuzzled her neck. We approached the bike and I stepped toward the back and she toward the front. I had my bike custom made to be able to have her sit nestled into me versus exposing her back and having to hold on. Just didn't sit well with me.

They are definitely close, Pix I can feel the displacement in the air. I am going to keep the link open just like we like it.

Pixie smiled at me and I grinned back. One of the benefits of training together for so many years and being connected by mind, which doesn't happen often in our world, was the ability to fight in tandem and cohesively beat the shit out of people by taking them out together.

I sent an undetectable extra shield to my motorcycle lover. He couldn't get hurt after all, I mean c'mon, Shadows lurking and Beast damage? No, thanks.

LEDD approached us from the shadows. *What the fuck was up with the whole melting in and out of darkness thing.* It was creepy.

"You know, boys, I thought we were getting some-where tonight. I really thought we were going to be besties and paint each other's nails and shit." I shook my head sadly. Dimitri took that chance to use his super speed to pull me away, thinking to distract me. Using a counter attack I learned years ago, I used his own momentum against him, quickly threw an elbow, grabbed his shoulder and flipped him over, pushing a little of my strength in the flip to make sure he needed extra time to recover. I suspected he had speed when playing darts, he gave up his advantage too early.

As he flipped, Luca was throwing a combination of kicks and punches at me that had me grinning from excitement at the practice, he was good but I was better. I saw him drop low for a punch, I turned as I knocked his fist to the side and countered with a swift kick to his low exposed neck. As he shook that off, Dimitri had approached my back, grabbed my hair, the fucking pussy, tugged my head back and tried to sweep my legs out from under me. I went with the momentum of the pull, turned and hooked my arm over his arm to disengage his hold and punched him twice in the face until his nose bled.

"Dimitri, really, hair pulling?! I was even going to save the black nail polish for you! Fucking ungrateful vampires. Shit! Shadows must be getting low on quality!" I quipped as I went on the defensive stance as both Luca and Dimitri growled. I felt Pixie at my back throwing a few hits to either Etienne or Dante, or shit both, knowing Pixie.

Luca narrowed his eyes. "Little one, what are you?" he said in a sing-song low voice. I turned my head. "Is that some kinda nursery rhyme? Sounds kinda hot coming from you, who knows maybe I'll call you papi in the bedroom after all, if you play your cards right...although this plan was not a good start."

Pixie laughed while she fought, and quipped, "We are a package deal, sweetheart, we will both be screaming their names. That is if they are better in bed than they are at fighting."

We laughed, getting the boys worked up. I heard Pixie take a few hits to her face and side, but we kept laughing.

The men stepped back watching us warily as we all ignored our magicks reaching toward each other and tried to stay focused. We needed to up the stake and show them something that would make them want us on their ranks, we needed those damn invites. Women rarely, if ever, get invites and last I heard there hasn't been any female invites in a few years. I considered for a second, while deflecting attacks.

Pixie, make Etienne and Dante start twerking on each other. Mind manipulation for the win, and I'm going to knock these two out with speed and then use water and create a little water fortress to keep them in place.

I felt Pixie use her powers in response instead of replying. Before Dimitri and Luca could react, I ran forward with a burst of speed but still had to dodge a kick to the head from Dimitri. Then, I caught a kick to the pussy as he scissor kicked. Fuck, that hurt! Angry now, I turned around to face him and before he could react, I gave him a few well-placed punches to his ribs and heard a satisfying crack. I felt heat building behind me and I used that moment that Luca thought I was distracted to mentally tell Pixie to step away as I pulled deep and used a shit ton of water elemental magick to wrap around Luca, Dimitri, Dante, and Etienne, who were looking pissed as they tried to stop from dancing with each other. I bit back a laugh as I continued and created a little water tornado that settled into a water fortress. A water palace? A water cornucopia spinning thingy like in Hunger Games without the drowning! Anyways, fuck it, we won.

I looked over at Pixie and noticed a small cut above her eye but overall she was in good shape. If I couldn't heal, I'm sure she would be bruised and hurting for several days though, as I saw a few bruises already forming. I'm sure I have a few too, but my pussy hurt so I don't care about the other stuff. As they bickered inside the fortress, I healed Princess Peach. I cannot ride with damage, can I? Pshhh.

Pixie and I approached the bike, and prepared to mount it. Dante spoke up, my sweet sex on a stick sounded a little angry.

"What was that, Dante?" I asked.

"Are you really going to leave us in here?" he asked again, his accent getting heavier the angrier he became. The other three were too busy staring daggers at us and it was quite entertaining to see the big bad Shadows brought down a fucking peg. There is a reason why people become well versed in as much as possible, and it looks like the trainers at the Academy were too blind to see that, content in their little world to break the mold. Self-inflicted limitations stand in your way; I don't like things in my way, I like progression.

I shrugged. "Yup, you will figure it out."

I brought Pixie in for a deep victory kiss before getting on my Beast.

"When you boys figure it out, feel free to come find us, we will leave your names at the door. Bye, boys!"

Pixie quickly rattled off our address and we got comfortable on my baby, turning up the music so "Under the Sea" from the Little Mermaid played loudly. The guys groaned, and Pixie and I laughed all the way home.

How long do you think it will be until they get out? Pixie asked. I laughed. *Forty minutes top, and another hour until they get to the house. It felt good to knock them down a few pegs.*

I say thirty minutes and they will be at the apartment within an hour. I have a feeling they are going to be pissed.

I also sent a text to the receptionist to put some clothes that I think will fit them in the spare rooms. They are going to want to change, Pixie said.

Where is Usher when you need him? Because Pix, you got it bad.

She laughed. *Maybe I'm just a nice person.*

Luca

"WELL, THAT WENT WELL," I said as I looked around the damn water walls, keeping us in here.

Dante took a deep breath and just glared at the rest of us while pacing.

"I knew something was up with them, but fuck I did not realize they would fight that way. They kicked our asses, when the fuck was the last time that happened?" I said as I shook my head. I lost count but it seems that Ellie has a lot more powers than normal. Is that even possible?

"Etienne, did that satisfy your curiosity? Because I'll be honest, that was mind-blowing. I didn't think getting my ass kicked would ever turn me on, but here we are, the enforcer has a hard-on. We are going to their place, right?" Dimitri said excitedly. I've never seen him excited, angry maybe, sullen definitely, but excited? I admit that actually scared me more than him being angry. It was weird.

Etienne rubbed his hands over his face. "I was right for sure, but now I'm not sure if that satisfied my curiosity or piqued it more. I admit they are something else, I don't even think they used their powers to their full extent either. That is impressive. They were barely winded. So yeah, I say we go over."

71

Dante snarled, "How about we try to get the fuck out of here first? How the fuck do you get out of a water fortress?"

I laughed. "I will evaporate the water but it may take a while."

❧ 6 ❧

An idea that is not dangerous is unworthy of being called an idea at all."- **Oscar Wilde**
"So you agree. Phew, I'm glad, because shit is about to get real."- **Charlie**

C harlie

WE PULLED into the underground garage and smiled at the security guard. They were so used to seeing us come in and out at odd hours, and it always felt good to see a familiar face. Most of the staff live in the building with their families, or in our other sky-rise at the far side of the city. I figured if there is space, why make them go through the trouble of looking for apartments somewhere else. They were loyal and they were family.

"Hey Johnny, we are expecting four surly Shadows

showing up soon in a black truck. Dante, Dimitri, Etienne, and Luca." I laughed.

Johnny raised an eyebrow. "I assume by four, they are part of an Elite squad? Oh man, I would love to knock them down a peg or two."

"That's what I said!" I exclaimed. He chuckled and returned to his post while we went up the private elevator to our penthouse. It was so cool, if we were inside the apartment and someone was coming up, and we wanted the door to be opened for the guests, we would give a voice command. It helped that the elevator door to our apartment served as a bulletproof, two-way mirror, we could see who was there but they couldn't see us. Even cooler, it was a smart house, it sensed emotions and picked up on certain trigger words. So of course, I programmed it to play different songs as it picked up on those emotions and words. It was hilarious. Sigh, I loved magick and all, but technology was just so fucking cool. If only the Council would embrace it all.

The doors opened and we were greeted by the system as "We Are The Champions" by Queen started to play. We laughed and went to our shared room and stripped. While we each had our own room, we never used them really other than to store our extra clothes and things. I sighed as I thought about the whole shared room, it needs a better name. Team Room? Group Room? Love Room? Mighty Room? Lots of Licks R Us? We couldn't figure it out.

"What's wrong, thinking about naming the room again?" Pixie laughed as we padded toward our bathroom, comfortable in our nudity. We rarely ever wore more than underwear. Anyone who says they like wearing clothes in their home are filthy fucking liars. There is nothing like free boobs and no underwear.

"The room needs a better name, Pix! We should really make a list and take a tally."

We stepped into our own little oasis. I loved this bathroom, it had warmed floors, a jacuzzi fit for at least ten on one side of the room, and a huge fifteen-by-six glass shower with the rainfall shower effect and side jets. It felt like swimming standing up, and you could adjust the steam and the power of the jets on the side. On one side of the shower, there were warmed benches with cushions under, where we would sit if we just wanted to steam and turn on the aroma therapy, or kneel and make the shower a little more... interesting. The entire room was painted in light greens and purples, and soft music played in the background when you stepped into the shower, from the speakers that we had installed, all waterproof. With triple sinks and two water closets, it was just heaven. Best room in the house, easily.

I sighed deeply in satisfaction as we set up the aromatherapy and turned on the rain fall option and started to lather our hair. The system picked up on my needs and started playing 90s love songs. As Babyface crooned over the radio, we washed and scrubbed the day's dirt off of us. I sent healing magick to Pixie and she moaned in appreciation as all the bumps, bruises and injuries faded away. I made sure I did a close inspection of my Princess Peach when I got through with washing everything. It sucked getting kicked there, but fuck if it doesn't sting extra when you have your clit pierced. Pixie and I got ours done the same day, our nipples too and triple tongue rings. Healing was a bitch, unless you had magick, a little healing and we were good to go. We vetoed the bellies so they couldn't be used against us in a fight. Only difference in our body modifications was that while my back was a huge tink tattoo, hers was a huge female avenging angel with barely discernible features and huge purple wings that wrapped around to her sides and looked extended when she held her arms out. It was some good work overall, our friends were quite talented.

We finished up, brushed our teeth and combed out our hair. We figured the men would be here soon, there was no way they wouldn't let their curiosities win out. So we threw on some sweats, tight tank tops and fuzzy socks, because who doesn't love fuzzy fucking socks, and sat down in the living room. Another favorite of mine as the couch could also be warmed.

The sun was peeking up, but I felt wired. I said as much to Pixie.

"It's like my magick is excited even to see them again, is that weird?" I asked Pixie. She moved over to sit closer to me and I put my arms around her and lightly rubbed her pierced nipples through her tank top. She didn't need a bra or magick; her breasts sat up naturally and they were fucking amazing.

She squirmed and I could tell she bit back a moan as she replied, "No, I feel the same way. It's only ever been us two, isn't it strange for our magick to like four others too? Not that I care much but what are the chances, not to mention the complication of trying to infiltrate and essentially go against the Council they are sworn to protect."

We sat and mused. Magick chooses, we can ignore it but it's very hard. I can stop the connection for us, I'm strong enough. Like a mental block of sorts, but I could tell from the way our magicks entwined and flared up that it didn't want that. It wanted the boys.

I sighed. "A complication for sure but in all seriousness, it would be an instant in. It's also slightly dangerous, which makes it more fun." I considered Pixie and I being caught slim, we were effective and quick but a party of six? Not as likely to get a seat at the restaurant as quick, if you know what I mean.

After a few moments, Pixie drawled out, lightening the mood, "You knowwww, we read a lot of those reverse harem books and there is ever only one girl with multiple guys. Imagine switching it up a bit. That would be fucking awesome. Even better since it's us." She laughed.

"Damn good point. No internal bleeding either when you have someone to share the pounding. My peach will not be a pulp, damnit," I said, as the system started to play "Peaches and Cream" by 112, and we laughed uproariously.

I stood up to grab us a glass of wine when the elevator suddenly dinged and asked us if we wanted to let in our expected guests, approved by the security guard, Johnny. Did I ever tell you how much I love technology? Fucking amazing.

"Elevator, allow entrance," Pixie said, sitting up on the couch. The men trudged in looking a little rough but pretty good, all things considering.

The music changed to "All My Life" by KC and JoJo.

Pixie and I stared at each other. *Traitorous little smart house.*

Dante looked around, confused. "Did the music change when we walked in?"

I cleared my throat. "Yeah, um. It's a smart house. It picks up certain emotions and pheromones and changes according to what it senses," I finished off quickly.

Dante smiled widely. "And it chose All My Life?

Very interesting." God, he had a beautiful smile, some-where angels were crying.

Luca looked at us, rolled his eyes, and got straight to the point. "How did you do that, it takes some serious skills to best us and you guys look like daises." Until he made eye contact and actually took us in, giving us a slow perusal. His eyes heated with desire.

I smiled slowly and winked at him. I turned around and took in the other men, looking delicious, I might add.

"Hello gentlemen, welcome. Would you like anything to eat? Drink? Maybe a shower? I have a change of clothes here for each of you if you need it," I said cheerfully.

Dimitri groaned. "Why are you so cheerful when the sun is coming up?"

"Oh yes, babe, we forgot, he is a vampire. He needs to sleep under the bed, hurry." Pixie cracked up in laughter.

Etienne and Dante stood a little too far apart from each other, I looked at them and I tried to hold it back. Scouts honor. I really did. "Etienne, Dante, what about you two? Maybe some sausage?" I and Pixie howled at my own question, hard. The men immediately started muttering under their breath about mean women, and we both made our way into the kitchen. Then the grumbles from the men suddenly stopped. We knew why. The system started playing "I Wanna Sex You Up" by Color Me Bad. Pixie and I started laughing again.

Luca, ignoring the music playing, cleared his throat and started off again, "How did you two do that to us? We figured you were hiding something, shit, we figured you had some power but fuck, you fought with more skill and precision than most of the fighters I know. You two think when you fight, you have strategy." He walked to the kitchen and leaned up against the counter, his muscles flexing. "How the hell did you best us and get us stuck in a water dome—"

"Water fortress," I interrupted.

"What?" He looked confused as I interrupted his line of questioning.

"It wasn't a dome, it was a fortress, get your shapes right, they don't teach that at the Shadow Academy? Can't imagine they teach much really, if their Elite guard got taken out in less than ten minutes by two women!"

"Sexy women," Pixie added from beside me.

"Yes, sexy women." I nodded enthusiastically.

Luca looked between Pixie, bending over her ass, stretching the material, and me, a smirk on my face, and bit out, "I will take you up on your offer to shower, I think we all will. Where are the bathrooms?"

"There are seven Rooms. All rooms have an en-suite. The bigger bedroom can be ignored as well as the first two on the right, they are mine and Pixie's rooms, but you four can each grab one of the other rooms. There are a few different options for you to choose from when it's time to get dressed, the clothes are in the dressers," I said as I got food prepped for breakfast, from what Pixie was handing to me.

Dimitri stood up with a groan and a glare. "Why do you even have sets of men's clothes that would fit us, we aren't exactly, uh, average-sized?"

This time, Pixie licked her lips slowly, showing off her own piercings. "Ooohhh baby, we are counting on it," she teased and turned back to the stove.

"Right, well, umm, I gotta grab that shower," he stammered and they all pretty much ran out.

We chuckled.

Pixie and I whipped up pancakes, eggs, bacon, toast, and a fruit shake for each of the men.

As they walked in, they grumbled appreciatively and devoured their food.

After a few quiet moments, Etienne looked at us, confused. "Aren't you two going to eat?"

Fuck, that French accent is going to make my fucking clit piercing start to dance.

All four heads popped up and stared at the apex of my thighs. Pixie started laughing. I groaned.

"I said that out loud, didn't I?" I cleared my throat. "Right, anyways, we aren't eating because we already had our protein shake, and I'm not really hungry for food." I gave a heated look to Pixie, making her blush.

All the men quietly groaned.

Dante grumbled, "I'm going to need another cold shower."

I laughed, drawing Luca's stare.

He looked at us. "You never did answer. How did you have a bunch of clothes our size ready? Not that we aren't grateful," Luca asked.

"We texted ahead on the way home and had the receptionist bring clothes for some well-built, tall, gorgeous men, I forget the exact wording," Pixie said airily.

Dante laughed and shot us a wink. "She meant me, you guys were just lucky to reap the rewards of my good looks." I shook my head at him and smiled.

"Right, so you boys finish up and clean your dishes after. We are heading to our room." I took turns, looking at them dead in the eye. "The doors to our personal rooms and offices cannot be opened without a biometric scanner so don't even bother snooping. The gym door does open if you need to work out. The elevator will not open without my direct command and eye scan." I let them know. Their eyebrows shoot up.

I laughed and continued, "The rooms have the ability to be soundproof, so if you need them to be, just speak the command into the room. Certain trigger words will trip the system and cameras will start recording. So I highly suggest not doing or saying something stupid."

Dimitri spoke up this time, "Jesus, why in the world do you need such a sophisticated system? This is like a prison."

I scoffed. "Hardly. I just like to feel safe in my own home especially when inviting Elite Shadows into my home when I barely know you all. Just be grateful."

"So, why did you?" Luca asked softly, with a confused look on his face that I wanted to kiss away. I shook the idea away.

I want to kiss him too, its' disconcerting. Even more so because it doesn't necessarily feel wrong, they fit, Pixie spoke into my mind.

I will have to do more research but it is disconcerting, a magick harem with six people. You know I'm not a big fan of things I don't have control over.

"We control the narrative this way. But...that same narrative wants you a little closer to figure out why Pix and I feel drawn to you." I bit my lip in confusion, but quickly let it go. The men made eye contact with each other but remained silent.

"Anyways. Bed time. I would hurry up, boys, I haven't soundproofed our room, and we aren't tired...yet."

Collective growls echoed around the kitchen as "Invented Sex" by Trey Songz started to play.

"Ohh! Before we forget, we have been trying to name

our shared room. The Love Room? Banging Room? We cannot figure it out!" I exclaim, frustrated.

"Why do you have to name your room at all," asked Etienne.

As she tugs me into the room, Pixie answers for me, "It has a bed that is about three kings together, has two dancing poles and bondage toys, hanging from the ceiling. Perfect for groups...we just can't figure it out. Be a doll, would you? And come up with something...fitting." She winked and closed the door behind us as another chorus of groans went up. Torture at its finest.

7

*"You don't have to live a lie. Living a lie will mess you up.
It will send you into depression. It will warp your values."*
— ***Gilbert Baker***

*"Sometimes, it's better to embrace the unexpected than to
turn it away. It's made my life worth living."- **Pixie***

Charlie

WHEN THE DOOR to our room closed and locked, I turned
around, and slowly stalked toward Pixie who was already
sitting in the middle of the large bed. When we came
home, after all the bullshit, after all the stress, we recon-
nected in the best way we knew how. It went beyond
stimulating conversation or casual sex. We reaffirmed our
bond. We opened our links and became one. In a way, it

was our safety blanket. There was something powerful with being completely vulnerable with the person you love the most. Someone who was made for you, someone who has shown you that despite everything the world throws at you, you are never alone.

Her eyes were dilated and she bit her lip as I pushed her down and straddled her. I took my time taking off her tank top and kissing my way from her throat to the dip between her breasts. I ran my hands lightly over her body as I kissed, making her shudder and moan loudly. When I finally came to her breasts, they were pebbled and looked delicious. I palmed both of them, reaching over to give her a kiss, letting our tongue rings play.

Still fully dressed, I leaned up from our kiss, and tugged my tank top off and pressed myself against her. Grabbing her sweats and tugging them off as I reached the end of her perfectly toned abs, I looked down at her freshly waxed soft pussy, and the tattoo right at the top of her lips. *Alohamora*. We were Harry Potter lovers, and it seemed fitting to put that spell on our pussies at the time.

I kissed and then dragged my tongue up her slit, and then just like she enjoyed, I grabbed her legs and closed them over my head as I dived in and sucked at her clit. Her moans increased, and I backed off as she growled in frustration. I tugged off my pants as I looked at her spread on the bed and bent over to blow some air on her clit and used air manipulation to make her feel filled, as if I were fucking her. She arched off the bed.

"Fuck, Ellie, yes baby," she pants out.

Hearing my name, I grasped her hips roughly, pulled her hair and made her moan even louder, my name should always be on her lips.

I focused on her clit, licking her softly, alternating

between quick and slow flicks, keeping her on edge but not letting her cum.

She moved her hips in frustration and I growled against her pussy and bit her clit gently, making her jump.

You come when I say you come, I whispered in her head.

I flipped her over, smacking her ass as I bent her over and eat her from behind. I dragged my tongue across her pussy and started to tease her ass with my tongue. She whimpered and pushed her ass softly toward me. Groaning deeply, I give her ass another lick, then I reached over from my position behind her, pulled her hair and tugged her up to her elbows to give her what she wanted all along.

I positioned her directly on top of me, focusing my attention on her plump ass on my face as I swirled my tongue around her clit, letting my piercing tease her. She threw her head back and moaned as I sucked her clit between my lips and suckled. I looked up at her, in the throes of passion, and lust shot down my spine as I took in her perfect breasts, plump pussy, thick thighs, the small curve of her belly and the blush taking over her entire body.

When she threw her head back, her short hair tumbled down her back. Reaching up to cup her own breasts, she moaned my name in a thick Spanish accent as she started to shake. I reached up to grab her ass pushing her pussy firmly down onto my lips. I worked her into a frenzy. Her moans became longer, her accent more pronounced as she cursed and tried to pull away from my onslaught. Holding back a grin at the effect I have on her, I grabbed her thighs, wrapping them firmly around my face, working her clit over until she screamed my name and begged me to stop. I chuckled as I grabbed on more firmly to keep her in place as I continued to lap her up. She looked down at me, her face flush, her lips plump from biting them, and she reached for my head to try to get me to stop. I shot her a warning glare that had most people running and her eyes dilated even more as she instead grabbed my hair and rode my face harder. She screamed as she came, her juices pouring down my neck, and whimpered as I held her in place.

I licked every last drop, still fucking her slowly with my power, filling her as she whimpered. But I didn't stop, I quickened my pace and reached over to pinch her nipples, pushing her over the edge again and she tightened her thighs, keeping my head firmly in place while I tease her clit.

"Ellie, fuck baby, Ellie, por favor, ay Ellie," she screamed as she came again. You know you're done when your partner starts speaking another language.

I leaned back, making her sit up and as I took a look at her dazed face, I sit on her lap with my legs wrapped around her as I grab her neck and kiss her deeply. We moan as our shields drop and our magick sparks and lets off purple streaks into the air from our sweaty bodies.

I climbed off of her with one last kiss and tuck her into bed as I go wash my face, and take a quick shower to rinse the sweat off my body.

I REACHED into the closet and grabbed a random robe, threw it on, and went to get a bottle of water before I crawled into bed with Pixie.

As I stepped into the kitchen, I saw that the men had cleaned up their breakfast. As I leaned over to grab a bottle of water, I felt electricity shoot up my spine. I looked back and saw the men sitting on the couch instead of being in their rooms, eyes completely focused on me.

"Umm. Hey, don't you Shadow people sleep?" I joked.

Etienne said thickly, his accent more pronounced, "It was hard to sleep with all the...noise."

I laughed, really laughed. "Yeah, Pixie is a screamer. I warned you guys to head to your rooms and make them soundproof with the command. Why didn't you?"

They looked a little embarrassed as Etienne continued, "Well, we weren't tired yet and sat down in the living room instead, then we heard the screams, and when it got..." He cleared his throat. "When it got intense, we tried to go to our rooms and then purple sparks were shooting around," Etienne finished.

Wait, what? I cleared my throat as if it was a daily occurrence. "Ah, well, the first part is your fault for being creeps, as for the magick, I'm sorry, Pixie and I have always let off magick when our bonds fully open. I did not realize that I would affect you, I'm sorry," I said simply. It's like, the magick... is looking for something more. I didn't say the last part but it hung in the air. Heavily.

The men all looked at each other and I knew they knew more than they were letting on. I have cracked all council records on magick and bonding but there is nothing electronically based about it. I wonder if it is something that is hidden in their vast libraries. Yet another reason I need to get this invite.

"Well listen, I'm sorry, she is sleeping. I'm going to catch a couple hours of sleep. Meet us in the back gym area on the other side of the hall. At 4 pm." I paused trying to lighten the mood. "Unless you're scared after last

87

night." I smirked and laughed, as Dante started cursing in Spanish and Etienne in French. Luca and Dimitri just glowered.

I went into my room, grabbed my phone, sent out a quick text to our front desk guard, held Pixie, and passed out.

Dimitri

WE WATCHED Ellie walk away in a sheer robe, I don't even think she noticed what she put on. But it definitely caught our attention. Her nipple piercings on display and her curves so close enough to trace. Hearing Pixie scream her name made us all want to pull our teeth out in need. I don't think there are enough cold showers in the world to survive this attraction. I kill shit for a living and I couldn't murder this, it was stressful. We really can't deny that there is certainly a connection there. The magick keeps tugging us closer and closer. I don't want to fight it either, what Dante said was true, we needed to really take this gift and go with it. We don't want to be like our parents, married for connections, never finding our bonded. Fuck that.

"We need to figure out this fucking mission and lock them the fuck down," I declared.

A chorus of approvals went up. We walked to our rooms to take a nap but I don't even know how to fall asleep, knowing my future is sleeping a few rooms away.

8

"You're gonna be happy," said life, "but first I'll make you strong."- **Unknown**

"Our strength comes from how far we are willing to go, to make sure we accomplish everything we set our hearts out to do. Anything else is not laziness, it is weakness."- **Pixie**

Charlie

OUR INTERNAL CLOCK set for our daily workout routine dug Pixie and I out of bed. After we carried out our morning routine of cleaning up and dressing, we made our way to the kitchen to make our shakes. We made enough for all the men and who shortly after came out of the spare rooms and grabbed a cup, all grumbling their thanks.

Yeah, I hated waking up too. The only perky one in the morning was Pixie, and even she seemed subdued. I had shared with her about the boys being affected by our magick and she was just as confused as I was. I picked up on her trepidation before I closed our mental link, if she wanted to tell me, she would soon. I wouldn't intrude.

Stretching my hands over my head, I started walking toward the gym. I noticed all the clean uniforms on the couch, and weapons cleaned and sharpened. I had sent out a quick text last night to make sure it was handled for them. Figured being a little extra nice might be useful. Worst case, the ass kicking they are about to receive certainly will be. "Boys," I said. They were still stuck on stupid even though they finished their shakes, and didn't hear me. A ringing phone snapped them out of their stupor.

Luca picked up his phone and immediately took on an authoritative air. "Yes sir, we will question the witness, we will be there in fifteen minutes." He closed the phone and looked at us apologetically, "We have to go, apparently a witness has come forward about the vigilante, and we are being called in to question her."

"Awesome, good luck with that. I was actually trying to get your attention earlier to let you all know that I took the liberty of sending all your dirty shit to get washed and for your weapons to be cleaned. Everything is laid out for you on the couch."

As the men walked over to their uniforms and picked them up, they quickly went to get ready. Now, my mind was somewhere else. Instead of working out, I was going to do more research instead, I had certain alerts set up for certain keywords and I'm thinking I should expand those searches wider. I also needed to run my numbers system because if our magick was purposefully searching for one another and wanted to bond, I needed to calculate how that will affect our plans, short term and long term. Most magicks yearn to bond, it fulfills a deep need one never knew they truly had until that point. I didn't want to deny them that, shit, I don't want to deny myself or Pixie that either, but they are the enemy. *Aren't they?* I shook my head, I'll figure it out later.

They stepped out of the room looking ridiculously heartbreaking in all black, their imposing figures just knocking the air out of my lungs.

"It's pretty fucking nice that you guys have a tip on the vigilante, any idea who the informant even is?" asked Pixie, while I finished my shake.

"Something about a redhead from a bar, apparently the guy she was with was killed about a week ago," Luca replied.

Pixie turned her head to the side, confused. "So why wait a week to come forward?"

Etienne spoke up this time, "No idea but we intend to find out."

"Hmm, well, good luck, take our numbers. Let us know when you want to come back and we will re-add your name to the approved list," I said.

"Why don't just keep us on?" Dante asked, confused as if it would be fucking obvious.

"Um, because the only people allowed free range are me and Pixie. Period. Hey system? Program Pixie and Ellie into the phones of Dante, Luca, Etienne, and Dimitri please," I commanded.

"Numbers programmed, Madam Ellie," replied my system.

"How did you do that, our phones are encrypted," asked Etienne suspiciously.

"You are really going to have to learn to stop asking me how I do things. You'll never like the answer," I replied as I walked to the elevator and allowed them access to leave.

"Don't Leave" by BlackStreet started to play in the background, and I groaned.

"Bye, boys," Pixie and I said as the doors closed around their laughter.

We paused.

"Right, so research time?" Pixie asked.

"Yup!" I reply as I head into our security room, hidden behind an undetectable panel near the workout room. We stepped in, take the steps down a level and scanned our fingers as we walked into our oasis. This room is every spy's dream and it's where I do the majority of my work and research as I only go back to my parents estate once a year, on my birthday. I did convert the hidden section of the home into a panic room just in case I ever came under fire, and Pixie and I were in danger.

Before we get settled, Pixie picked up her phone and called our contact to inform them of a possible redheaded snitch that needed to disappear in five minutes and gave them the coordinates that the system picked up from the person talking to Luca. Yeah, Exousia is not to be fucked with and she won't be found unless she wants to be. Pixie waited and after everything looked completed, she cleaned the cameras. Five minutes. All it takes. I gave her a high-five and we settled in to really work.

We sat down at the computers and started to hack into the Council's records for information about the boys, their parents, and everything we could dig up about their histories and their connections within the Council. We ran this search on nearly every Shadow in the system but we needed a more in-depth search, we needed to get more information.

I searched again for information about my parents and those who replaced them but those were the only two names I could not locate in their entire system. I growled in frustration. What the fuck are these people hiding? We did, though, find more information about purple sparks by trying a different combination of the words purple, magicks, and sparks in all languages. Apparently this type of connection is considered mythical, which didn't make sense because Pixie and I had the same colors when we met. Apparently, regular connections are gold. That's all we found though, nothing about what the difference in colors actually meant.

Sigh, after a few hours, we had compiled information about all the potential Shadows that have already been recruited and given invitations for the Academy two months away. We learned their history and calculated possible weaknesses. Also interestingly, enough it turns out our four guys were actually four out of six instructors that will be teaching the students. The curriculum will involve, hand to hand combat, weapons training, defensive magick, offensive magick, tactical training, and apparently a course dedicated strictly for outdoor survival, which meant obstacle courses, let's be honest. These people aren't going to spend much time outdoors, surviving shit.

I smirked at Pixie. "This shit is going to be fucking cake. Now just to get this fucking invite."

❧ 9 ❧

"I never insult people, I only tell them what they are." -
Unknown
*"That would be an accurate representation of me, yes. It's
not my fault that everything they are is, indeed, insulting.
To humanity. To themselves. To us. To the French."* -
Etienne

L uca

As we took the elevator down to the parking lot, I slid
my well-practiced façade in place. I knew that in order to
deal with whatever shit was coming, I had to fake it until I
made it.

"That may not work that well this time around, boss,"
murmured Dante.

"What are you talking about," I snapped. We got to the lower floor and stepped out, heading to where the car was parked.

"I'm saying, your cool face of indifference doesn't mean shit. You are as affected by them as we all are." He rolled his eyes. I bit back a sigh and ignored him.

The garage attendant nodded his head, and smirked. "Those girls put you on your ass?"

"They definitely did something alright," I muttered.

"Those girls are the best thing that has ever happened to this Magick Community." He narrowed his eyes. "Although they can be quite intimidating to a lesser man." He chuckled at that, and Dimitri scowled. At my expression, he added, "No worries, no worries. Ellie and Pixie have every man within a 500-yard radius conflicted. At least you didn't leave in a body bag. It means they like you," he said jovially.

"Hmm, it was a pleasure meeting you again. We will see you soon." I nodded at him, walking toward our truck, not even bothering to grin as it would probably look more like a wolf ready to attack.

We piled into our respective seats and turned out of the lot, heading to the coordinates provided.

"I don't like leaving them. I demand we go back, tie them up, and make them love us," Dimitri growled.

"Dude, that was ridiculously illegal and kinky." Dante held his hand over his chest. "That's all my job. Don't tell us you're a changed man! Who else will torture, maim, and murder. We cannot have the same roles in this relationship."

"Let's joke around after we figure this out. My father hasn't stopped borderline harassing me since we arrived," I grunted out. My dad is such a prick. I'm not sure when he became that way but it was when I was younger. He suddenly came home one day with a new passion for uniting the Council families. Ranting and raving about allies and takeovers. I think he had officially lost it then. I just did what was expected of me, excelled in my studies and became Elite. Anything to keep him off my back.

Etienne scoffed. "Your father harasses everyone. That is not a surprise."

I gave a rueful smile. "You've been quiet, brother. Granted, it's expected, but this is more than usual. Something on your mind?" I asked, knowing what the answer would be, what the answer for all of us would be. Despite the mission, there were two people on our minds. Two women who made sparks fly, literally when we were around them.

"I'm considering the danger here," he started, looking pensive. "The sparks that fly when we are around. Can you imagine what would happen if the Council got wind that this was more than just a myth? But an actual possibility. They thirst for power and control, think of what they would gain if we were on their side. But more realistically, think of the threat they would perceive us as."

"You know your father will not stand for something he cannot control," Dimitri added.

I sighed as we drew closer to the Magickal Law Enforcement office.

"What do you suggest? I cannot deny us the chance of being truly bonded," I said plainly, pulling over, and turning to face the rest of them all.

"After you bond, normally, the visual aspect is no longer there. We can assume that the same thing will happen with us all. But..." Etienne paused. I know the sparks were a source of contention when bonding. With normal users it was an exciting time, boastful to show those sparks fly before the bonding. For us? It would be potentially lethal.

"But?" I prompted.

"That is assuming they want us. We know the urge to bond is difficult to deny, to ignore, and we may never get the chance again, but it's possible," he finished quietly, his accent thick with frustration or sadness, but I'm sure it was a combination of both. Etienne thrived on knowledge and control, without either, he was...lost. Shit, with this, I think we all were.

"Let's shelve this conversation, all this emotional shit is making me want to punch someone. Let's go and fucking do that." Dimitri jumped out of the car, and strode purposefully into the office, everyone parting as he walked in. We chuckled as we followed suit.

Two Hours Later

"What the fuck do we do now?" Dante growled, his rare but deadly, angry side peeking through as we got back into the truck. I blew out a breath, punching the steering wheel. I completely understood his frustration. We got to the MLE and waited for fifteen minutes only to be told that the witness was missing and then another hour to review all footage and even that looked to be scrubbed clear. Then another pointless forty-five minutes, listening to the excuses of the useless MLE. Honestly, I don't even understand why we go through the motions of having that pointless organization when the Council had us.

No, that was a lie, I knew they needed someone to appease the ever present weight of the Council in the city. I heard my father discussing it when I was younger. To him, the law enforcement was a way to show the people that they have a hand in their own protection, fostering a sense of community. If only they actually hired beyond the higher castes and that they weren't pretentious fucks. People complain about the Shadows, but at least we showed up in all castes, these fuckers wouldn't even do that.

"We call the Council, but knowing my father he will want us to report in person. So I say we skip the middleman and just go directly there," I responded. The men grumbled but otherwise stayed silent. They understood the dynamics. I sighed and rubbed a hand across my face and pulled off from the curb.

Soon the city turned into forest and we approached the capital city. The over exaggerated opulence always pissed me off. Especially when you took in the status of the lower castes and how they were being taken care of, or not taken care of, in this case. I parked the car and we stepped out. "Well, let's get ready for this shit show," I growled out.

"As long as I get to punch something I don't care," Dimitri grumbled.

Ignoring the other buildings, we strode straight to the Council building, ignoring everyone else. Here? It was dog eat dog, and we were on the top.

Dimitri

WE ARRIVED at the Capital a few days ago and after being chewed out by the Council, we were told to stay for some bullshit version of a debrief. I wanted to be debriefed alright, by Charlie and Pixie. These days have left me with a burning need to just say fuck you to this stupid ass farce of a Council and get to the women who are meant to be ours. It was blatantly obvious, the sparks were indication enough, but from the moment we left, they have weighed heavily on our minds. I, for one, intended to sweep them up into my arms and kiss them senseless. *Hopefully more.*

"Can we fucking go now?" I asked, striding into the room Luca was sleeping in. We were in our apartment but after we were fully debriefed last night, I was ready to fucking go.

"Yeah, let's grab a few of our things and head out," Luca responded sleepily.

Dante came to the room on my heels. "Dude, cover your fucking morning wood. Unless that meat stick is pointing us in the direction of the best asses I've ever seen, I'm not trying to stare at it."

"You stupid fucks wouldn't have to look at shit if you wouldn't barge into my damn room," Luca muttered. Still in bed.

"Or you can be like the French, and wear full suits to bed. In case we have to meet the Queen," Etienne tossed in as he walked by the room, fully dressed, on his way to the kitchen. I shook my head and laughed, idiot.

"I'll get packed, let's fucking go back to our women, assholes!"

Charlie

It took a week, a motherfucking week for the men to text us that they were coming over shortly. They were lucky we took the day off.

Fuckers, at least we spent the week being productive, I thought as we went to take showers after another grueling training session. As it was, we had increased our physical training to help with the frustration thrumming through our bodies at not being around the guys. Which was ridiculously annoying enough.

"Were you able to finally get in contact with James?" I asked Pixie, pulling a towel off the warming rack and drying off. Pixie had been trying to get in contact with James to let him know that she would be leaving the club and focusing more on working from home.

"Yeah, he said to come by and get a few drinks whenever we want and that he will keep his ear to the ground for any drama in the castes." She grinned, snatching the towel from me.

I rolled my eyes. "You two gossip more than the Golden Girls, I swear." I tossed over my shoulder, walking into the room and toward the closet to get dressed.

"Accurate." She walked in behind me, swatting my ass.

Laughing, I reached over to grab my phone to make sure the guys' names were on the list and threw on some blue jeans and a neon pink crop top, while Pixie threw on a stretch jean mini skirt and green crop top.

We took each other in.

"The good old distract and conquer routine?" Pixie laughed, walking to the kitchen to pull out a few pots and pans.

"You fucking know it," I grumbled, taking out the ingredients for a simple Latin dinner.

"Why do you think it took them a week? Intel says they found out and left the scene after a couple of hours," Pixie wondered out loud. We have been tossing back ideas all week but without hacking their phones and going full blown stalker on them, we just didn't know. It's bad enough we both felt really down this week. Yeah, we had each other but we were slightly aching. We tried to avoid talking about what the reason was, *tried* being the key word.

"You know," she started pointing the knife at me in between chopping peppers. "We are going to have to figure this purple ass connection out."

I sighed and avoided rubbing my eyes while I dealt with cleaning the chicken in lime and vinegar, before rinsing it. "I know that, Pix, but we know what it meant for us. So can we try to ignore it for just a little longer?" I pleaded. She hummed in response, and I rolled my eyes.

We quickly made the Pollo Guisado, white rice, veggies and brought out some wine. It was a typical dinner but it felt like more. We may not have bonded with the men but our magick was not happy about that shit, and was taking it out on us like some fucking high school bully. Well magick, this isn't some strange lifetime movie set in fifties, damnit, we had choices.

By the time the elevator dinged, Pixie and I were in the kitchen, one wine bottle down, dancing salsa, and laughing when we tried to sip from our glasses and spilled everywhere instead.

"Allow Entrance!" We said at the same time and kept dancing to the music blasting on the speakers. We laughed when the guys paused dumbstruck but laughed even harder when they split us up and started spinning us between them. Dante and Dimitri dipped and turned us perfectly right into Luca and Etienne, who didn't miss a beat and finished off the song with an over the head hand turn and dip.

Our cheeks bright red, Pixie and I regarded them. Luca still had me in his arms, and Etienne held on to Pixie like a life preserver. *Fuck. Abort the mission, abort the mission*, I chanted through my head. But for some reason my brain wasn't listening and Princess Peach was like 'fuck you, Charlie Mario, I'm tired of you ruining my sex feast.'

"Well, I'm very impressed. Thank you for the dance gentlemen." I stumbled out while their stares became more intensive. Then suddenly, Luca's lips were on mine and dammit I didn't stop him. I couldn't. I wanted it. I could blame it on the magick, but fuck, this week was something out of a sad hallmark movie.

He started slow, testing and teasing but I opened my mouth and sucked his tongue in my mouth. My tongue rings rubbed up against his tongue and he moaned and gripped my ass, bringing me closer. I ran my hands down his back and up again to tangle into his hair. All of a sudden, a huge burst of purple streak jumped between us and around us. We pulled back, trying to catch our breath.

"Fuck," I whispered. He looked down, his eyes on my lips, and caressed my face and replied, "Yeah, fuck."

I didn't have a chance to catch my breath or gain a semblance of control as Dante grabbed me, picked me up and pushed me up against the wall with my legs around his waist and kissed me as if he was drowning. He was grinding his dick up against Princess Peach, as the purple magick spiked and jumped. He teased my tongue and ran his hands up under my top, squeezed and pinched my nipple, and I moaned into his mouth. You would think he had something to prove, but I'd be lying if I said I didn't want more. The magick didn't care that we barely knew each other, the bond knew we belonged together. The bond was like a grandma who wouldn't stop trying to hook you up when even you told her you had a tinder app.

Suddenly, Dante stepped backward so Luca could slip in behind me. Working in tandem, I sighed as Luca wrapped his hands around me, tugging my heavy breast out of my bra making me moan into Dante's mouth as Dante continued to fuck my mouth with his. Feeling completely lightheaded, I let Luca take my weight as he kissed and licked his way up my neck to tug at my ears.

"I'm going to spend my life teasing you, until you are always begging to have me deep inside you," he growled into my ear, making me groan right as Dante slipped his finger below my waist band and I jerked in their arms.

We were completely engrossed and the magick just kept wrapping around us, squeezing us tighter. We lost control, and the magick took over.

Pixie

As I WAS SPUN around by Etienne, his hands were making his way up my short skirt. When Luca kissed Ellie, Etienne looked into my eyes as if asking for permission and came close and captured my lips with his. The moment his lips touched mine, I lost my control. I grabbed him, moaned into his mouth and grabbed his hands to wrap them firmly across my ass. I didn't want space between us. He bit my lip and brought my arms up over my head, and spun me around into Dimitri who captured my lips as Etienne continued to palm my ass and groan softly in my ear. He kissed my neck and made me moan into Dimitri's mouth.

Dimitri caressed my tongue rings and brought his hands under my crop top to squeeze, pinch, and knead my breasts. My hips bucked, my nipples so sensitive I could be brought close to the edge with the stimulation. Etienne whispered in my ear in French, grinding his dick against my ass. He could have been making an order for dinner and I wouldn't even care. Dimitri put his hands under my skirt, moving my thong over and played with my clit, swirling his hands in circles. I moaned uncontrollably, making him growl into my mouth. Etienne reached down and pulled my skirt up higher and slid a finger deep inside me, making me clench around his finger. Dimitri worked my clit over in perfect tune to Etienne's ministrations but when Etienne added a second finger and used my pussy juices to slide one finger into my ass, I came. Stars burst through my eyes as I shuddered and screamed into Dimitri's mouth.

The purple sparks were going off around the room and it was as if we were being pulled even closer. Dimitri ripped my panties off and put them in his pocket with a wink as he slowly licked his fingers. He came close to me and whispered "delicious" into my ear. Etienne fixed my crop top and pulled my skirt down, and licked the fingers that were in my pussy clean, and whispered, "This isn't over, Chérie."

Fuck, you promise? I thought to myself.

❧ 10 ❧

"Strong women don't play the victim. Don't make themselves look pitiful and don't point fingers. They stand and they deal." – **Mandy Hale**

"Fuck, I hate when quotes are right sometimes. Time to buckle up and jump on this bond-wagon. Get it?" - **Charlie**

C harlie

THE PURPLE STREAKS can no longer be ignored. It was just stupid to do so. As the men set me down, I adjusted my top and Dante pouted. "Not fair, I want to see them all night." I laughed and gave him a quick kiss. Fuck trying to maintain distance that all just felt too right. *Way too soon, too. You should really try to calm that hoe shit down,* the rational part of my brain trilled.

I took a look at Pixie and we both went to grab our wine from the table as the guys looked at each other with slight smirks on their faces as "Sexual Healing" by Marvin Gaye started playing.

"Fucking hell," I muttered.

Etienne winked at Pixie and strolled into the kitchen to wash his hands.

He, uh, fingered my ass, she whispered into the mental link, her face fully tinted pink.

I burst out laughing, and spit my wine out.

Fuckkkkk Youuuuuuu.

I laughed harder.

"Guys, we made dinner for you, would you like wine too?" I asked.

"Thank you, ladies. Over dinner, maybe we can discuss what's going on a bit more?" Luca cleared his throat.

"Yeah that's a good idea," I replied as I set the food on the table while Pix grabbed plates and glasses, and Dimitri hunted down the wine.

We tucked into our food, and after a few bites, I couldn't hold it in. "So, thoughts? And no, don't do that look thing where you all stare at each other like this is High School Musical and you're all down to the last basket. Why the fuck did we just Halloween Town the house? I said calmly, I was pretty proud of myself actually.

Dimitri's lip quirked up. "Did you just speak Disney?" We gaped at him.

Pixie, I'm sucking his dick first. Called dibs. I failed to keep the smirk off my face.

He fingered me first so I guess you can swallow his dick first.

Yeah, I mean he speaks Disney and then I sparkled over there with the Sullen one.

Suddenly multiple voices started speaking at once.

"While I'm amenable to getting my dick sucked, why can I hear you in my head?" The voice sounded like Dimitri.

"Fuck, this is going to make shit complicated, wait, sullen one?" Luca.

"I want to glow purple and get my dick sucked too. FUCK, I gotta watch more Disney." Dante.

"This is going to be a cluster fuck now, I feel it," said Etienne softly.

We all stared at each other and then we put our forks down. The food forgotten at this point.

"Okay, so what in the world is going on," I murmured, rubbing my temples. I mean logically I know what was going on, but still there has to be someone who asks the obvious question with the most obvious answer.

Still, someone was going to give me those answers. They kept doing that weird-stare-at-each-other thing, and I, for one, hated not being ten steps ahead. Hated it. Never knew how much until now. Research was my baby, research never lied. But these Council motherfuckers, have to have books that will explain a lot of shit. I want it all. Because mind-melding, or rather the ability to speak in each other's minds, typically happened after a full, sexual bonding. This? This belies everything I know, and it's pissing me the fuck off.

They all looked at each other.

"Talk, and stop doing the damn staring thing!" I barked at the men as I picked up my fork menacingly.

Luca starts, reaching over to take the fork out of my hand, "Okay, so we suspected something was going on when you mentioned how the magick between you two exploded, when"—he swallowed thickly —"um, but somehow it got to us in the living room. At first, we all thought it was because we were uhhh..." He trailed off. Luca, ever the strong one and a control freak, looked uneasy.

"For goodness sake, Luca. Listen, we thought we were just horny from all the sex and we wanted you both but when the magick hit us in the living room, we knew something was up. When the magick sparked between Luca, me, and you as well as Pixie, Etienne and Dimitri, it just confirmed our hypothesis and fears," Dante finished.

Oh hypothesissss, science words made my proverbial dick hard.

I drummed my fingers on the table. "So that means what? Because guess what, I'm a smart bitch, and that must mean that we are perfectly matched to be bonded. But I'm bonded to Pixie. Also regular bonds are gold. Ours is purple. Now it's sparking purple again, with you four in the picture. So, all six of us? It's crazy. Don't get me wrong, the sexual logistics work, I never understood harems with hot guys and one pussy hole, it just doesn't make sense. Her pussy would be broken, and no one is breaking Princess Peach!" I stop my rant while I make eye contact with them, getting up from the table and walking to the living room. Everyone moving as one.

"Fears," Pixie spoke up as she narrowed her eyes, sitting on the couch.

"What fears?" she continued, asking Dante, "It seems to me like we are the ones that would be cautious, no? You all being the Council's little bitches, who does all the grunt work to make them more powerful and leaving the lower castes to shit. No, no fear here." Her voice kept getting quieter and steadier. Well, nice Pixie has left. Welcome, Dixie, the dick of the Pixies.

"Little bitches? Little bitches? We are a mother-fucking Elite squad who handle high profile cases and bring justice," Dimitri snapped back. I scoffed, who the fuck does he think he is? Captain America?

We both laughed at that. Freaking out the men in the process, who at this point had gotten up and stood around us.

"Let me tell you about justice, word on the street is you are out looking for a vigilante, you mentioned that part so cool, but what is bothering you is that this person is catching the bad guys faster than the Shadows on patrol and the useless Magickal Law Enforcement fuckers. Right?" Pixie spat out.

Oh shit, it's getting real.

Dante nodded, and Luca stared at us with rapt attention while Etienne tried to pick up on any slight lie. *Good luck with that.*

"Would this vigilante be known to have a reputation for not giving two fucks and being an overall ass, yet no one would have been willing to give information, or the information has somehow been muddled in their minds, and no matter how hard you search, the cameras are clean?" Pixie raised an eyebrow.

"How would you know *classified* information?" Etienne asked suspiciously.

I scoffed as I turned around, walking out and bending over to get the vodka out of the liquor cabinet in front of the TV; wine isn't cutting it anymore. Purple sparks light up the room and the men struggle to adjust themselves despite the conversation at hand.

Right, don't bend over around the men.

I tip the bottle into my mouth and chug while I continue my pacing. Her ranting does things to me, dangerous and sexual. I don't like when my mate is upset. Then, the more dominant side of me wants to spank her. *It's a tough life I live.*

"So," Pixie continued, snapping me out of my guttural thoughts, "the Council sent you to get someone that is killing people, nothing on specifics on what or who is being killed. The vigilante had to build an image, one with the people she cared about, which is everyone she can protect, and make enough waves for an Elite Guard to show up. Genius, right? Anyways, those people killed? Not the high ranking members of society that are listed on your paperwork, nope, they are rapists, murderers, child-killing monsters. You guys were sent here to pick up someone because the Council couldn't stand having someone run the city better than they can and not be able to trace it. Could not deal with not being the one everyone turned to, just to eventually be turned away. Yeah, that person you're hunting, who is an untraceable vigilante, has been hiding in plain sight. You've been hunting Charlie this entire time." I bowed graciously as she finished her statement.

Dimitri, Luca, Dante, and Etienne's jaws dropped.

I picked up where Pixie laid off. "When you look at me, what do you see? Purple hair? Curves? A snarky mouth? When you look at Pixie, do you see the stripper? It is funny really that you guys are *so Elite*. You mentioned at the club that people seemed to fear me." I shrugged. I knew who I was. "You should have picked up on the fact that other than those, who disrespect me and get their shit rocked, that is just who I am."

I paused, taking a deep breath. "Now magick users have pretty good senses. The others who don't know of Exousia, well, they have no idea why they respect me, they just do, because of what I do. Even if people haven't been helped by me directly, word travels quickly. Those homes falling apart in the lower castes? I fund to rebuild them. Magicks who are too low on the Council's radar? I bring them food, provide safe shelter. Anyone who steps over is handled quickly and efficiently. So who am I, boys, hmm?" I then waited for their reply.

"24601?" muttered Dante.

I blinked and laughed. "Hot, very hot, but yes, I am essentially Jean Valjean. I brought hope and gave jobs, except I didn't go off and fuck over some lady who ended up with an STD and adopt her baby or anything... I have read the documents given to you, the ones in the hidden dashboard of your car. I have seen why you came into the city way before when I hacked into all the Council networks and saw the fake names and positions of the supposed people murdered. I knew you were going to come, what I didn't know was that we would be destined by some fucking magickal jokester, to be bonded in any way, but here we are." I give a dry laugh while I take another chug from the bottle.

"Wait, when did you get into our trucks?" Luca asked.

I looked at him and laughed. "Dude, did you seriously think you were going to park in my private garage, and we weren't going to take advantage?" I scoffed. The nerve that he truly thought we would not be breaking and entering.

The day their fresh uniforms were brought up, a nice little stack of documents were put in the kitchen cabinet too. I felt the need to laugh maniacally but I held myself back. Impressions and all that.

"Oh and Pixie? Worked at the club to get information so we can figure out how the fuck to get closer to the Council. We knew we needed to join the ranks of Shadows. She is, like me, one of the best hackers and an encryptions specialist. You couldn't find me because I didn't want to be fucking found. Now we know there is a recruitment going on for camp in five weeks and you motherfuckers are going to give us an invite."

"So you're telling us that not only did you concoct a plan to draw Elite Shadows to your area to hunt you, you're also the one who has been helping the city, and in turn, confusing everyone on the Council. Fuck." Luca joins in my pacing. "What the fuck are we supposed to do? We have to bring someone in, it's what we were here for."

I just kept pacing, and Luca snapped, "For fuck's sake, Ellie, I cannot think while you're strutting around like that."

"I do not strut, asshole, I glide. Cannot handle seeing your intended bonded saving the world, deny the bond," I snapped back. If it was any quieter, I'm sure it would be because we were in Dimitris' hidden coffins.

"Deny...the...bond?" Luca said softly, and sat down with his back against the wall.

"Magicks can spend their lifetime without feeling the purity of the bond, and to deny that would be like ripping someone in two. Is that what you want, Ellie? Pixie? To deny what magick is telling us is right?" Etienne said softly.

I sighed. "Listen. I am a very logical person, I say fuck a lot, I'm a fucking badass, I kill people. Not the easiest person to love under all of those conditions, but Pixie and I have been bonded since we were fourteen. I have no idea how to live without her. I would never want to. I know what it is like to be bonded. To be loved, made love to, I do not want to deny any of you that. Pixie?" I looked at her.

"No, I do not wish to deny the bond, but give us another alternative. Plain and simple, we need invitations to get into the Shadow ranks, you cannot deny our fighting skills. Those skills, alone, would make us a perfect fit. How the fuck are we supposed to hide purple sparks?" Pixie said quietly.

Dimitri's head snapped up at that. "How did you know about the recruitment anyway? It's by invitation only, and no one but the Shadows know about it."

I spoke up at that, "So you know I said I was stronger than Dante? Well, when I met Pixie, she was stronger than me in that department. We have trained and we are strong, we got her a place at the club so she can read the minds of officials to glean information." I smiled.

Dimitri looked taken aback. "Stronger? I'm going to get back to that because I have a shit ton of questions, but you're saying you picked it up from the club? Not even they would know."

I looked at my now empty bottle, *nut-fucking, magick liquor-burning-fucker upper*, and went to find a new bottle. Luca looked at me strangely to look for any effects of the alcohol. Fuck it, I wasn't hiding, not from them, they either accepted the bond or they fucked off, and I erased all their shit. Like a fucking Ellie Virus.

"Ah hah! Another bottle!" I exclaimed. I took my time opening it, drinking deep and giving some to Pixie too. "Where were we, oh yeah. No, not the patrons at the club, those nut-scratching sack-lickers didn't know shit. Do you know how many jaws...anyways back on track...I picked it up from you boys," I said cheekily.

They all started talking at once.

"Ah...ah...ah, bad boys," said Dixie Pixie with a stern face.

"One at a time. I'm sure you all have the same question, but then after that I'm taking a fucking relaxing jacuzzi dip with my magick wife," she said saucily, and winked at me.

"I'll go first," said Dante. "How did you know we would even come to the area? You also mentioned reading classified documents. How the hell did you do that, let alone hide your trail so well?"

I sigh and sit down on the floor ignoring the sparks from being near Luca. "I knew because I have been studying the Council for years. I am the best hacker and no one can bypass my encryption. Those programs built to hack encryptions? Yeah, I built them, sold them, bought the company and I'm the silent and never seen CEO. I'm young but I'm a baby genius. I knew the Council would send a group of Elites once the tales of the vigilante rose. They tend to be some conceited, corrupt, pretentious, stupid fucks. So I hacked, I read, and now I know shit. Next question."

Dimitri went next. "Why do you want to get into Shadows so badly? I'm assuming it is to make an Elite team and get close to the council, but why?"

I smiled darkly. "The Council doesn't keep everything electronically, they have paper files, books, knowledge hidden, and I want it. I need information and I'm going to get it. They killed my parents, and I want to fucking know why."

Etienne went next as Luca was still sitting, looking like someone kicked his puppy. "How did you amass such a fortune? This shit looks like a fortress, you save lives, yet you also are known as a vigilante, who are you really?"

"I am all those things and more. I am Ellie Elimentis, the daughter of the last known, most powerful Water and Fire Elemental ever on the Council of Magicks."

Shocked gasps broke out across the room, and Luca's head snapped up.

"My fortune is my family's legacy. I invested. I learned to fight. I learned to hack and encrypt. I learned to love again," I said softly, looking over Pixie's face, taking in the soft features and my heart grew. "But I never thirsted for revenge, this isn't about that. I have accepted my parents' death. I just won't accept that someone got away with it by hiding information. I want the information and I want the murderer or murderers brought to justice in front of his people that is all. Revenge is trivial, it gets in the way of clear thinking and logical results. I just want to know," I finished.

It was quiet for a few moments. It was nice, telling people about me. Then, hurricane Luca came.

Luca finally spoke up, "You know my power is to pick up on powers, and yet I could never get a proper read. You've shown Air, Fire, Water, Speed, and Strength. That's just fucking insane and unheard of. So my question is, what powers do you have?"

I stood up, stretched, grabbed Pixie's hand to head

into the—Bang Bro's Room? Fuck, I really needed a name for that shit. I made eye contact with each and every one of them, and finished with Luca. Just our eyes caused purple sparks to crackle. Fuck.

"All of them."

❧ 11 ❧

*"Happiness can be found, even in the darkest of times, if one only remembers to turn on the light."- **Albus Dumbuldore***
*"Are you making a dig at me? I'm not a Vampire!"- **Dimitri***

L uca

As ELLIE and Pixie walked away, my heart clenched in my chest. Even though, logically, I knew they were a few feet away, I hated not being able to see them. Fuck, I rubbed a hand down my face. *All of them.* Those words kept bouncing around in my head. I knew she was someone special, magickally, but fuck, bombshell after bombshell, just made my head spin.

I looked up and realized the boys must all be thinking the same thing. "What do we do, boys?" I refuse to break or deny the bond, fuck, when she said those words, I just felt like my heart was ripped out of my chest.

Dante stretched out his legs in front of him. "Well I'm not giving them up, sorry, boys. Chicks before dicks."

Etienne laughed. "I'm sure it is the other way but I will have to agree we cannot just deny it. Not everyone is lucky enough to bond once, but to bond twice, to a bonded pair? That has to be something special."

"Everything about them is special. Amazing, even, there is no way we can possibly deny this bond, and I don't think they really want to either, Pixie looked sad, and Ellie is just... difficult, too analytical sometimes," Dimitri added.

"So we issue them an invitation," I said and held my hand up to stop the arguments. "They are two of the most powerful magicks we have met and they sure as fuck are the strongest fighters, if anything, we could stand to learn from them." I chuckled.

"How do we stop the bond from showing? This shit isn't exactly normal. They won't see gold, they will see purple, it will paint a target on their back and while I'm sure they can take on the world, being noticed by the Council won't be a good thing, no matter how powerful they are. We have suspected corruption in their ranks but the murder of the Elimentis was the biggest news in our time, Ellie's information puts things in perspective." Dante leaned over and put his head in his hands.

"You all know the lore as well as I do, purple sparks is the strongest bond anyone can possibly manifest, it means a melding of power and minds, not just souls as is typical.

This hasn't happened in several hundred years and even then, it was considered a myth. No, this is the best way to protect our girls. We need to accept the bond and we need to accept it tonight," I say with finality.

"Let's go take a shower and then talk to them."

We all get up and head to the same rooms from last night. When she said bedroom, I expected a small room with a regular shower. No, this room was huge, floor-to-ceiling windows, a king-size bed so soft, I was so pissed when I had to wake up. Even so, nothing compared to the bathroom. There was a glass shower with aromatherapy and jets coming off the side and rain effect from above. The bathroom was more masculine, with grays and blacks but still felt open instead of the darker colors, making the room feel smaller. I took a quick shower and threw on some fresh gray sweats and underwear from the dresser. I skipped the shirt. I did throw on a pair of fluffy socks though. Because, I mean, fluffy socks.

I stepped out of my room the same moment the boys did and we walked over to the girls' shared room. The door had been left open, purposefully, I'm sure. Probably Pixie, she's going to be the balance, I can feel it. I knocked but there was no answer.

There was music coming from the room, and it sounded like "Motivation" by Kelly Rowland, so I'm sure she just couldn't hear us. Taking the open door as an invitation, we walked in. And we froze. Fuck.

Charlie

. . .

Pixie and I relaxed in the jacuzzi for a bit and then threw on some underwear and a bra, and called it a day. We will talk to the boys in a few. Right now, I needed to get some energy out. Pixie and I turned on our sex playlist and started dancing around the room and sneaking kisses. Then "Motivation" came up and we fell into the tempo as we made our way to the poles in our room and climbed up and started doing a routine we learned on YouTube. We turned upside down and let our legs open slowly. Suddenly, I felt the door open but just kept going. We wrapped our legs around the pole at the same time and slid down into a split and bounced just enough to make our asses jiggle. It cheered me up to be such a sensual fan-fucking-tastic beast.

I turned around to face four shirtless, muscled men with gray sweats on. Fuck, gray sweats should be illegal. But I liked what I saw, and one look at Pixie, I knew she did too.

I cleared my throat. "Gentlemen, what's up? And I don't mean the obvious." I smirked.

Dante spoke first, "I would ask you to cover up but I'm sure you won't, so I'll try to keep eye contact here. We want to extend the invitations for the recruitment but..."

"But?" Pixie prompted.

He sighed, and Etienne stepped further into the room. "Ladies, bonding is not something that happens often and I...*we* do not want to give the chance for that up." He emphasized the 'we,' and looked at the guys. I looked at Pixie and we sat down on the bed, putting a pillow on our laps while the guys said their piece.

"When it does happen"—Luca stepped in—"a regular bonding only has gold sparks but still does its job and

connects the souls, melding magick and heart rhythms."
He looked wistful when speaking, and my heart started
pounding in my chest.

"Purple sparks are something that even hundreds of
years ago was considered a myth. The fact that you two
bonded that way was a miracle, the fact that our bond is
manifesting that way is downright mystical," Dimitri said,
his voice gruff.

"Are we getting to the 'but'?" Pixie said. I bit back a
smirk.

"This type of bonding is said to come from pure
magick. To even have this type of bonding shouldn't
happen to us. Unless one of us is..." Luca looked nervous
then, looking around the room as if he was being watched.
I frowned.

"One of us is..." I prompted.

"It's really silly but one of us will have to be a direct
descendant of someone who is pure magick. But those
beings do not really exist," he finished.

Dante rubbed the back of his neck and muttered,
"Clearly."

"I'm interested in how you guys know all of this,"
Pixie inquired.

Etienne paced. "As you reach certain levels in your
training, we are let into certain archives. Let's just say,
these beings more than exist, our Council was having
clandestine meetings years ago. According to something
we were able to snag from the forbidden archives."

"Forbidden?" I inquired.

"Just that. Forbidden. We never did find those papers
again and we knew better than to ask. The point is, if the
Council even suspected someone here was a direct

descendent in anyway"—Etienne looked right into my eyes for a second—"we wouldn't be alive long enough to even whisper a goodbye."

We took a deep intake of breath and the room felt heavy with questions, fear, and something else. Something that I was too scared to put a label on, but my magick knew it already.

"That's not the end. Our bonding would not only be a melding of souls, but also a melding of magick, minds and skill sets. It is, according to those archives, so strong that those who bond this way are an unstoppable force. Just like those entities they reference. Even more so, the love they share is completely irrevocable. A love that is so bone deep that we are all perfectly aligned and our souls are truly one," Luca said gently. The look of longing was clear on their faces. I knew in my heart we could never deny them the chance. We may have just met physically but our souls have been dancing with destiny for a long time.

"We want that," Dimitri finished.

"Okay, so now can we touch the 'but'?" Pixie said huskily, as she was completely transfixed by Luca when he was speaking. I, on the other hand, was eye-fucking the shit out of my vampire.

I tore my eyes away from temptation and laughed. "Nice Nemo Reference!"

Dimitri beat Dante to it. "We want to extend the invitations for the recruitment, but logically we cannot walk in shooting purple sparks around all Willy Nilly and expect for people to not freak out, so we would need to accept the bond. Tonight."

"You all want to have sex tonight?" I asked. I mean Pixie and I bonded without sex since we met so young but it was the moment we came together, *see what I did there*, that sparks finally stopped happening.

Dante and Luca looked like they were about to choke, and Dimitri and Etienne smirked.

"No, there is no need for sex, not right now at least, we can complete the bond through touch," Luca said.

"No offense, Luca, but the first time me and Ellie had sex was when our sparks went away, so we are just a little confused here," Pixie said just what I was thinking.

He sighed. "Listen, in theory, sex works to solidify the bond, like snapping a rubber band in place. What I'm proposing is more like a Band-Aid, we would hold hands..."

I couldn't help it. I barked a laugh, and had to interrupt, "Like pre-coitus kumbaya?"

Pixie and I fell back on the bed laughing, breaking the tense moment in the room. Luca looked peeved so I tried to sober up to let him continue. "I'm sorry camp guru, continue."

"As I was saying we would hold hands, drop our mental barriers and let our minds become one," Luca finished.

I spoke up, "Logically speaking," and they all groaned. "This idea of purple sparks hasn't been around for hundreds of years, so I don't think I'll trust a kumbaya moment, when I know for a fact what worked for Pixie and I, also keep in mind—our minds touched—when sparks hit us in the workout room and we heard each other's thoughts, and yet here we still are, thunder barneys."

"So what are you saying?" Dimitri asked thickly.

Pixie piped in, "Everyone, drop your mental shields

and connect. Breathe and focus on the emotions, sensations, and the wants and needs of others in the room."

"What I'm saying is," I continued as me and Pixie got off the bed at the same time and snapped off our bras. "We start"—we slide off our panties—"you watch."

Then I whispered in everyone's mind, *Then you join, when I tell you to.*

❧ 12 ❧

"Everything in the world is about sex except sex. Sex is about power." - **Oscar Wilde**
"Or the melding of said power." - **Pixie**

Charlie

I FELT RATHER than heard the men take off their clothes and get on the bed leaning on the head board.

I turned to Pixie, grabbed her ass, and moved her sideways, so the men could see everything. I smacked my lips on her mouth, controlling her, while she slide her hands over my body, tangling one hand in my long purple hair, and wrapping the other hand around my neck.

Baby, you start getting rough and you won't like the

consequences, I whispered to her, knowing everyone can hear and feel what we are feeling.

Try me, she responded.

I pushed her back on the bed and made her lay right in the center. I straddled her face and she took two fingers to spread my plump pussy lips and gave my clit a soft kiss. I threw my head back and moaned, as the men groaned in tandem. Fuck, if we are going to feel each other during sex, this is going to be insane. Pixie snuggled her face into my pussy and started to eat me out with vigor. God, I can't stop moaning, it's like everything I feel is multiplied by all the sensations in the room. I looked down into her gorgeous eyes, challenging her silently to keep eye contact as I start to slowly ride her face just like she likes me to. She gripped my ass, urging me over her soft lips and sweet tongue. Never breaking eye contact, I used a combination of my air manipulation and strength to thrust into her just the way she liked it. She screamed into my pussy and started to hump her hips in time with the thrust. I kept my gaze locked on her as she licked, sucked, and kissed my slit until I came down her chin. I moaned and whimpered, as she gripped my ass firmly to lick me up and I finally let her come. The chorus of groans around the room reached their peak as it looked like the men came when we did.

I slid down her body and captured her mouth with a kiss.

Pixie started to pant, and the men looked on curiously as I started my particular brand of sexual torture.

Pixie likes a little pain, gentlemen. I'm going to give her that pain, isn't that right, baby?

Yes, mi amor, she whispered in everyone's mind. The guys cursed and were hard already.

I leaned over her body and kissed, nibbled on and rubbed everything until she was over sensitive. I opened her legs wide so her piercing glinted through her pussy. I pulled my elemental fire and sent a lick of flames over her engorged clit, soothed it with my tongue, and healed the ache. I bit down on her clit, and she screamed. The men hissed in pain and pleasure. I used my healing to stop the pain and did it over and over while I used my fire and wind to press against her tight ass with a warm presence.

I flipped her over, and propped her ass up with a pillow. Taking a second to admire the view, I reached over to the side table for our small leather whip we liked to use from time to time. Without warning, I lashed out on her ass, and she screamed, hard. Don't ask me how, sex sounds are unexplainable sometimes. I whipped her and healed her over and over, mixing pain with pleasure.

"Sit back and get on your knees, Pixie. I want you to watch this," I said, barely recognizing my lusty voice.

The men were moaning uncontrollably, and I was shaking as I was overcome with an overload of sensations but I was going to keep up my end of the promise. I was going to make her see stars. Using my mind manipulation, I kept them on the edge of pleasure, and I leaned over and took the closest dick I could reach. Making sure the mental link was strong, I looked up as Dimitri fisted his hand in my hair and his hips bucked into my mouth. I let him use my mouth for a few seconds before I jerked out of his hands, licked his balls and shoved him down my throat and hummed. His eyes rolled back as he came, and the men jerked, experiencing the same sensations and pleasures he did. He looked at me completely dazed and I winked, as I turned back to Pixie.

"Did that turn you on baby, watching our man's dick

in my mouth? Do you want to taste his cum on my lips?" I asked as I roughly grabbed her head and kissed her passionately. She moaned in my mouth and I pressed her back onto the bed as I leaned over and wrapped her clit with my plump lips. I quickened my tongue and reached up to choke her lightly. As my hand closed over her throat, she screamed and came, and came, and came. I came too, it's like I felt everything she did. Holy fuck.

The purple crackling in the room were like fireworks at this point and we were all on fire for one another. This mental connection opened up the floodgates of emotions, needs, desires, passions, and at this point, stamina.

Let's move to a side of the bed not covered in cum, although by the end of tonight we may end up with it everywhere. I laughed. *Also don't worry about protection, I put a flexible shield inside of me and Pixie, you cannot feel it but it's there.*

Thank God, magick users couldn't contract sexual disease. That made this all the better.

Gentlemen, we need you, Pixie whispered in their heads as she got on her hands and knees on the bed.

I followed suit as Dante slid over and placed a hot kiss on my lips while Luca lined himself up behind me. I didn't bother looking and comparing dicks, they were all perfect from what I saw. At least we will be sore but not split in two with walking portals to Narnia.

All thoughts left my head as Luca slammed into me holding my waist with one hand and grabbing my ass with the other. I gasped, and Dante took that chance to slide his dick all the way down my throat. Pixie and I researched this shit, we could suck some fucking dick.

I looked over as Pixie had Etienne stroking her face with a look of adoration, until she sucked him in completely and started humming as his dick touched the back of her throat, and he threw his head back and moaned loudly. Dimitri grabbed Pixie's perfect ass, and smacked it while he was fucking. She was held up by his hips and Etienne's dick.

The men jerked when they heard our voices in their heads, losing control quickly as moans echoed throughout the room. We felt each other's pleasure, all thoughts blending into one, all of us about to come with the overload of sensations.

Dante gripped my purple hair in his fist and shoved his dick down my throat and threw his head back with a hiss as I used my air manipulation to make my mouth more pressurized. Then I used the same tactics as Pixie, and hummed hard over his dick. He was trying to hold out but with a wink at Pixie, we tightened our pussy at the same time, hummed harder, and I threw in a little airplay to stimulate the men's prostates. They all bucked, and yelled at the same time as they emptied themselves inside of us. I swallowed Dante's cum, and Pixie swallowed everything Etienne had to offer.

The purple sparks were almost gone. I already felt the bonds falling into place.

The streaks are almost gone, guys, let's take this into the shower and switch. But I have something a little different in mind if you guys can hack it, I whispered into their minds.

I sent a mental picture to everyone and the boys ran into the bathroom.

I gave Pixie a deep kiss as we walked in after them.

After getting in the shower, Etienne quickly scooped me up for a kiss just as Dimitri pressed up against my back and dropped kisses to my neck and lower back. I moaned. I made sure to grab lube on the way in and slathered Etienne's dick with it before tossing it over to Pixie to work over Luca. Thank goodness, the boys were pretty much the same height for this work. Etienne picked me up and lined himself up with my ass. After a pop, he slid in, and everyone groaned. Dimitri kissed my neck and sucked on my pierced nipples before lining himself up and sliding all the way in.

FUCK, FUCK, FUCK.

Then they started to move and fuck if I didn't roll my head back against Etienne and started saying nonsensical shit. Pixie wasn't faring any better as all I kept hearing from the mental link were several 'oh my gods' and 'what the fucks.' Was she speaking Greek? The fuck? The guys chuckled and started to fuck us harder. I sent air to play with Pixie's clit while she was being fucked and she came so hard, Dante let out a choked gasp, and we all groaned. Their paces got more frantic, and I realized Pixie was keeping us from coming with her manipulation.

Fuck, this feels so damn good, Etienne. Fuck, Dimitri, yes, just like that...

She then let go of her manipulation and sent us spiraling into the most intense orgasm of the night. And we all let out a hoarse yell. *Now that* is how you orgasm together, folks—magick. None of that porn shit or romance book shit. MAGICK.

As we laid in the shower to recover, the purple sparks reappeared but this time it wrapped around us, tightened, and burst inside of us, and disappeared. Suddenly, our hearts beat in tandem.

❧ 13 ❧

"The path is smooth that leadeth on to danger." -
Shakespeare
"Don't foreshadow in the middle of the book. That is just rude." - ***Charlie***

E tienne

THIS IS QUITE HONESTLY the happiest I have ever felt. When the magick burst, I felt like I was complete. As if I can do anything. I felt...power?

Dimitri

. . .

131

THIS IS EXACTLY what I was hoping for, all the other complications can come later. The big bad enforcer found his bonded...or bonds...What's the multiple term for bonded? Mates? Whatever, that was the most intense sex I have ever had. It is true what they say that sex between those with the bond is the best ever. I want to do it again.

Dante

I LOOKED at the woman next to us sitting as the rain shower kept us from falling asleep from exhaustion. "So this bathroom is amazing but where else can we do that again?" I joked. Then "Anywhere" by 112 starts blasting in the shower, and I laugh. *Touché, smart house, touché'*.

Luca

DANTE IS AN IDIOT, but he's not wrong. How do you stop yourself from wanting to be bonded over and over again, how long does the obsession last? Does the strain get easier? I find myself getting hard again at the thought. There is an undercurrent of power that is filling me that I have never felt before, it is exhilarating being connected like this.

Pixie

. . .

I LOVE ELLIE, she has been my world and my heart for years, the thought *of multiplying that feeling is incredible. I feel so content and... hungry.* I must get food.

Charlie

I DON'T THINK it hit these fuckers yet that we can hear each other's thoughts yet. Everyone's thoughts bring me such a feeling of deep satisfaction. As if pieces of a puzzle have come together. This is right... this was destined.

"RIGHT, so let's rinse off and actually get dressed again; fair warning, Pixie and I rarely wear a whole bunch of clothes, you're all gonna have to get used to it. Pixie is hungry so let's make something to eat since we left our dinner uneaten."

They groan as they stand up. "Goodness guys, here," I said as I filled them with healing power and fixed all the aches.

The men gave us each kisses as they headed over to pick up their discarded clothes that they had thrown off earlier and go to make sandwiches since we made dinner earlier. It was sweet. Pixie and I threw on the best form of night clothes we had, see-through silk nighties and fuzzy socks. Listen, I'll be damned if I wear anything remotely constricting unless I absolutely have to. Fuck that. We walk out into the kitchen and the men turn to stare. At least the sandwiches were done. I grabbed mine and Pixie's, went to sit on the couch, and settled in to eat.

"So how long did it take for you and Pixie to be in the same room without wanting to rip each-other's clothes off," Luca said huskily, his eyes slightly dilated.

I laughed. "Oh, about a year or so." I winked at him.

"Fuck," he bit out.

"You get used to the yearning after, but you'll have times where you give in to the call, like when I was in the club that night." I shrugged.

"Well that's going to make things difficult at the Academy," Etienne admitted.

"Yup, but at least there won't be sparks and we have to weigh the benefits, besides the obvious feeling of completeness, we can feel and hear each other so if anything is ever going on, we will all know first-hand," Dante spoke up.

"You know about that whole melding of powers after bonding, how do you all feel right now?" I asked curiously, savoring my food, seeing if they have figured it out yet.

"Powerful, more than usual," Dimitri said with a confused look.

"I noticed the feeling of power in the shower," added Etienne.

"Okay, but how do you feel? Reach into your soul, into your reservoir of power, what do you feel?" I urged, suddenly excited.

The men closed their eyes for a moment and so many emotions and reactions were being projected into the room.

"Wait, how is that possible? I don't feel an ending, how can someone have an unlimited reservoir, does that mean I can use magic and literally never stop?" Luca asked.

I nod. "You should also be able to use all my powers too. Pixie and I dabble here and there but have never fully practiced using all of my abilities. Although clearly that has to change now. "

"How did this happen?" Dimitri asked.

I knew he was referring to the source of my powers so I answered honestly. *Not like we can keep secrets anyway. Mind barriers though? Totally a must. No one needs images of tupperwaring pussy.*

"My parents had a really tough time conceiving. They were able to get their hands on a potion that allowed them to finally bring me around. But instead of surging into my magick when I was twelve, I surged at birth. On my way down the vaginal slide, I used elemental fire and she was never able to have children again.

"Regardless, it wasn't as if they could ask around to see if everything was okay with me. They knew a baby like me would raise too many eyebrows. So I was kept hiding away on our property."

I smiled, leaning back on the couch as I recounted a few stories fondly. "Growing up was uniquely different than I could imagine someone else's childhood would be. I would throw water balls when I was in my bath and my mom would laugh. The house was full of toys, and the bright hallways full of photos, always felt warm. It had been a big house with just us three, but there was so much laughter, hugs and whispered dreams that would fill my heart till almost bursting." I laughed. "A lot of those pictures were of a mom or dad smiling and me doing something out of the norm. I pretty much read every book in that entire house by the time I was eight, my powers also gave me increased intelligence and abilities. They would bring me home new books and I would just devour them all. They were on the Council, their seats set in stone from our family name. They were the strongest fire and water elementals in the capital, and were loved and treated so well."

I cleared my throat and wrapped my arms around myself, suddenly cold. "On my thirteenth birthday, they didn't come home. I taught myself everything from that point on, furious. I studied for hours gaining knowledge on hacking. My encryptions are extremely hard to crack because of my mental capacity. I read through everything the Council had and has on their networks but I was never able to find out anything about my parents, however I learned about everyone there. When I met Pixie, I helped her learn and we researched and trained together. There is something missing in all of this and it drives me insane constantly. They replaced my mom and dad with other people but their names were never on record, but they were listed as low level power and I never understood that. It didn't make sense. No, I have a feeling they were digging for information or found something they weren't supposed to and were killed for it." I finally stopped and the guys all stared.

I sighed. "So yeah, the first part is how you have my powers. I'm an unknown variable for now, although this mythical aspect makes me want to do some more research on that part. Even though I have a feeling not much will come from it, if what you all said is correct. But the bright side is, you will have full use of my powers now."

Pixie sighed and laid back into Etienne's chest as he maneuvered his way behind her. The image was nice. Despite knowing the reason for bonding may have been a little selfish. Okay, a lot selfish. *I can't infiltrate and glow purple.* The bonding was still fate, it felt right. It was destined and regardless how it came out, it did. Might as well make the best of it.

"You know we should use these weeks to try to control those powers because you don't want to be the hot sexy instructors in the academy that have new abilities that they cannot control. I'd rather not be killed on my first day there. Preferably," Pixie said softly from Etienne's lap.

"Before you ask, I did research on all of you and we knew what your positions were." I stuck out my tongue, and Dante chuckled.

"Always a few steps ahead. I like that in a wife. Especially the head part," he growled pulling me closer to him. I laughed and batted his hands away.

Luca was silent for a while and sighed deeply. "Ellie, this isn't on the computer files and I'm not sure why, but your parents were replaced on the council by my parents. It was when I was sixteen, my parents pretty much married for political connections, not because they actually liked each other. They even stay in separate houses. I joined the Academy as soon as possible to get away from those crazy fucks."

I steepled my fingers beneath my chin and leaned forward. "Interesting. Do you think your parents may be connected to their murders?" A clue is a clue.

Luca

"No IDEA," I answered honestly.

"The guys would tell you we have been suspecting corruption for quite some time, they have more funds readily available and they seem to have more in clandestine meetings, and my parents, not that they were decent before, are more pretentious as if they are untouchable. It's strange really," I admitted.

"The Council is generationally run, historically. However, when members pass, new members are voted in by other members. So what we have been trying to figure out is how the hell his parents were voted in. They are high society but not enough to be on the Council. Money talks, but their name would not have certainly disappeared from all records," Etienne tossed in.

"It is true. Money talks and while we had money, it was not enough to grease up an entire Council and get two members murdered," I said.

"How about magick child trafficking? Would that get them rich enough?" whispered Pixie.

"Wait, what?" I replied.

Pixie

It's FUNNY, I have always come off as more easy-going, and when I'm side by side to Ellie, I am. I don't murder, I research. I had survived quite a bit of my own bullshit before meeting Ellie and other than with her, I didn't feel the need to share my background, until now.

"I grew up on the human side of the border. I didn't know I was magick at all. I grew up with human parents who loved me at first, I guess, or at least they may have wanted me? But one day I got really sick, felt like I was on fire from the inside out, I must have been eight or nine. I didn't realize until later, after moving to Darnika, that I had gone through the surge and apparently I went through it early." I gave a sad smile. "I woke up with my parents, fretting over me and I kept hearing their thoughts and responding to them. They were confused as to how I knew what was on their mind. They freaked out, and they started to take me to church, thinking I was possessed." I gave a sad laugh. "Soon it got worse, they started bringing home holy water and would make me chug it in the morning, then they figured they could beat the demons out of me. It was my daily routine. I started to get used to it."

"I am so sorry, Pixie," said Luca. Dante, Etienne, and Dimitri seemed to shift closer.

"I was thirteen when I met Ellie, we are the same age you know, nineteen. So that was about four or five years of holy water martinis and beatings." I shifted uncomfortably and closed my eyes. Did you know that water is usually blessed by a priest dipping his hands in the water and that that water is touched by hundreds of people at the church? Between dirty hands and regular bacteria, holy water was poison. I started to get sick. Lost weight. My parents at that time became almost obsessed with the idea of finally winning against the Devil. I lost count how many times during the years that I would throw up, my throat was always raw, my teeth in the back of my mouth started to decay." I sighed and got up not being able to bear touch anymore and stood against the wall. The concern coming from our emotional bond was overwhelming and I threw up my shields. "I started getting so ill that I was taken to the hospital and put in a medically induced coma due to swelling in my brain. I was ten at that time. Turns out drinking contaminated water for long periods of time and ignoring the symptoms can end up with liver failure, especially for someone with an already weak and broken body. Then when my parents were asked why I was so weak, they told the doctor I was bulimic." I snorted a laugh. "Fucking bulimic. The stupid doctors released me back into their care with instructions to get me to a therapist for help. I started to believe I was cursed. Surely, I had to be right? Crazy ass parents, mind reading. I mean, fuck. Not even something that should be a gift, felt like it was one."

I got off the wall and hugged myself. Dimitri stood up and ran his hands on my shoulders, offering comfort but let me finish, and I shot him a grateful smile.

"Do you know how hard it was to know when the beatings were coming? To hear the thoughts of hatred justified by some religion? I hated myself. I hated everything. Everyone. I needed to get out and do more, be more. I was so very tired of being weak. I started to sneak out when they were gone. I found a gym down the road and the owner saw the bruises and let me train for free. I just wanted to protect myself. They didn't allow me to go to school, I had no friends, I didn't know how to be social so I just didn't speak. Ellie noticed me and I felt...seen. Understood. We would spar together when I was able to sneak away, it was my only moment of peace. One night after a particularly bad beating I could barely walk the next morning but I knew if I got up, I would see Ellie, and I didn't want to miss a day with my only peace. That same day she offered to take me to a place that was for people like me, that she would stay with me, help me. I didn't ask how she knew, I just knew it was my chance to leave. I knew that eventually they would kill me. We left that day and I never looked back."

Dimitri grabbed me, hugged me, and kissed the top of my head. "You will never be weak again. I know you are strong already. Well trained. Powerful. Loved and able to love. You are incredible and we will be grateful, to our core, every second for the rest our lives, that you are with us. That we found you, that Ellie saved you. We all have a past, some of ours is darker than others," he said gruffly. "But we have each other and we swear to you, people will fucking die before they hurt you or Ellie. I don't give a fuck who gets in the way. Yes, we know you can handle yourself, but fuck it, you don't have to do it alone."

"How did they get a magick baby over the border," Etienne mused softly. "The only ones allowed across the border are Shadows who have to hunt murderers who cross illegally, and even then that border is highly protected, yet Ellie crossed everyday—I'm assuming with her powers—but how did anyone else get out, let alone smuggle a baby born in Darnika?"

"Listen to what you just said, Etienne, the only ones allowed to cross are Shadows, the border is highly protected. I grew up on the human side, it's where Ellie found me. She used to cross over every day when she was younger to go to a bunch of different martial arts classes, yes, with her powers. Point is, someone was able to sneak me out. When we started researching more, we wondered if everything was connected. So we not only looked into her parents and the Council, we looked into money trans-actions, people who had babies and suddenly lost them. We looked into the Shadows. Ellie's dad was insistent that they were under the Council's thumb, she said he would consistently call them the Council's little bitches. The

Shadows on the border were getting paid a lot more than any of the ones on patrol, in fact those assigned to the border who didn't have a raise increase, suddenly died on patrol. The Shadows are dirty, boys. You're training a bunch of magick human traffickers and kidnappers for the Council."

❧ 14 ❧

"A strong woman builds her own world. She is one who is wise enough to know that it will attract the man she will gladly share it with."- **Unknown**

"You realize that magick did all the work right? Okay, just making sure we are all on the same page."- **Dimitri**

Charlie

I FELT an overwhelming sense of sadness, disgust and guilt coming from the men.

"You know it is interesting, I can pick up on lies, literally observe and pick up on peculiarities. We figured the Council was dirty. We have been in position for years to figure out why but we never looked further into the Shadows. This time we will have the opportunity to have the girls in place at the Academy. With all six of us we will be able to fix this shit," said Etienne.

"Hey," I said gently, "we aren't blaming you. We are getting you on the same page so you understand everything we are up against, so stop the fucking guilt trip. I feel it coming from you all. The Council is dirty and they are corrupting the very people they have protecting us. I mean, fuck, they even sent you out here under false pretenses to kill Exousia, with a fake ass list of victims. All that just to stop someone from being helpful to people in the lower castes. Well, that particular plan is a bust so we need to move on," I said.

"Fuck," Dante started, but paused. A million thoughts and expressions flitted through his eyes. Anger, confusion, distrust, pain, wariness, and finally his face cleared. "I'm not saying all of this isn't a lot but I believe in you. I feel the conviction coming from you. So... what is the plan?" finished Dante, his signature grin warming me. His belief in our mission driving me even more so.

"Our plan? We train, we infiltrate, we solve. Simple really, we have been training for years, you boys only got a taste of what we can do. You really need to get on our level. For more reasons than one. First, you're all now bonded to two sexy as fuck women. Well, that's actually one and two. So then three, we can literally wipe the floor with your asses. As trainers, you cannot let new recruits show you up." I smiled, then laughed as Dante got up and sat on me.

"Show me up now, princess," he said, then stuck his tongue out, teasing. I smacked him but wrapped my arms around his waist and mindlessly rubbed his abs and sighed in contentment. I could get used to this.

"We do not hold back for anyone period. That's for pussies," I said.

"We have five weeks," I continue. "We need to practice and then make sure we can attempt to be in sync. Hmmm, maybe pick up the moves we have learned over the years."

"You won't have the muscle memory to be perfect but we can start and then as much as it is going to suck after training all day during the Academy, we will have to practice after hours too," Pixie said as she groaned and snuggled in closer to Dimitri, who looked scared for a bit before he wrapped her up like a lettuce leaf.

I cleared my throat. "Not the kind of practice I wanted, ugh." I pouted, eyeing Dimitri's body up and down, while Pixie stuck out her tongue at me and smirked.

"Right, and what kind of practice did you want?" Luca asked, his eyes flashing.

"Oh, you know the open leg kind." I smiled at him, and he leaned over to give me a kiss. "Mmmm." I savored his slow kiss.

"Hey, get your own bonded chair!" joked Dante, and Luca smacked him in the head after one last kiss and laughed as he danced away from Dante's fist.

"Let's head to bed, the boys and I will have to go get your names in and bring you the official slip. Ellie, what surname are you going by now? Pixie?" Luca asked.

"Charlie Laurel and Pixie Luci, keep in mind people may recognize us from the city once we get there but the names are clean," I reply. "Dante, get off of me, you ass, you're going to crush me until my curves flatten!"

He let out a shocked gasp as he stood up. "No, not the curves," he yelled dramatically, and he bent down to pick me up and throw me over his shoulder. He smacked my ass and ran toward the room, and I couldn't stop laughing.

.   .   .

Pixie

I LAUGHED as Dante ran off with Ellie dramatically. Luca shook his head and asked me where we put the sheets for the bed and went off with Etienne to prepare the bed, ever the charming leaders. I cuddled a little closer to Dimitri.

"I try not to talk about my past. You have made me a little braver and soon I will share more of myself with you as well. Thank you for being so brave. Thank you for surviving," he whispered.

For the first time since Ellie, I truly melted. This was only the beginning and I was so grateful. There are books that always talk about finding mates and falling in love right away, I always said that was bullshit. I have always been firmly on the side of building before falling. Truth is, finding your bonded was special, you will be connected and cherished? Love will develop naturally just from that alone because, just like everything else that was worth it, love took time.

The bond helped but it didn't mean we all suddenly would fall in love right away. We would all get there though and that gave me more joy than I could explain. What I felt with Ellie was intense, multiply that by four more bonded, and fuck, we were just so lucky.

Charlie

.   .   .

DANTE SET me down in the room and kissed me gently, wrapping his arms around me.

"I have always wanted to be bonded, this feeling of contentment of peace is different. Training, arrogant recruits and bullshit missions, I'm used to. This is new, but fuck, if it isn't what people would whisper it was like," he said softly. He kissed me gently and let his hands roam all over, teasing, caressing tenderly. Like he couldn't believe I was real. It felt amazing to be in his arms, my six foot four, Latin jokester.

"Mmmm, it does feel fucking amazing." I looked up at him and into his eyes. "You are so fucking sexy it is distracting. Let's get these sheets changed, even this horny bitch doesn't sleep on cum," I joked.

Luca and Etienne walked in at that moment with the fresh giant sheet that was custom made for the bed. "Ellie, why did you ever have a bed made so large? Especially if it was just you and Pixie?" Luca asked, then started stripping and changing the bed.

Pixie and Dimitri chose that moment to walk in. I winked at Pixie and grabbed her hand. We looked on as they finished, Dimitri joining in to help as they wrestled the sheets and looked like they were losing. We fucking hated changing that sheet so huge win.

When they finished and put all the pillows back, I finally responded, "Well, honey pie, for the orgies of course." Then, we ran out of their reach and jumped onto the far corner of the bed as the men gaped and started to come toward us.

~

I woke up a few hours later and as comfortable as I was, I still had a company to secretly run and encryptions to update, to make sure they were at the peak of superiority. I also had to prepare for time at the academy, do my patrols and make sure my security team understood that we would be leaving for a few. Most importantly I had to make sure the castes were safe while Exousia was out playing hot school girl.

I snuck out of bed, took a quick shower, brushed my teeth and threw on some sweats and a tank top and made my way to the kitchen for some elixir of life.

"Yummmm, coffee, gimme gimmie," grumbled Pixie as I poured a cup, then she snatched it from me.

"Bitch, I will fucking cut you."

She stuck out her tongue and threw me the middle finger. "Not before I rip off your fucking tits if you stand in between me and my fucking unicorn blood," she retorted.

"I'm glad it's unicorn blood; you will live a half-life, a cursed life from the moment that shit passes your mother-fucking lips!"

"Fuck it, it was worth it. Least I still have my nose, more than Voldemort had. I will send your ass through the veil like Sirius." She had the balls to compare.

"Not my Sirius, you bitch," I shrieked. "You take that shit the fuck back," I launched myself at that traitorous coffee stealing bitch but was caught mid-air by Luca.

"What the fuck is going on?" he asked. I looked around and the men were all standing in the kitchen dressed in their Shadow gear, looking ready for battle.

"Bitch took my coffee, then mentioned Sirius Black, she has to die," I grumbled.

Dante burst out laughing. "Well that makes sense

now, we thought there was a war going on but that is a reasonable reason to lose your shit," he said as he came around, poured me a fresh cup, handed it to me and gave me a kiss. I looked up at him adoringly. He gave me coffee, he's gorgeous and intelligent.

"Okay, so this was all just because of coffee and Harry Potter?" Etienne said, looking very confused. Poor guy, understanding behavior was his job, he was so out of his element with us. *Wait, did he just say?*

Dante and Luca groaned, and Dimitri just stepped to the side.

Pixie and I narrowed our eyes and looked at him. "Just? Just coffee? Just the most amazing book series in the entire world? Etienne, we will cut you."

He grumbled something in French and walked away, but not before Pixie threw a loaf of bread at his head.

"I love you," I said as I leaned over to give Pixie a kiss.

"So, uh, safe to say coffee is important in the morning?" Luca scratched his head.

"Clearly, Luca."

"Okay, good to know but next time don't try to kill each other, or at least wait until we get back. We will be dropping off the invitation names and bringing your entrance passes. We should be back in a couple hours, we will text you when we are on the way," Luca said as he leaned over and gave me a kiss, then Pixie.

Having finished our coffee we were much more amenable, hell, we even walked them over to the elevator door and gave them all hugs, kisses, and sensual promises. All domestic and shit. Now if I could only get the motherly thing down I would be a shoe in for bonded of the year, next to Pix of course.

As it was, the bond is incredibly difficult the first few

months. The craving to be with one another is strong. Having to train, then heading to the Academy soon, will be quite difficult to say the least. Not that I will back down from the challenge. Sounds like clandestine sexcapades. Fuck yesss!

❧ 15 ❧

*"Once you eliminate the impossible, whatever remains, no matter how improbable, must be the truth." -**Arthur Conan Doyle***
*"The problem with the Council, is that you must first go in assuming that nothing is impossible."-**Etienne***

D imitri

"How much fucking longer until we fucking leave this shit show?" I asked Luca for the hundredth time. He stared at me drolly. Fuck his look, he couldn't blame me for wanting to get back to the girls; he wanted to leave too, he just had to always be the epitome of control at all times, his father being who he was.

"Once my father gives us information, we can go," he said as we strode through the main Council building, aiming for his father, Sergio Ignis', office. One of the strongest fire elementals and the current head of one of the founding families on the Council. Every time, I was in his presence, I wanted to throat punch him. He was arrogant and there was something off with his thirst for power. It was an addiction for him. He was constantly looking for more power, I'm sure that is why he set us out on this mission to find this vigilante. Granted, it was a Council decision, but we all had a suspicion that Ignis was beyond the move. While I understood the reason for the hunt, I'm sure it went beyond the need to actually help the caste. It wasn't a secret of his disdain for anyone who wasn't at the top of the food chain, no, the thought of anyone undermining his control was beyond anything his narcissistic personality could possibly fathom.

We paused outside of his office as Luca knocked.

"Come in," Ignis said from the other side of the door. I bit back a sneer and I fought to keep my face impassive as Luca let us into the painfully ostentatious office. There were accolades on every wall, Lucas and his combined. Photos of every major event over the past several years, but what really caught the eye were the two giant fireplaces on either side of the room, his large desk situated right in the center of the room, covered with paperwork and old worn books.

"Ah, Luca, Dante, Etienne, Dimitri. I'm glad you took the time to come see me before heading back over to the castes," he sneered the last word. Glad indeed, considering he sent us a missive that pretty much said 'come or else.'

"Yes, well. You had something to tell us father?"

He stood up and walked around his desk, looking every inch an Elite warrior, muscular, tall, with a carefully placed blank expression. Not that it hid his dark soul.

"Yes. As an Elite guard who is on track to bring in the Vigilante, you four will be quite the catch for political alliances and you are not getting any younger." He reached over to pour himself a few fingers of a dark liquor from a decanter.

The words he uttered settled over us like a thick suffocating blanket. This is what the capital was about, political and loveless marriages, intrigue, lies, all for the detriment of the many and the benefit of the few. There is nothing that could come from this that would bring us any joy, but that never mattered. What mattered is whatever aspirations the Council had.

"How do you mean, sir?" Etienne spoke up, an undercurrent of fury lacing his tone.

"I mean, Etienne, that you all have a role to play and you *will* play it well. Bring me the vigilante, and after the execution we will be having a wedding ceremony...for all four of you... and one of you will be marrying my daughter," he finished with a dark look. The silence was thick.

"I do not have a sister, what are you talking about?" Luca broke the silence.

"Oh, you do, she just didn't have a purpose until now. So she was kept well protected but away. But now? I see the value of her marriage to an Elite guard who has brought forward the vigilante. I will even let you decide which one from your team gets to have her." He chuckled, walking around and sitting back at his desk. We simply stared at him. Luca looked like he was about to lose his shit when he raised his hand and effectively dismissed us. Closing the door behind us, I held my hand up, indicating that we needed to move further before we started to discuss any of this.

We started to head over to the car when the snark of some Elite Shadows that were drinking whatever koolaid they had in this place, reached our ears.

"Wow, the Elite of the Elite. I hear you're having a few problems tracking down one vigilante in the lower castes." One of the dickheads laughed.

"I guess the real Elite team has to be sent in now," another threw in. I was done being nice. I looked back at Luca, he gave me a slight nod and I grinned. I strode over to the men talking shit and swung, hard, breaking his jaw. His friend tried to put me in a headlock and I shifted my body, flipping him over my head and tossing him to the floor. A few dozen punches to their faces, and I felt the boys start dragging me back.

It wasn't nearly enough to satisfy my need to make someone bleed, but it will have to do. Now, back to my women.

Charlie

"THAT CAN'T BE RIGHT," I muttered as I looked at the screen in front of me.

"What can't be right?" Pixie looked over her shoulder and her eyebrow popped up.

"Exactly," I responded to her expression. "I have

refreshed the system, double checked the names, and it doesn't make sense. Why now?"

For the first time in several years there are more than a few female recruits, in fact other than us, there were four more. I went into the system a couple hours after the boys left to make sure the invites were processed, and to manipulate the sleeping arrangements to have Pixie and I next to their rooms. As trainers they were given special sleeping quarters in the building next to us, so we just needed to be closest to the exit. It worked for two different reasons, the wet-spot-on-the-bed kind, and the bring-down-your-entire-operation kind.

"Pull up their names, families, histories, medical information, and pictures. I can't speak about the timing because we have no idea if they were going to be put there with or without us, infiltrating this year." She shrugged. "No one knows about us, but at least there will be more than a few buffers between us and the meat market," she teased, but the slight concern in her eyes was clear.

"I wouldn't be so sure. Looks like all of these women are daughters to the members of the Council, pretty ones at that. Why the hell would they put high caste girls in the training academy when they were usually used for political marriages and alliances?"

Pixie pulled up the information on her screen and she catalogued all their details away. I took note of all of the incoming females, Aliya Gi—daughter of the Earth Elemental, Raegan Leigheas—daughter of the Healer, Maitie Myalo—the daughter of the Mind reader, and then Laikia Ignis—daughter of the mysterious unlisted Fire Elemental. The last one threw me for a loop, Luca didn't mention having a sister, and I don't think he would hide that.

"Luca has a sister, that's interesting. We still cannot find his parents on any of the databases either so it makes sense we missed her too. I mean the only reason we knew of Luca was because of the Shadow Academy registry. Hmmm, it looks like the girls inherited one power though. Not too strong by the looks of it. Nothing here indicating any formal training in fighting, not that that is surprising since they aren't allowed to learn. What is the Council playing at?"

"I have no idea." I steepled my hands on the table. "Realistically, even if they were strong, there is a physical component to the training. Why put their girls at risk? I don't think they would. No, they have to have been trained for hand-to-hand, secretly or something. I mean if they want alliances, putting your daughters in danger wouldn't be one of the ways to do it."

"Well, lookie here." Pixie pointed out something on the screen. "They were added literally thirty minutes after we were put into the system. Wanna bet the Council daddies panicked at the idea of two unknown females near their high caste instructors and warriors."

I laughed, joke's on them then. *Is there a song for we fucked, sucked, and bonded to your men?* I need to add that to my list of to-do then.

We printed out their profiles and then spent extra time hacking into all cameras in the academy and erasing our trails. I had ordered four additional tablets and computers brought up for each of the men, and spent time encrypting all eight devices to keep them from prying eyes if any room is hacked. In fact if anyone were to get nosy, they would think the boys had an addiction to unicorn porn. I didn't even know it existed.

We needed constant eyes on the property and extra

devices if I needed to do some updating to my systems, but overall we were set technology-wise. Despite the bond and our abilities to connect and sense general locations, I also ordered tracking devices that would get here later today that I will also have to hack and encrypt. The life of a vigilante spy is never dull. I stretched and looked at my phone and frowned. The boys had yet to text or call us, and holy fuck, we have been here for four hours. I told Pixie as such and her pretty eyes popped open in surprise. It was always a little shocking when her full gaze hit you.

"No wonder I have to pee," she grumbled, and we secured the room and headed upstairs. "We might as well get into something to workout in, when they get here we need to start, besides I'm wondering what this roster is all about and how it's going to affect our plans we need to run numbers and come up with some possibilities and solutions."

"Maybe that is what's keeping the guys so long? Debriefing? I feel that they are pissed about something but fucking figures they get full access to my powers, and motherfuckers start to block out thoughts first. If this is some bullshit way to try and play alpha male, I'm going to kick their asses," I grumbled as I dressed into my workout gear, and walked over to the kitchen to get a protein bar and prep some shakes for the guys and Pix. As Pix came out of the room, the elevator announced visitors, and we peeped in through the glass wall, since the boys didn't even text us.

"Allow Entrance."

Luca stormed in looking pissed, Dimitri had blood on his hands, Dante had no hint of smile on his facial features, and Etienne looked deadly furious. We gave them a wide berth and after a few moments of silence we walked toward the workout room and let them know to follow when they were ready and where to find it. When they wanted to talk, they would, I'm not harassing anyone for information, they aren't a mark, and to be honest, if they want to shut us out of their thoughts, then they need to man the fuck up and talk. We are their bonded, not their babysitters.

THE MOMENT I walked into the room and took a deep breath, I felt a deep peace resonate inside of me. Sparring with Pixie was always an adventure to let our shields down and try to react before our brains can pick up each other's incoming movements. Besides, this was as much for Pixie as it was for the men. In that we needed to increase her control at this point too. The stronger, the better. I needed to make sure she had a grasp on everything as well. Although with her mental prowess, she would pick it up faster.

"Hey room, play 90's punk rock," I commanded softly to the room.

We started to stretch and get warmed up by jumping on our Pelotons to do our spinning classes. These instructors were funny as fuck and any instructor that can curse and train is my soulmate. We pushed ourselves for a forty-five-minute class, before hopping on our treadmills to cool down. Drenched in sweat, we groaned and went to drink water before starting our sparring sessions. I threw my ponytail higher and wiped the sweat out of my eyes.

"Spar then magick, or magick then spar?" Pixie asked as we walked to the center of the room.

We felt the men walk in but we didn't spare them a

glance. We were here to train and we were on limited time. We didn't have time to coddle and honestly, I was pissed that they stormed in clearly upset, without actually telling us what was going on, and then blocking us out. I don't like that shit.

"Let's aim for magick and sparring later, we need to let our heart rates calm for a bit. Let's approach this differently and see which magicks you can start to pull and use." We sat and crossed our legs in front of each other and closed our eyes, and dropped the shields between us to speak freely so she can feel how I pull different forms. "Breathe deeply, and look deep down inside for a blue string of power and pull it up like an anchor. I want you to visualize it taking form as a ball of water and see how you feel as you manifest it." I felt Pixie reach and concentrate, and seconds later, her shocked gasp fills the room. I opened my eyes and a giant water ball was floating above us. She then made it take the shape of a rocket, then a fish, then a penis, and I started laughing and clapping.

"Good shit! That's amazing, Pix! Now go ahead and look for a red string at the same time but hold the blue one and do not let it go."

Pixie shifted her concentration a bit and with another breath created a huge flaming ball next to the water. The water started to steam and quickly I sent her a mental request to throw a shield between the two elements to prevent them from affecting the other. At this point, ridiculously proud, I saw the level of concentration and determination on her face as she tried to control three powers at once. The shield went up and the two elements remained pulsing with power.

"Now keep in mind you don't have an end to your powers. You can maintain this as long as you need to. I want you to remove the shield and use the water and fire together to take each other out. It can be simple evaporation or just dousing the fire. Whichever you choose, of course, will have the same effect. Difference is, steam will cause a visibility issue and it tends to burn skin more than fire. So the uses will depend on the amount of damage you wish to make. For now we just want the fire out, so focus on making the fire decrease, let the string go just a bit and then throw the water over the fire."

Without skipping a beat, the shield drops, the fire is smaller, and the water douses the fire ball. I started clapping and leaned over to her on my hands and knees to give her a kiss. "I am so proud of you, that was badass!"

"It was awesome, concentrating on three took a bit more than I was used to but I really felt like I could keep them up forever. That was incredible." Pixie sounded excited. We really should have been doing this more often.

"Yes! Okay, let's do it again! I want to get those down before we add another power and try to do four at once, then we want to be able to use the powers while sparring. Then I'm considering having you try practicing when you're at your most vulnerable. The mind reading can be useful if you're able to extend that to not just reading thoughts but more so to pick up if anyone is near you. Like a tracker can smell scents and pick up a trail, you will be picking up mental signatures. That will be way more difficult, the mind isn't meant to take on so much at once, so we'll go slow to avoid any neurological damage. Mental workouts, so we just need to keep flexing it."

Pixie sat back and did the same exercise four more times. Each time the elements got bigger, and the concentration less noticeable. Which is perfect, we didn't want anyone to even notice what was coming their way. Rather be taken by surprise at the ease.

I felt rather than heard the men finally step a little closer to sit around us as we practiced. Either they talk or get ignored. I shrugged.

"Okay, so now let's throw in a little curve ball, Pix. I don't want you to hold the elements up. I want you to make them move. This isn't just by using the power to make the water and fire and shield take form, that is easy, I want you to make them move around you by manipulating the air around you."

She looked at me confused.

"Fair expression." I laughed. "Maybe I explained that poorly. Close your eyes and feel the air around you. Breathe in and breathe out. When you breathe, the air is going in and out of your lungs. It is natural. It is around you. You control it. You can stop breathing by holding your breath and you can start simply by giving into your natural instincts. Just like me, magick is your natural instinct. There was never a moment where it wasn't part of me. Tap into that. Dig deep and get to know each portion of your magick, let it fill you, become you. However, remember you are still in control, it's natural to you but it *is not* you. The moment you forget that, you forget who you are and can lose control. Your mind will break. Just like depression can break the mind and soul, the loss of yourself to your magick will have the same effect. Do you feel it?" She gave a quick nod and a smile.

"Good, build the water but this time throw a shield around it instead, and do the same with the fire. Now they are two separate and powerful bombs that can be thrown and used, because the moment you let go of the shield should be at the point of impact, which means you need to feel where your magick is being sent. Stand up now."

She stands and faces me and I throw up a shield around me.

Practice makes perfect, even if you have to be the dummy for a bit.

❧ 16 ❧

*"If you want something said, ask a man; if you want something done, ask a woman." –**Margaret Thatcher***
*"We made waves. We make moves." - **Pixie & Charlie***

C harlie

THIS ENTIRE TIME, the men just sat around and watched, not saying a thing. After Pixie and I came down from our high, we put our hands on our hips and stared at them.

"Hi, welcome home, how are you? Okay, cool. Wow, that is such an interesting story. I'm so glad you decided to share." I rolled my eyes dramatically. "Seriously if you're trying to actively piss me off, you are succeeding."

"You have your minds locked down pretty tight,

what's up?" asked Pixie as she sat down in front of them. Well, I wasn't in the mood of having a kumbaya moment, so I grabbed a Gatorade from the gym fridge and leaned against the wall while I glared at the men.

Luca

Fuck, they were so beautiful and powerful and amazing. We were so lucky to have them and now we had to deal with the fucking mess the Council had put on us. I rubbed my hand down my face. We had to take a few moments to calm down when we got here, Dimitri went to wash the blood off his hands, and we switched into workout gear. It was impressive to hear Ellie describe magick and control, she was a natural, and Pixie just absorbed it all and kept going. I was in awe to be honest.

I felt Ellie's stare, I knew she was pissed, I could lock down the thoughts but the emotions still came through. She looked like she was ready to just walk out and say fuck it; Pixie had a tighter hold but I could tell she wasn't too happy either.

"So obviously we went to the Council and we put your names in. We were ready to go but the Council decided that they needed to see us. They are not too happy about us not catching the vigilante and that the informant we had suddenly disappeared." Pixie and Ellie gave each other a look and a smirk at that.

"What was the look for?" Etienne demanded and stood angrily; we were all a little on edge.

"You don't get to ask me jackshit, until you finish explaining why you all came here acting like a bunch of dicks, blocking us out, not even calling or texting us, and then on top of that, Dimitri comes in with blood on his hands. So I suggest you be very fucking careful. I don't care if we are bonded, I don't care if you are a foot taller than me. I will beat the ever loving shit out of you. Don't fuck with me," Ellie said in a dark voice, a shiver going up my spine and partially to my dick, and I can see why Exousia was feared. I smirked as I picked up Etienne's similar reaction.

"We caught a lot of heat for not finding the vigilante, they think we are incompetent, questioned our ability to be trainers, and be a team. As for Dimitri..." I trailed off.

Truth is we keep him centered as much as possible but he thinks with his fist.

"Someone ran into his fist until they were unconscious," I finished.

"That's fucking hot," Ellie whispered, and Dimitri smirked.

"There is also a small issue of four other females being put into the academy this round and they are all daughters of the Council members, color me surprised when I found out I had a fucking sister." I rubbed my head, fuck, I had a headache from all this bullshit.

"There is another small issue. We need to bring someone forward as the vigilante by Friday before Shadow training," Dante piped in, also rubbing his head.

"Oh, that's it? You fucking men are so extra. Follow me," Ellie said and walked out of the workout room and stood in front of a wall. She pressed a combination on the wall and a scanner popped out, took her eye scan and her finger print, and it even looked like a bit of blood for her DNA and then the wall opened to reveal a set of stairs. At the bottom of the stairs was another system with a combination and scan. The door opened to reveal a large room with computers, books, and chrome walls. It looked like a lair for a fucking mastermind criminal. Pixie brushed passed us and said out loud into the room, "Pixie and Ellie, plus four." Until that moment we hadn't even realized there were red dots on our chest. Holy fuck. *Did she make super suits too?*

Charlie

MEN PANIC TOO EASILY. Tell them who I am, what I can do, my history and they still thought that... what? They couldn't just come to me? I mean the bond should at least assure them they can trust me, that they can rely on me. It kind of hurt. I didn't like that. I don't like weakness. So we needed to tighten up and lay everything on the table. I gestured for them to sit down around the table.

"There is all the information needed on the four additional ladies. Added exactly thirty minutes after you initiated our invitations, which means they were placed there for a reason, I'm hoping the reason you are upset is because you know that reason, which means we can start calculating risks and countermeasures. As for the missing informant, we tied up that loose end minutes after you left that day. I don't do loose ends, I protect my castes. It sucks it affected you but I am not sorry about it. She was taken, killed, and disposed of by an inside man. Snitches don't get stitches here... they die."

They looked taken aback by my statement, well Luca did. Etienne gave me a calculating look of respect, Dante looked proud, and Dimitri looked turned on. So different, so perfect. I sent affection through the bond to let them know that even though they sucked, I cared about them. They gave me a small smile.

"So how did you get information about the women so quickly, and is this pretty much everything about them?" Dante pried further.

"Everything is relevant." I waved my hand around. "We have a suspicion, so now we want to ask you what you know. What's up, and how can we work together, you know since we are bonded and all, to fix the problem?"

At least they had the decency to look slightly ashamed as if they just realized that we are in this together. *Idiots, all of them.*

"Well, it looks like the Council would like me to be married for political connections. My parents being in the Council makes me valuable to them. The other ladies are there to marry other high ranking Shadows and build those connections. It seems that, to them, it would further solidify the Shadows as the force of the Council and ensure that the Shadows are, even more so, tied to them. It's a cluster fuck and it doesn't make sense. We told them as such. We were built to protect Darnika, that includes everyone. It is a conflict of interest to tie the Shadows to the Council in that way; it's one thing if it's a bond, but completely another if it's seen as a political move. There is already unrest in the lower castes and the only reason they are thriving and becoming stronger is because of you ladies and the work you do. They may be hiding it, but the crime rate is pretty much non-existent but they are saying it's because of the MLE and strong Shadow presence."

"I picked up several lies, but from their body language you can tell there is something else going on. Something they are hiding. They know of my abilities and they tried very hard to hide certain tells, even as far as putting on too much perfume to hide the scent of deception. I am rarely wrong, we knew of corruption, but this all smells and feels of a deeper plot. Well thought-out, calculating. Dangerous," Etienne said softly.

Pixie and I looked at each other and turned around and started typing rapidly on the computer. "Pix, once you are in their system, look up the following keywords: wedding, invitations, union. I will pull up the search for strength, force, power, and allies." The men stepped closer, intrigued as our hands flew over the keyboards and our eyes quickly scanned and dismissed information, kept the needed information, and became engrossed. After about forty minutes and several fucks, motherfuckers, and shits, we finally came up for air.

I walked over to the side of the room and pressed a button that brought down a punching bag. What? After several years of research I hated going up to the gym and coming back down so I had one installed. Don't judge me. I started to wrap my hands and punch the bag while speaking.

"This shit never came up in our searches because we never looked into political unions or allies within the stupid Council that would come from marriages. Even if we did logically, it wouldn't be something that would affect the castes, bring up information on trafficking, or connect dots to my parents' death." I punched harder and harder until the bag became my bitch.

Pixie picked up, staring at me with a look full of amusement, love, and exasperation. I loved that woman.

"Looks like they have been planning a self-inflicted revolution of sorts. We hacked into emails and encrypted files and as it stands the Council wants to join the Shadows with marriage because they need to make a political stand. They want to show to castes that the Shadows aren't just their protectors but their leaders. It is like a psychological mind fuck. Shadows will not only have more power on the streets but they will no longer keep to the shadows, they will show force by whatever means necessary. They plan on using the narrative that the vigilante has been captured and now the higher castes will be told that they are safe, because they have been fed lies of murders, and the lower castes will start to crumble because their savior is gone." Pixie shook her head as she finished and wrapped her hands to join me at the bag.

"As if that's not the best part, the Shadows being married? It isn't only Luca. It's you three as well. The bringers of the vigilante, the heroes will be commemorated and given honors, and married to these daughters as a show of some sort of fucked-up, dystopian novel fuckery. I mean really, what does this stupid shit do? You guys get married and the Shadows are further under the Council's thumb? You already work for them. It isn't logical, a lot of this defies logic. My people are kind, they just needed someone to show them that someone cares for them. No more abused women, children or even animals. Homes that are actual homes, food on their tables, building up businesses and improving everyone's livelihood. I have been doing this for years. My last mission? I saved a little girl named Ambrosia from a gargoyle shifter serial killer. That shit wasn't even on the news, the MLE kept it under wraps except for some boasting at the strip club, they didn't want to do anything. I solved that case. I saved and healed that little girl. I took her home. I even patrolled after. I mean what the fucking fuck is the Council even doing?"

Oh. My. God.

I flew to the computer and typed in the words 'shifter' and ran a full database search.

I leaned back in my chair. I scoffed as the results filtered through the screen and I shifted through relevant and irrelevant information. *All a fucking ploy.* Every night an older child was attacked and a baby was also kidnapped. There was slight unrest in the middle and higher class castes, because of the kidnappings of newborns. The problem was, why. Why children, what did they gain from stolen children. It would cause anarchy when the Council couldn't protect its own people.

I racked my brain and really tried to focus but was struggling to piece this together. Married Shadows, militant Shadow force. Outrage at stolen children. I sighed. None of this made sense.

The computer dinged and I peered at email communications and bit back a curse. The shifter had two purposes, attack the lower caste and torture information about the vigilante before they had to make a formal show of sending an Elite team. Seems like I was really putting a wrench into whatever plans they had, and they were out of options. Their planning seems like a fucking cluster of stupid ass ideas thrown together to bring dissent to Darnika. But why?

I took a deep breath and faced the men. I took in all of their features; Etienne's handsome face and his calculating look making his blue eyes brighter, Luca's piercing green eyes and a bit more than five o'clock shadow, Dimitri's vampire-like scowl struggling to maintain his anger even hours later, and my sweet Dante no longer laughing but sullen. Fuck that, these are my men, our men, and I'll be damned if we let them be used for some fuckery too. I knew they wouldn't marry, they aren't weak pawns but the Council didn't need to know that. I needed a curveball, we needed a new target for them to focus on and I felt my power roll, I felt it awaken in levels I haven't felt since the day I knew my parents were gone or the day I finally brought Pixie home. My rage blasted through me, Pixie shot me a panicked look and the men's eyes flickered in alarm. I slammed down my shield and locked it up. I protect, I plan, I calculate, and I kill when necessary. Something is coming and my blood lust felt it. Except this time I wouldn't tamper it down.

Etienne

THE COUNCIL DOES nothing but lust for power, it is disgusting. Luca has been trying to deal with having a sister, being told to marry, and having to bring down someone who we bonded with. He took his phone and threw it when we left the Council room, smashing it into pieces, and when that other soldier was being a dick, we didn't even give a shit when Dimitri walked up to him and punched him repeatedly. Luca rarely loses his cool, he's more personable, more political and to be honest, it is the only reason I defer to him, despite being more calculating and controlled myself. I don't like people or pretty speeches, and I damn sure don't want to have to speak to the Council more than necessary. When we got in the car, we were silent and said nothing until we were at the penthouse.

Watching Ellie and Pixie train was impressive. It soothed something in me and filled me with affection for them. Ellie calling me out on my bullshit and challenging me set me on fire. Hard work, patience, and perseverance was sexy and it was alluring to me in a way that spoke to my nature. But when we were led down into their hidden private research office, which to be honest, looked more like some type of lair, and presented with the information we were told a few hours ago, I was glad I had to sit down because I got hard immediately. I am not getting married, I am bonded. I have more than most people have, the chance to fall in love with my actual matches. Fuck that. The Council is supposed to lead but they are melting from the inside from twisted corruption, and here are these two women about to take them on with information, inner fire, power, and sheer will.

I felt rage fill the bond, pure anger and fire, and my eyes flew to Ellie's face, and Pixie's expression of panic at the feeling. The look in Ellie's eyes sent a shiver down my spine, I picked up on the combination of anger in her gaze and her relaxed posture. She was comfortable in her anger, and unlike Dimitri who tended to live in it but was unable to rein in and let it loose when provoked, she accepted it and wielded it like a weapon. She was going to take the Council on and set it on fire. Strangely enough, I have been feeling on edge since leaving the Capitol, but now I have a strong feeling of peace. I shouldn't have.

*"Nothing in the world is more dangerous than sincere ignorance and conscientious stupidity."-**Martin King***
*"Dangerous, yes. Because now, this fury has to be directed somewhere and it just keeps building."-**Charlie***

C harlie

"THE COUNCIL HAS BEEN ATTACKING its own people," I said as I threw the freshly printed papers in front of them. A chorus of fucks filled the room.

I took a deep breath and closed my eyes, I have to go. I need to patrol early and warn the castes of Exousia taking a leave and to be vigilant. A few people in the community had a direct line to Exousia for emergencies, everything else was monitored by my cameras and security systems. I needed to expedite the construction and prepare my team for possible issues. If the Council plans to make the Shadows more of a militant presence, I needed them warned and prepared to take people in. Mentally, I made a list and slightly panicked.

Maybe I can set up panic buttons around the city but I don't think I can accomplish that, and the downside is that I would have no idea who is calling because of a need or because of a set-up.

Fuck me. I may thrive on action but realistically, I cannot leave the academy every time I get an alert...it would draw too many eyes. Knowing all the shit I do now and the possible dangers concerns me. Warning them and taking the Council down from the inside will have to be sufficient, for now. But I just cannot promise to stay on the academy grounds if shit becomes too much for them to handle over there.

I sighed. I am not sure when I started to think of them as my people but I knew that a part of me would die if I ever let them suffer because of the callousness of the Council.

I opened my eyes to everyone staring at me. Pixie understood, she always did. Now I need to explain to the men and hope that they don't give me shit. I understand the bond, if I could, I would wrap Pixie in bubble wrap, but you don't do that to someone you care about. She is tough, trained, and this angry bitch will always have her back. That is the way our relationship works. However, we haven't really developed a dynamic with the men. They knew how I was and now they know who I am, they understood it, I hoped. In the end, it wasn't about me anymore, hell, it never really was, it was pretty much Pixie and I; now it was Pixie, Etienne,

Luca, Dimitri, and Dante. I needed to respect that, didn't I?

"Okay, I need to patrol early. It's Monday, which means we have the rest of today and until Friday, five weeks from now, to train as much as we can, however I have a responsibility to the people I chose to protect and I won't leave them defenseless."

My vampire spoke up, "What does that mean? What's the plan and how can we help?"

"Well, two things here, Vampire." I resisted a smile when he scowled. It lightened the mood and we needed that. We needed to take as much happiness as we could get. "Okay, so Pixie and I are going out on patrol earlier than usual this entire week, we need to make sure people are extra vigilant. That means we need to still fit in training, sex, food, sex, drinking water, and more sex." I rubbed my head and started up the stairs with everyone following.

"When can we get to the sex part?" Dante said excitedly, finally smiling again. I couldn't help but laugh at his smile. I dropped my shields and winked at Pixie. A barrage of thoughts and banter entered my mind, but my vampire stuck out the most.

Dimitri looked at me angrily before launching himself in my direction, tackling me, and pinning my arms above my head. Let's be honest, I totally let him. You would too, Damon Salvatore is hot and this man was his fucking doppelgänger with muscles and height. Fucking gorgeous. His eyes locked with mine.

I whispered in his ear, "You know baby, if you just wanted to get on top you could have said so." I nipped and sucked on his ear, trailing my tongue down his neck letting my piercings tease his throat, while rolling my hips

175

into his. He groaned and reached to hold my hips in place and I turned my face to his and captured his lips, and sucked his tongue into my mouth.

You play dirty, Ellie, but I can get even dirtier. His voice sounded husky even in my head.

I flipped him on his back and rode him through my shorts and his pants, while nipping his neck and capturing his lips again.

We separated breathlessly. "Mmm, vampire, you promise?"

"Fuck yes." He gripped my ass and slid his hands to take my shorts off. I jumped up, and moved away.

"Uh, uh, vampire, we need to train first, then patrol, then I will let you do whatever you want with me."

He huffed, while adjusting himself and stood up. I looked back to the other guys and sauntered up to them. "Mmmm, Pixie and I didn't get a kiss yet. If you're going to get married, you're going to have to practice how to please a woman. Wouldn't want to leave them dissatisfied." I grinned.

Luca grabbed my waist while Dante stepped up behind me, and Etienne snatched Pixie up while Dimitri went over to grab her ass and kiss her neck.

Fuck.

I laughed, and reached my arms around Luca's neck while Dante pulled my head back to bite my neck and Luca kissed me like he wanted to fuck me, rough, slow, fast, deep. Fuck. Then he turned me around and smacked my ass. Dante picked me up and I wrapped my legs around him while Luca put his hands in my bra and played with my breasts, God, they felt so heavy as he caressed them, bit my neck, and smacked my ass again. I cried into Dante's mouth and I was completely melting into a fucking puddle of need over here. This man could kiss. Holy fuck.

Yes! Fuck. Mmmm, Luca, you turning into an ass man, baby, because I have plenty for you, I panted.

I'm turning into an Ellie and Pixie man, baby, you two are all that matter, Luca grunted in response.

I heard them all murmur in agreement while continuing to drive us fucking crazy.

I heard Pixie moan as Etienne put his hands into her shorts and played with her pussy while kissing her deeply and Dimitri licked and sucked her neck.

Fuck, Etienne, baby.

Chérie, you keep calling me pet names and I'm going to take you right now.

Turn her around, I want to feel her pussy clench in my hands.

I heard Pixie panting, while Dimitri took over her lips and her pussy, and Etienne grabbed her ass and bit between her shoulder blades. Ahh, he learned her spot, and she came apart in Dimitri's hands and screamed into his mouth. When she came, she forced it through the bond and we all came apart. The men yelled hoarsely and I ripped my mouth from Dante and moaned into his ear. He shuddered more and put me down gently.

We all looked at each other. Well, that is how you greet your fucking bonded.

Pixie and I freshened up a bit and headed back into the gym. We started to warm up but realistically, we couldn't get any hotter if we tried. I opened my mind to everyone, I was going to have to get used to us being connected, we could still have our private thoughts if we learned how to erect a wall around them, but still share everything else. In this case, I wanted them to understand how I felt and what I thought. I sighed. *I sighed more these days, more than a fucking helpless lass in a highlander romance story.* I rolled my eyes. I heard the laughter in my head.

I know the bond makes us closer than normal couples. However, if what we discussed about the purple magick is true, then it makes this six way bond hundred times stronger than normal. Other bonds had a basic melding of powers but the connection of minds and power reserves was a new one. I mean, shit, regularly bonded pairs were lucky enough to even be connected as it was, that soul binding feeling is incredible. The pairs felt closer and developed a profound love that was so strong that it felt impossible to survive if one passed. With Pixie, we were friends first; we trained, flirted, even kissed but when we finally completed the bond, it was as if the entire world stopped. With the men, we didn't have the time to build our relationship like Pixie and I did but, I admit, the world, the moon, the stars, the galaxies and even super novas stopped when our bond was completed.

Now I have four others, and granted we skipped straight to the end for various reasons, I knew we would get to that point. They spoke to different parts of me. Etienne being analytical, Luca needing to lead, Dimitri needing to feel the blood and bones under his hands, and Dante with his humor. Overall? What really is sealing the deal? Is it the idea of them being offered up as marriage bait? It spiked my more possessive side and made me want to punch someone in the face repeatedly, poke their eyes out, and eat their brains out with a fork. I would even share and have Dimitri suck their blood. Good clean up, right?

I felt him laughing and scowling at the same time as he picked up on my stray, murderous thoughts. *The other men are suspiciously quiet in here. Well, you know, less brain cells and all.* Growls echoed in my head.

Pixie came to me and caressed my face. "Baby, don't overthink it. Just feel. Just let the bond work the way it's supposed to. It's new but this feels just like we felt. It feels right. They feel right."

"Ugh, I know, Pix, it's just one day, I'm killing shit and eating pussy, and then the next day, I'm sucking multiple dicks and half in love with a vampire, an angry French man, a fucking classical music loving general, and a guy who wants to eat my pussy until I die. So forgive me for just freaking out just a little bit."

She laughed at me, shook her head and tapped her head, indicating that our conversation wasn't as private for that particular thought. Ah, mental link. I groaned as the men filed in with smirks on their faces.

"So, half in love, huh? Looks like I need to up my game if you're only half in love with this Latin magick." Dante did a little spin and hip dip, and gave me and Pixie a kiss, and Luca followed suit, sans spin and dip. Can't lie, I was disappointed by the lack of the dance moves.

"I don't know, Dante, I'm still stuck on the sucking multiple dicks part, the idea has merit, do you think I can command it as the general?"

"We all know vampires get all the chicks..." Dimitri grinned, running his hands through his dark hair.

"Ah, but the French invented the only way to really kiss," Etienne said with a smirk.

Pixie put her hands on her hips. "Well, we Latinas

have you wrapped around our fingers already, so I don't know who's worse. Me and Ellie and our attraction to you all, or, you four and your attraction to us. I'm going to venture and say you four, at least, me and Ellie aren't cheating on our fiancés." We chuckled as the men scowled.

"We are not getting married!" Dimitri said dismissively. I rolled my eyes, ignoring him.

"We still have the problem of actually bringing in a vigilante," Etienne said thoughtfully.

"Bringing in the baby-snatcher really is the best decision at this point. It can help us discover who sent him and it's a Band-Aid while we are gone." I shrugged.

"Is that even ethical, Ellie?" Luca said reproachfully.

"Do we even care at this point, we have to bring in someone. Might as well be a criminal," Pixie tossed in.

Exactly my point, also sweetie, if you haven't realized yet, you will. I'm not ethical or moral when it comes to protecting what is mine. This city? Mine. Let's train.

❧ 18 ❧

"A wreck on shore is a beacon at sea."- **Proverb**
"In other words, always be prepared for a shit show and
immediate cleanup." - **Dante**

Charlie

DANTE LET OUT A LOW WHISTLE. "This is your workout room?" It looks more like a state of the art gym." Last time, they just walked in looking all sullen and watched Pixie and I train with magick, *now he is actually looking around.*

I shrug. "We like to stay fit." I took a look around the huge room and zeroed in on the boxing ring, sparring floor, workout machines, running machines with heart monitor attachments, spinning bike, rowing machine, multiple punching bags set in a circle to mimic multiple opponents, my weapons wall, and a full range of weights and lifting sets.

"Impressive, this is very well put together," Dimitri said as he walked over to the punching bags. "I never would have thought of this. This is for multiple opponent simulation right?"

I simply nodded while wrapping up my hands, I would fight dirty anywhere but here there is no need for extra blood cleaning. That shit stained like a bitch.

While the boys walked about and started on their machines, Pixie and I headed over to the sparring zone. It's part of our routine usually, to get out any extra energy and today, we certainly needed it with the men around, causing all this fucking emotional confusion.

"Same playlist?" I asked Pixie. She nodded with a smirk. Our fighting playlist makes us focused, gotta love it.

"Hey room play 'Fuck This Motherfucking Bitch Up' playlist," I said loudly. The men all burst out in laughter as they stopped their machines and stepped closer to see us spar. Eminem's angry lyrics came over the speakers as we circled each other. We go at it for about twenty minutes before calling it. We were so evenly matched it was ridiculous.

"That was impressive, but you guys know each other's patterns, maybe it would be best if you spar with one of us instead?" Luca said.

I chuckled softly and looked him dead in his green orgasm-inducing eyes. "Okay, I'll take on two of you. Pixie can take on another two. When sparring, anything goes. Then we can move on to practicing controlling and fighting with your new magick. We can work on combining the two tomorrow."

Dante stepped up next to me and wrapped his arms around me, nipping my ear. "Sure gorgeous, anything goes, in that case weapons good too?"

Pixie read my thought process, or saw my face and bit her lip to stop herself from laughing.

Biting back a moan, I caved in. "We can do weapons too."

I looked at Pixie. "There has to be a switch to turn this attraction off." I threw up my hands, exasperated, as I walked to the weapons wall muttering under my breath, arming myself.

Dante chuckled, and the men armed up.

Etienne paused and looked at a spelled sword hesitantly. "What is this, it has interesting markings and magick?" Looking over, I noticed he was referring to the sword I typically used when patrolling and doing stabby things. It was also the sword that took magick from creatures and passed it on to me.

I sighed, staring at my sword lovingly. Well as lovingly as one would look at sword like on the same level as a new, cute, murderous puppy. "Ah, so that sword I had spelled by someone I know in Pajila, before I learned to spell myself. If I kill a creature with it, it gives me some of its strength and sometimes it gives me a feature I may not already have."

"Like what?" He looks at me curiously.

"Like if I kill a shifter..." I trailed off. It took a moment but then it hit me. *HOLY FUCK. I have wings. Yes! I can fucking fly! Well maybe, but I will be training with them for the next few days until I can actually fly. Can you imagine the benefits in combat? Man! Wait, do they make wing shields?*

The men look at me. "Baby, your thoughts are moving fast as fuck, what do you mean you have wings and you can fly, are you okay?" Luca looked at me curiously, and even the vampire looked concerned.

"All I heard was penetration and I'm happy to oblige," Dante said excitedly. Pixie and Etienne rolled their eyes.

Instead of responding, I stepped to the middle of the sparring floor and concentrated on the feeling of the wings from that night that seemed so long ago; before everything changed. After a few moments, the gray and blue gargoyle wings appeared from between my shoulder blades. They were bigger than I remembered, and in the light, they seemed almost shimmery; and as I flexed my back, they moved with me. Woah, they were heavy as fuck and I had no idea where to even start with trying to fly with these. I sighed, adding another thing to my ever growing list of shit I need to do.

"Fuck!" Both Luca and Etienne looked shocked.

"She calls me vampire but she turns into a fucking bat," Dimitri glowered.

"So hot, I wonder if she can fuck and fly." Dante looked deep in thought.

"Holy shit bat girl, I know we spoke about it but I have yet to see them, that's so fucking cool."

I pulled them back in, and smiled at Pix. "I honestly forgot I even had them. And fuck you, vampire, I'm not a bat. I killed a gargoyle shifter."

"Wow, I can imagine it will make you very sore to learn how to control them. May not be best to start now when you'll be at the academy training non-stop in a few weeks."

My French man was so sensible, I blew him a kiss. "Yup, Pix and I will be too busy kicking ass and smacking fiancés around to focus on these." He stepped closer to me and wrapped his arms around me.

"Okay, so back to the power of the sword." Luca stepped in, his voice filling with authority.

"Yes, well." I grinned, and turned to explain. "The sword takes the power of whichever creature I kill and fills the spelled blade, transferring those powers to me like an extension. It also makes the blade stronger in battle."

"Sick, does it give powers to anyone else?" Dante asked, staring at the blade with a critical eye.

"I had it spelled directly for me." I paused, considering. "But I do wonder since we are now all connected whether it would work in the same way if you were to kill someone with it."

"Well, that just means we take it with us to the Academy, just in case..." Dimitri grinned wickedly.

We stepped up to the mat and split up, Dante and Luca faced off with me, while Etienne and Dimitri faced off with Pixie.

"Okay, so, um...weapons are being used. Do you gentlemen want a body shield to prevent being stabbed in the heart?" I asked as I palmed my knife.

The men nodded and I threw up a shield for everyone and it shimmered, then went invisible. I nodded. "We will be practicing shields this week as well, it is a handy skill to always have on the go."

Gotta make sure I keep those abs safe from harm, I thought to myself lustily.

"You are shielded from blades but I held back enough to make sure you nick. This is till first blood. Loser steps out, the other remaining two will disarm and go into grappling instead," I said firmly, everyone nodded and we got to fucking work.

Pixie and I launched at the exact same time, throwing our short knives in quick succession as we got closer to our targets. Dante walked around to my back while Luca took my front. Wrong move, so predictable. I threw up a wall of water in front of Dante and had it circle him while I pressed my advantage with only one of my men. As Luca used his short sword to come closer, I quickly brought up the same sword I had strapped to my leg to parry. He quirked up his lip, and used his knife to stab my gut while I was distracted by the sword. Smart. At the last moment I manipulated the air and the knife flew from his hand. He raised his eyebrows in surprise, but countered quickly using air to bring him back the knife quickly slicing upwards drawing blood up my arm.

I growled, "Keep going," ignoring my previous rule. The rush from the pain filled me with a need to push myself. Training with someone who knows you and someone who knows there shit is going to be good for us. We needed it.

I let the water around Dante dissolve and felt just a brush of wind as Dante attacked my back. I launched my body back into a light flip. This caused Dante to almost cut Luca and Luca to cut Dante as my sword knocked his to the side during my flip. With Dante out, we paused. I heard Dante muttering about liking me first and wanting to grapple with me.

Baby, how about you and I grapple after. I sent him a

mental picture of us on the bed and his pupils dilated as he licked his lips.

"Fuck yes, deal. You win, Luca."

I laughed and we focused on the battle next to us.

A light sheen of sweat covered the other trio, their battle getting intense. I saw Pixie throw herself on the floor between Etienne's legs to avoid what would have been a killing blow to her stomach. At that moment, Dimitri side-stepped and brought his sword down to her head, but she used her mind manipulation at the right time as he tossed the sword and started dancing instead. He was actually pretty good. Etienne smacked him upside the head while performing a series of kicks and punches that Pixie blocked right at the last moment, while she smirked. Dimitri shook off the manipulation which was impressive in and of itself, and while Etienne pressed her back toward the wall, Dimitri used his speed to stab her sides as she focused on Etienne. Only Pixie 'heard' him coming and side-stepped another one of Etienne's punches while rotating her body to the right, effectively making Etienne stabbed by Dimitri's instead.

...

I laughed lightly and clapped. "Go team! And by team, I mean me and Pixie. So now we move on to the grappling, I assume you men know how to fight on the floor? So it's me and Luca, and Pixie and Dimitri. Need a water break, boys?"

Luca and Dimitri looked at each other and declined at the exact same time, and took off their shirts. *Holy abs, holy sex gods, thank you for this moment of joyous celebration.*

I raised an internal eyebrow because they wanted to fight dirty. Okay, fuckers.

"Let's take turns this time, that way we can observe different techniques. In our world, magick rules, fighting hand to hand is very useful and there are so many forms of fighting. Each form builds certain strengths, so we need to bring those forms together cohesively. Luca, would you like to go first?"

Stepping into the sparing section, I winked at him, and he rolled his eyes, and we faced each other. Without warning, I quickly grabbed his neck with one hand and his arm with another, and crossed his arm against my chest and swept him to the floor. I hooked my leg over his opposite leg in a scissors sweep. He fell hard. None of that mattered though. The moment our bodies became flush, skin to skin, we had to fight hard to focus as the bond worked its magick and passion flared between us. Shaking out of it, Luca leaned forward, grabbed my leg, pulled and turned with it effectively, tangling our limbs but leaving me on the floor underneath him, then gripped my hair back. From this position my neck was vulnerable so despite the pain I jerked my head to the side and maneuvered my elbows out to hit him repeatedly to dislodge his hold. Grunting, he let go. His eyes heat at the contact but he held my gaze and turned to pin my hands over my head, but instead of caging me in he let off my shin just enough for me to push harder and essentially bend my knees to launch him off of me. He breathed deeply but instead of attacking everyone stood at attention as alarms blared through the house.

Fuckk.

I jumped off the floor and ran to the security room/lair as quick as I can to see what was setting off the alarms. Pixie and I got into the computers.

"Building secure, perimeter secure," she yelled.

"Fuck, it's not the buildings, it's the lower castes, there has been another child abduction and a murder. This alarm came from Burns, he called in Exousia." I banged my head on the table and we quickly run up stairs, the men on our heels as we quickly dress into our gear. Sensing the panic, the men start to dress as well.

"No, you cannot come with us on patrol or on an investigation. You stand out like sore thumbs in your gear and hummer. Pixie and I will take our bikes and shield our presence until it gets dark. We need to figure out this SOS and verify its credibility," I said as I quickly tied my hair back.

"We are going whether you want us to or not, we will dress down and take another vehicle. This isn't up for negotiation, this is us being your bonded and having your back. You have both done this alone. We know you're capable, that's not the point," Etienne said halting my objection. "This is us also figuring out what the fuck is going on as Shadows and as your mates." The men quickly move to put on jeans and dark tees instead of standard gear. I didn't have time to argue, although I admitted jeans on those muscular thighs and asses should be illegal. So should tight shirts for that matter. The men threw me a smirk as Pixie laughed.

"Fuck, your phones. Turn them off and I will destroy them later. I have new encrypted phones for you programmed with the same number. I don't want your messages, calls or location tracked." I ran and grabbed their new phones, secured the rooms and passed them out. Etienne looked at me with pride.

We didn't think of this, thank you.

Don't mention it, we have a lot more things to focus on. Pixie and I have been working all morning.

We made our way to the garage.

"Johnny, lock this down tight and call all of the families. I want everyone accounted for and safe. I will be back soon," I said as I locked eyes with our security guard. Pixie and I, after a while, suspected that the guards knew we not only patrolled but that I was Exousia. I mean they were a smart group of people but they never asked and we didn't talk about it, but they knew that when I issue a command it's for everyone's safety and they never hesitate.

"No problem, Ms. Ellie, Ms. Pixie," he said as he nodded to us both. "Stay safe." He glanced at the men and started to issue orders on his walkie.

Pixie stopped the men as they headed to their car. "No, too obvious, we said that. You boys can take midnight instead."

"Midnight?" Luca looked around confused. I let down the illusions and their jaws dropped as they took in my fleet of cars, bikes and even my war tank. I admitted I got that last one out of sheer impulse.

"A fucking tank baby?" Dante laughed and shook his head.

"You never fucking know when you might need to fuck someone up." I threw my hands in the air and walked over to my Beast, and Pixie walked up to her purple and black, almost identical bike, except hers wasn't customized to have me sit in the front if needed, same shit applies. I had her back always.

"Grab Midnight, they all have name placards, keys are in the car. I will cast the illusion as we pull out."

Holy fuck.

I smiled as they finally located Midnight. Yeah, that baby had that effect on people. A deep purple, almost black, four-seater Bugatti I snagged before it hit the market; it reminded me of a midnight sky during a thunderstorm.

We pull out of the garage and into the street and head into the lower castes.

We pulled into lower castes and our first stop was Burns' bar. If there is anyone who knows anything right now it would be him, well, that and he called the alarm. The lower castes didn't talk to outsiders, Pixie and I had proven ourselves we are part of the entire community. Burns was also one of those rare people that pretty much knows but doesn't know. There is a fine line between knowledge and suspicions; one will save you, the other will get you killed. Pixie and I pulled up and quickly hopped off our bikes. We tell the men to stay in their car and we head inside, making sure all lines of communication are open.

His eyes widened when we walked in and he nodded his head in understanding. He knew why we were here. "Ellie! Pixie! It is great to see you, come on back. I want to show you both the new pool table I'm setting up this weekend."

"Oh yes! A new table!" We headed to his back office and he closed the door behind us. The office was large, painted black, with a beautiful wood desk toward the back wall, and he had an entire bar set up behind his desk. The office reminded me of a MC club, and I often joked that he was secretly a President of the Magick Sons of Anarchy. He sat down behind his desk and set up three glasses and poured some whiskey and handed it to us while he chugged his in one swoop.

"Listen Elps," he said affectionately. He started to combine our names when he always saw us together a couple of years ago. "A child was taken about an hour ago... a newborn, her mom was a low level water user, Rassie, and was murdered for interfering." He shook his head sadly and leaned forward in his chair. "Rassie's apartment was a few doors down from Mary's and she called the alarm." He sighed deeply and headed over to the bar behind his desk. "No one saw much but what we do know is that a hummer was seen leaving, and they headed east."

"A hummer? East? Toward the border?" I drummed my fingers on the desk. "Fuck."

Pixie was able to string along more words than I was though. "So what? A Shadow kidnapped a baby and headed toward the border, separating us and the human side. This is a suspicious time, considering the Council has sent out Shadows and have been after Exousia to bring her in."

Do you guys know of another team being sent out after your meeting? The timing is too close.

No. Luca's voice floated through. *We don't know if anyone was sent out but it would be unlikely as they want us to bring them in. It is more than likely a trap of some sort but no idea by who.*

Hmmm, I'm sure we can guess considering they kidnapped a child. They would know I would swoop in and save the day.

Burns nodded. "I thought so too, I honestly think it's a trap to catch her." He held my gaze for a minute before continuing, "I know she is too smart to get caught though, however the Shadows complicate things, it's going to cause upheaval."

"Honestly, Burns, there has been enough unrest as it is. This isn't the first child stolen. It is just the first baby from the lower castes to be attempted to be taken over the border. It's been high castes for years. But you add that to Shadows having to give special recruitment invites, it's like the Council is switching up tactics. Possibly preparing for something? I mean you know as well as I do, they do not care about the lower castes. So others are trying to possibly draw me out, why all the attention now? It's been years in the making?"

Burns looked taken aback by the news, but quickly masked his features. If there is one man who would burn the midnight oil to get answers, it was this one.

"I'll learn what I can and buckle down the lower castes. You know Exousia has been preparing us for a long time." He smiled softly.

I smiled back but right now we needed to shut the threat down. We couldn't stop the plans we had to infiltrate now, things were rolling and honestly that *had* to be the end game right now. Everything will get better from then. I felt it.

"Burns, can you call your contacts and see if they actually left the city limits? If this is a trap, they wouldn't keep driving, they would pull over. Also, if you can spread the word that Exousia will be using contacts and cameras to patrol, starting five weeks from Friday." Pixie asked.

"I did, they didn't. It's a trap." He smirked. "As for Exousia, I will spread the word. The lower castes band together, you know that. I will keep the lines open though for emergencies. When the baby is saved, Mary will watch over her. We will all lend a hand." I loved them for it. It's amazing how an entire community can grow when they are treated fairly and given a chance to thrive.

Our timeline was closing in, I don't know how I knew that but my gut was never wrong. I was excited though.

We are going to fuck shit up. The men's amusement was clear through our connection. I thrive on this shit, they have no fucking clue how real shit was about to get.

We stood up and headed toward the door of the office. I hesitated at the door and looked at Pixie. We had to tell Burns about our plans. They welcomed us and they needed to know that things may not be as they seemed once we infiltrated.

"Burns, Pixie and I will be going undercover at the capital, under the guise of Shadows.. If you need to reach us for any reason you have our cell numbers, it's encrypted, so no worries. I'm letting you know because things may not be as they seem. We need you to keep your eyes open and report anything that may seem out of the ordinary. Extra patrols, militant like behavior, any detail is important," I finished off, looking him in the eyes.

He looked at us and shook his head sadly. "I won't ask why, it's not an old man's place but be careful. The Council is...well I'm sure I don't need to explain it. But I will let you know if anything is amiss. Thank you for telling me, when you come back as Shadows, it won't be a surprise to us. We have your back."

He gave us a warm hug and we filed out of the office, back into the bar, then off into the darkening sky. Perfect. Exousia thrives off of darkness. Let's fucking do this.

We will be heading east, boys, let's figure this out. I send out as I swing up onto my bike and take off.

Luca

·   ·   ·

Hearing the conversation inside the bar set us all on edge. A murder, a kidnapping and now we are going to save the baby, and corner what may be a team of Shadows. Or Shadow impersonators. I'm not sure what is worse at this point. I rubbed my temples as I felt a headache coming on. Ellie and Pixie have led some interesting lives, it is inspiring really how they both took what was thrown at them and thrived. It was going to be an adventure being bonded to them.

"I really have to wonder how the hell Ellie and Pixie gained so much respect down here. They see them as family almost, I don't think I have ever seen such solidarity among magick users."

"It is mutual respect and the desire for change. They have a common ground and same enemies. Clearly, the Council is seeing it too, and knowing Elps," Etienne said with a smile, using their friend's nickname for them. It was cute, fitting. "Knowing Elps, for even a few moments, has been eye opening. Their strength beams through them," he finished.

"Eye opening, sure. I want to hit several things at once, starting with whoever motherfucker is trying to ambush Ellie and ending with everyone on the fucking Council," Dimitri piped up.

"Anyone else thinks it is awesome how they know who she is but don't at the same time. It's like she's a ghost." Dante chuckled. "It is actually hot how these two women work together to save the day and that Ellie always puts herself in front of Pixie and even tries to keep us out. Hell, she is ready to take everyone on to protect us four from the Council's desire to have us married. Out of everyone in the universe, we hit the mate lottery."

Yeah, they are definitely amazing and rare in their

characters. Gave me serious blue balls to be around them and not balls deep whenever I could. Just watching them on their bikes was an erotic experience. When they stepped out of the bar, our eyes roamed over them.

We will be heading east, boys, let's head out. Ellie said as she swung her leg over her bike and Pixie followed suit.

"Fuck, anyone else hard as fuck just from looking at them? They have curves for days, I'm going to fuck them on their bikes one day, mark my words," Dante whispered. We all nodded slowly as we took them in then pulled off after them.

FIFTEEN MINUTES AFTER HEADING EAST, I started to hang back at Ellie's directive and Pixie rode next to us. Ellie threw a cloud of darkness over her face and picked up speed. It was like watching darkness take on a persona, mystifying and creepy at the same time.

She looks like a fucking Death Eater. Dante chuckled.

I won't be sucking shit out, fucker. And Luca, I'm not creepy but I'll take mystifying, babe. Thanks. I see a Hummer ahead, pull over and I'll go the rest on foot. Having you here may be useful, you guys get to play daddy, seeing as me and Pix cannot carry a baby on the bike.

We groaned, we didn't think of that. Dante started to jump up and down. "I love babies. This is going to be awesome."

I'm glad you think so, my little Latin lover, because that means you can babysit ours.

We froze at Pixie's words and all started speaking at once.

I'm sticking to anal and throats.

The French do not have babies, we have full grown adults.

There is nothing little about my dick.

I'm team leader, I vote no.

As Ellie and Pixie started laughing, we suddenly saw an impact. Fuck, Ellie was being attacked.

❦ 19 ❦

"The world is a dangerous place, not because of those who do evil, but because of those who look on and do nothing."
- Einstein
"I'm done waiting and looking. I'm seeking to destroy." -
Dante

C harlie

I SHOOK my head at the boys' fear hitting me, they are afraid of babies. Well, imagine shoving one out of your pussy. Cowards.

I approach the car from the back, staying in the shadows, when something comes flying toward my head. I duck quickly and see an axe embedded where my head was just seconds ago.

FUCK.

I turned quickly, throwing out my shields and facing whoever the hell likes using axes. Kind of hot really, no one uses axes anymore. Such a shame. I looked over and saw a guy about my height but bulkier, who threw a fireball in my direction. I moved to the side and laughed.

"Really, a fucking fireball after an axe. I mean, I was really impressed by the axe, then you had to follow it up with a fucking pussy ass fireball."

"You won't be laughing when I take your ass into the Council," Axe man replied.

"Interesting to think you can actually take me anywhere, I mean I have standards and you didn't even ask nicely. Some date this is turning out to be. Last time I use Tinder."

I rushed him and punched him in his stomach and he reeled back and punched me in the jaw. Sometimes, I like to get hit. Then they feel like they can win. You know doing things for the underlings is always good. Boosts their self-esteem a little before you completely destroy them. I smiled at him and turned to the right and threw a roundhouse kick to his head and he flew to the pavement. He tried to throw up a shield but didn't have a chance as I followed up by straddling him and punching him in the jaw and using my magick to cut off his breathing slightly and wrap his hands over his head.

Pixie, grab the baby, honey.

I sighed as I stayed sitting on him, just crossed my ankles—Indian style. "Fuck, that was too easy. I wanted a challenge. Anyways, so you mentioned the Council wanna speak now or forever hold your peace?"

"I am not telling you shit, bitch!" he barely squeezed out.

Ellie, the baby is not here. Her panicked voice came through town and clear. I frowned.

"Well, that's not very nice." I looked down at him. "I am also done being nice. Where is the baby you kidnapped, you piece of shit?"

He laughed. Actually laughed. Cool, fuck this.

"Okay, this is going to hurt motherfucker." I started digging through his head. He tossed the baby about a mile back on the side of the road, and I felt rage choke me as I punched him in the jaw and neck.

Side of the road, mile back, boys, go. You have my power to heal now even though you haven't practiced.

I felt the boys take off while Pixie stayed to watch my back and I forcefully dug through this asshole's head making it as painful as possible. He screamed, I laughed. Doug here is not a Shadow, which I figured by the fact that he didn't give me much of a fight; he is, however, a mercenary. A shitty one, but one nonetheless, and BINGO, hired by someone in the capital trying to bring in the vigilante before the boys did.

That tidbit was interesting. Why would someone want to bring them in first. No name, no description though. Just a person in the shadows, a letter and a bag with half of the promised funds. No words were spoken, as if they expected mind manipulation. But he wasn't supposed to harm the child, he decided to do that on his own. The manipulator was smart and interesting, I admit. Protection against a mind user, which meant protection from Luca. Very interesting.

But the circumstances don't matter, the fact is we didn't have a face to who hired him, so this worked to our advantage. Best case scenario, bringing back Doug would make whoever hired him panic and show their hand, worst case, Doug dies. Either way Doug here was going to play Vigilante. But instead of my honorable name, Exousia, he shall be dubbed bitch ass motherfucker. Fitting, truly.

When the boys take his ass in they can look for anyone who may recognize him and it would definitely give them an edge, Pixie whispered in my mind after laughing at my thought process.

I picked his ass up and tied him up with some rope he had in the back of the hummer, presumably for me, and hog tied his ass to my bike. This was going to be so uncomfortable for him. *Awesome.*

Exactly. We will toss him into the cell under the building.

We pulled off, and headed toward the boys. Who had been very quiet.

Boys? Did you find the baby? Everything okay?

Dante

You HAVE to be a sick motherfucker to throw a baby on the side of the road. We fumed as we searched the darkness for any sign of the baby, splitting up to widen the search. I heard a little cry and ran in the direction of the sound, I really did love babies and the thought of one being harmed made my stomach sick. I looked in the grass and found a small bundled child, slightly blue in the face with some blood on his or her head.

I didn't know how to heal, but Ellie said we had her powers now and even if I didn't I would have pulled a miracle out of my ass from the pure terror I felt for this child. I held the child close and looked inside of myself like we were taught when first learning our powers, and I couldn't tell the healing from the other lines of power that were now in my soul. I felt helpless and choked on a sob as I kept digging and found a golden light that felt right. I pulled until it filled me and I gently pushed it toward the baby.

Luca

WE HEARD Dante choke back a sob and walked toward him expecting the worst. As we walked closer, we saw a soft glow of gold surround the baby. The blue cheeks going back to pink and the injured head healing closed. We felt the ladies pull up behind us on their bikes, we had been too focused on our search to answer their questions. They walked up as the baby fell asleep in Dante's arms and he turned to face us with a look of wonder on his face.

"I did it. I saved the baby."

He looked so proud and so infatuated with the little face. Granted this didn't fit the situation but I suddenly felt a little less terrified at the thought of one day being a dad. Of one day surrounding a beautiful baby and looking down with that same look of wonder. I looked back at Ellie and Pixie who looked toward Dante with such intensity in their gaze, and I felt a sense of peace that as long as we survived the oncoming madness, that I would love to have a family with them. We were already six, what's one more?

· · ·

Charlie

DANTE RELUCTANTLY HANDED over the baby to me while I dropped him off, who we learned was a him, over at Mary's place before heading back home. After shoving the stupid fucker into the prison, okay small cell, under the building and giving the guards instructions of bread and water three times a day, we trudged on upstairs.

Fuck, it's been a long day, the trackers I ordered had arrived but I figured we can implant them tomorrow. The smart system started to play lullaby music as we walked inside and I chuckled as the men groaned about smart houses and invasion of privacy.

"And yet you fuckers had no problem invading our privacies," I grumbled good-naturedly to Pixie and her laugh tinkered throughout the house. The guys looked at us with their eyebrows raised and we looked at them. "What?" We said it at the same time as we brushed past them on the way to the bedroom. I scanned us in, as Etienne cleared his throat.

"When are going to be added to the security system scans?" He looked so uncomfortable when he said it, that I threw up the mental wall Pixie and I had perfected over the years me and blocked them out. Eventually we would all be on the same level, but until then...

Wanna fuck with them?

Of course.

"Well, we thought about it and we figured maybe it wouldn't be a good idea since you may be working for the Council still. How do we know this mating bond would stop you from working with them?" I raised my eyebrow as we walked to the bathroom, the men on our heels objecting.

"Why would we do that? Also I would think you would know our intentions since our mental shields have been down pretty much..." I waved off Luca's explanation.

"Honestly though, boys," Pixie continued, "how do we realllyyyy know you want to be with us? I mean Charlie and I were tattooed and pierced together. How are you going to top that? I mean I can think of a few ideas that we have discussed but..."

Pixie and I started the shower and began to undress.

Etienne fought a smirk, damn, I forgot he picked this shit up for a living and Pixie and I were barely keeping it together. "Hmmm interesting, what ideas?"

"Jacob's Ladders," we said at the same time.

Dante's jaw dropped while the other men looked confused.

"You three looked confused, let us help you." We took down our shields and sent them a mental picture.

They looked a varying degrees of shocked and horrified. Dante though, looked like he was seriously considering the possibility.

Honestly I don't even think they realized we were naked and soapy in the shower. It was insulting and hilarious at the same time.

"Can we compromise? Maybe a Prince Albert?" mused Dante.

The men looked at him with the same look of disgust they were giving us. "What the fuck is that?" Dimitri demanded.

"It's a small ring at the tip of your dick that's supposed

to stimulate the G-spot when you're fucking," he explains.

"Why would I want to stab my dick with a needle?! Don't dicks work just fine without the damn piercings, how will that prove that we lov...want to be with you." He rushed to correct himself, blushing fiercely.

"Dimitri, are you blushing? Maybe that's why you need the piercings... the blood is rushing to your face instead of your cock," I said seriously.

He looked at us incredulously, and I just couldn't hold it anymore. Pixie and I started laughing so hard, thank God, the fucking shower floor was warm because we couldn't stand up.

Dimitri walked into the shower fully dressed, demanding we apologize to his dick and we just couldn't catch our breath. This was how we'll die, I was sure of it. Not being able to catch our breaths while apologizing to a dick.

We finally got off the floor and stumbled to the sinks to brush our teeth and moisturize, still chuckling. "Shower is all yours, boys, we will let you discuss the merits of dick piercings while you all sword fight." With that, we ran out of the bathroom while they growled at us.

Pixie

Fuck. Ellie and I would laugh all the time, it was never a dull moment with us but these men have certainly brought a lightness to our home. Our. That feels good to say. Their faces were just priceless and amazingly expressive. You would think being Shadows would have made them a bit more stoic, and when we first met them that was certainly their façade, but when they let their guards down it was incredible to witness. After a few minutes of getting dressed in our nighties we sat on the edge of the bed and stared at the open bathroom door, listening to the men argue about piercings vs. tattoos, and Dante declaring he is getting everything at once.

We laughed softly. "We are so fortunate to have them, Els, it's like they were made for us."

"They were," she said while "Must Be Nice" by Lyfe Jennings came on the sound systems. When Ellie had this system installed it was because we realized we had so many songs in our heads constantly and would always text each other lyrics about which song reminded one of the other. So of course she designed it and had someone modify to pick up on certain emotions and keywords. It was uniquely ours and soon the men would understand the importance of it. Music connected people, it expressed emotions that sometimes were too hard to say out loud, but here in our haven we didn't have that prob-lem, the system helped us sort it all out and gave us a different type of peace.

We smiled as we stood up and held each other dramatically and swayed to getting lost in the song after laughing. The shower turned off a while ago but we fell into the song realizing that it really represented us in so many ways. The song gradually finished and switched to "I Wanna Know" by Joe, and I pretended to sing to her. She laughed and kissed me softly. This is my Ellie, yeah she fights and tries to save the world and everyone around her, but this? Her laugh, her joy, her peace at home? Was her. I loved her so damn much, and it was mind-blowing whenever I looked at her.

Charlie

PIXIE WAS my center and despite the madness she always brought me back to earth. Her smile, her laugh, her joy just poured from her. I always felt like I have to take on the world and to be honest, I do. For her I will take it on and win, odds be damned. The men, they will be the same for us, the deep soul shattering love, we knew but in the end we loved each other first and that was so special. I traced her curves under her nightie and laughed as she sang to me. If she only knew, she didn't just take my breath away, no, I would give up all the air in my lungs just to look at her one last time.

I kissed her soft lips, leaning my forehead against hers, enjoying the moment. That's what we would all have, moments in time compounded by love and hope to get us through the future. I'll take all the moments I could, tomorrow could wait, the nights was ours.

I felt the eyes of the men behind us as they let us have our moment in time, the system switching to "Somebody's Watching Me" by Rockwell. Pixie and I laughed and looked back at the guys who stood behind us naked as the day they were born, dicks hard, looking casual as fuck. As if hanging around naked with their dicks out was something they did on any regular day while sipping coffee and probably stirring it with said dicks.

"All done, boys? Did you decide how to prove your

love?" I froze at the L word, but shook it off, waiting for an answer.

"Shush, we know you're mystified by the image in front of you. If you speak, you'll ruin it," Dante joked, breaking the tense moment.

"I admit we like the image. Actually now that I think about it, Dante, I promised you a grappling session and you promised to show me all the benefits of your tongue." I quirked an eyebrow and his eyes heated.

Si, mi amor, that's exactly what I said. How about we do that first, then we can move to the grappling? He walked toward me, his muscles flexing and his dick at attention. I licked my lips as he gripped my hips and laid me on the bed, all while taking off my nightie. Damn, he's talented. He smirks at that thought and I lose all forms of common sense at that smile.

Fuck yes.

Also, I want a baby and we should practice. I rolled my eyes.

Dante, no babies yet. I still plan on bleeding once a month for a long time. Gotta keep the resident vampire excited.

I smiled as Dimitri gagged. Yeah, it was gross but the rewards were awesome.

You know we talk about Dimitri but at least he just likes blood, this guy over here. Pixie points at Etienne and smirks. *Eats fucking snails as a delicacy. So I mean really who is worse here, the Kotex licker or the guy who sucks slugs.* I laughed.

The only one that's going to be sucking anything, Pix, is you, Etienne growled.

Promises, promises, French man. Are you gonna bring

that Baguette over here or do I have to go get it myself? Pix dropped a heated stare and walked over to him.

And you, General? Coming? She winks at him while walking back toward the bed and taking off her nightie. Seriously, I just think we should stay naked all the time.

This vampire has had enough of this shit!

You just said vampire! I win!

I laugh as the angry enforcer stalks toward the bed and I pushed myself further away. He prowled closer, giving me a slow kiss, and teasing my tongue rings.

I'm going to put that tongue to use while Dante eats that pretty pussy of yours.

Shivers ran down my spine and he trailed his hands down my jaw, to my breast, holding them and flicking my nipples before he bend down and caught them in his mouth. I moan, and toss my head back. He grabbed my head to force me to look at him and made his way back to my throat and lips.

I'm stuck, fascinated by his intense stare and his abs rippling as he held himself up on one arm while running his free hand to mine and bringing it to grip his dick and guide it to stroke him. He let out a hiss, and stared down at me setting me on fire. Fuck, I could have came from that look alone. Having this fucking badass, huge, muscled enforcer completely taken out by just a touch was intoxicating.

Dante, make her cum a few times, no mercy, Dimitri's gruff voice, flits through our heads.

My pleasure, he responds.

I cursed as Dante threw my legs over his huge shoulders and pressed his lips against my pussy, snaking his tongue through my fat pussy lips and flicking my clit gently, kissing it sweetly before winking at me and trailing his tongue down to taste me and back up to kiss my clit fervently. My hips bucked against my face as he gripped my ass, and licked and sucked my clit, switching back and forth, never on the same rhythm.

Fuck, Fuck, Fuck. Damn.

Fuck, I couldn't catch my breath and I damn sure couldn't keep up. Every time he would bring me close he would switch up the rhythm and start again. He sucked my clit in between his lips and brought my legs to close around his head, while he picked up his tempo running his tongue back and forth while sucking and licking with the tip first, then his entire tongue.

You taste so fucking good baby, I'm never coming up for air, fuck that.

At his words, I came hard.

Yes, baby, come for me, let me taste more of you, mi amor.

My eyes rolled back and my body got lost to the waves of sensation of being between them both. Right before I fell into a blissful sleep between both of their warm bodies, I heard Pixie's voice float through the link, *loving you all is just so easy.*

Luca

ETIENNE and I start walking to the bed after Pixie at the same time. She laid down on her back and crooked her finger and I settled myself between her legs, immediately running my tongue in between her lips before I latched onto her clit and gave it a gentle suck. She moaned and I felt her pleasure wash over me.

"You are so damn beautiful," I murmured as I settled her legs around my neck and continued to tease her. When she moaned again, Etienne crawled next to her, placing soft kisses from her neck up to her mouth before capturing her sweet lips in a kiss that made me harder. "So damn perfect," he whispered leaning forward and tilting her head up as he slid into her mouth.

Her lips tightened over him and he threw his head back. Her moans now muffled, I started to fuck her with my tongue before sliding up and putting pressure on her clit, flicking and teasing until her legs tightened around my face, and she started to shake softly before she groaned and came, screaming around Etienne's dick. Etienne grabbed her head and held her against him as her screams vibrated down his dick and he started to thrust into her throat.

Fuck my throat, Frenchie. Luca, I want you inside me too. Use me, I like it, papi.

Fenchie? Etienne raised his eyebrow, tightened his grip on her hair and groaned as she winked and started to hum on his dick. Fuck, I leaned forward and tossed her legs over my shoulders and slid into her warm, tight pussy, still clenching from her release. I let out a guttural moan as I grabbed her hips and tilted her forward as Etienne quickened his pace and started to tease and pinch her nipples. Reaching between us, I flicked and teased her clit, gently pulling on her clit piercing until I felt her tighten around me.

Luca! Yes, harder. She sent us a mental image and I flipped her over fast, Etienne's dick sliding out of her mouth.

She leaned over me, sliding me inside of her and we both let out a soft moan. *Fuck, she was soaked,* I thought to myself as she started to rock against my dick. I pulled her toward me in a heated kiss distracting her while Etienne settled behind her and rubbed lube on her tight ass and gently slid himself inside her until he was completely inside. She tossed her head back and let out a loud moan and made eye contact as we started to fuck her in tandem.

Fuck yes, fuck me harder please, rougher.

Etienne growled and grabbed her by the neck, squeezing gently, while one hand gripped her breasts. Her sounds becoming more frenzied, he leaned down and bit down on her shoulder. I reached down, pinched her clit hard and she let out a hoarse yell and I felt her pussy clench to the point of pain.

Yes baby, cum for us. You are so fucking beautiful, Etienne whispered as he thrust deeply, hand firmly around her throat as she came and started to tremble. Feeling her tremble, I came with a groan. Etienne let out a hoarse curse and I felt him pump into her and let out his own release.

I laid her down and went to the bathroom to grab a warm washcloth to clean her up. Pressing a gentle kiss to her head, I settled down with her in between Etienne and me.

Loving you all is just so easy. Her voice floats through our link.

My eyes snapped up to see her drift off and I made eye contact with Etienne, feeling her words echo through our souls.

🐾 20 🐾

"There is no magic that can resolve our problems. The solution rests with our work and discipline." ***Jose Eduardo dos Santos***

"I will train until my mind, magick, and physical capabilities are one. Anything less and I will not only be failing myself, but everyone who I have to protect as well." **- Charlie**

C harlie

I WAKE up before these fuckers again. Must be nice to sleep without an internal clock that always keep blaring inside your head. I sighed as I rolled out of bed and took a quick shower and threw on some workout clothes. I head out the room and grab a water, saving my coffee fix for later, to head to the gym.

I closed the door behind me and took a deep breath as I looked around my sanctuary. I loved the feeling of being in here, sweating out my demons and clearing my mind. I warmed myself up and wrapped my hands before walking over to my circle of punching bags and started to beat the shit out of the bags in front of me like they were everything that was wrong in the world.

"Last Resort" by Papa Roach comes on over the gym speakers and I breathe deeply as I land a flying roundhouse kick at one of the bags and follow up with punches and sidekicks. Training camp is going to be a sweet victory and a gut punch all at once.

Pixie's words from last night floated through my head. Fuck. The boys were unexpected but whatever, I can get over that, I am over it.

My problem is the fucking arranged marriages, I have a problem with someone hurting someone I love. I mean, fuck, I have been planning on the Council's demise when my parents didn't come home. Now I have to walk into enemy territory with my mates and four of them are going to have to deal with bitches pawing at them. What am I supposed to do? Play jealous angry mate and show my hand early? Fuck that.

It wasn't like we were going to walk in there and be obvious about our bonding, the plan was to infiltrate, but I damn sure didn't think we would have to walk in there and deal with this either. It was an unexpected complication, the complication being my heart wanting to jump out of my chest and beat the fuck out of these girls. I'm all about woman solidarity, on sitcoms and shit, not solidly sitting on my men's dick. Gah, say what you want but you know damn well, it's all unicorns and rainbows until someone tries to go where they don't belong.

I'm in the zone as "Only One" by Yellowcard starts to play, and I grab two swords from my weapons wall and start to flip them in my hands.

For the longest time the entire goal had been to infiltrate and kick ass, now I'm wondering if it could be and should be modified to fit our unique situation, but that just wasn't logical. But when was love logical. Fuck. Nope, no. Okay, fuck, well this can either make shit harder or easier. I will vote for easier. "Sugar, We're Going Down Swinging" by Fall Out Boy starts to play.

Decision apparently made by the smart system. I take a deep breath and turn to figure out where the fuck I put my water bottle, and notice five pairs of eyes staring at me.

Dimitri

I CLEARED MY THROAT, and tossed Ellie her water bottle and a towel. "Well, that was intense, are you feeling okay?"

She lifted her eyebrow and smiled, making my heart skip a beat. "Why wouldn't I be, vampire, I just kicked some serious ass. Those dummies didn't stand a chance and I disemboweled my imaginary friend."

I laughed and shook my head as I walked further into the room with the guys on my heels. We had walked into the workout room as Ellie ran at one of the dummies and took it down with her legs before kicking another dummy to the floor. We stared as she fought with imaginary opponents with her swords, using a complicated series of slashes, swipes, and hits.

My jaw dropped when she tossed the swords and caught them behind her back after doing a few punches and kicks. The music kept changing in the background as she fought, hinting at the inner turmoil she must be feeling. She threw up her mental shields so we could only pick up her feelings of anger, jealousy, back to anger, then acceptance. When her swords lit up with fire the men and I looked at each other and stared at her, transfixed. That particular ability was not known for the cities and only a few of the Elite knew how to fight with spelled weapons.

Pixie stood to the side with her head turned while she took in Ellie, a smirk on her face, of course she is used to this display of skills. My eyes widened when she threw the swords across the sparring zone, aimed true as they went through the stomach of the poor unsuspecting dummy.

"Yeah, we noticed that, care to share why you felt that you needed to murder an entire room of fake people," Luca asked.

"Not particularly, no, but I will say good morning before you all sit and meditate, you all need to practice with your new powers and tell them apart so you can use them quickly when needed. You will need them all soon and practice makes you perfect." She shrugged.

Pixie stepped around us to walk over to Ellie, who snaked her arms around her waist and gave her a kiss and whispered something in her ear that made Pixie's laugh echo around the room. My heart ached for the same reception and a look at the men's faces confirmed that they felt the same. She looked in our direction, her smile faltering when she saw our faces. She paused a second before walking towards us and stopped at Etienne first before she grabbed his face and kissed him deeply, following suit with Luca, then Dante—who prolonged his kiss—by grabbing her ass and whispering things in Spanish in her ear. When she finally stopped before me, her cheeks were flushed and she looked so damn beautiful, I tilted her head up toward me leaning down to press my lips against hers. I teased the outside of her mouth and she moaned softly as she opened her mouth and rubbed her tongue against mine, teasing me with her tongue rings. I pulled her closer and nipped at her bottom lip before giving her one soft kiss and pulling away before I ended up doing more.

She was so fiery and strong but the way she melted when she was in my arms gave me a thrill of power and passion. I wondered often how I was going to handle seeing her in training at the academy and not want to sweep her up, and drown in her kisses and moans. Between her and Pixie, my tough guy exterior was quickly fading. This shit happened all the time in movies, but I never pictured myself being that guy. Now, I see how easy it is to get swept up like it happens in the Disney movies my little sister used to make me watch when we were younger.

The Magick Community may be separate from the human side of the world, but we watched and listened to all of their shows and music. Same world, just different sides of the coin really and when it came to creativity and talent, the humans had it in spades, they didn't have to hide behind magick abilities, they simply existed and were talented despite not having powers. I envied that sometimes, the ability to be creative and growing in your own right without having to rely on magick to do so.

However, I'm sure that they would feel the same way about us if they knew more about our world. Grass is always greener, and all that.

"Mmmm, I love those lips, baby." I tossed a wink at her, watching her blush.

"Vampire, these lips are all yours."

I groaned as I shook my head and swatted her on the ass as we turned to walk to the sparring area to apparently meditate. Meditation sounded nothing like sex but fine.

Charlie

Love, Love, Love. The word kept bouncing around my head as the men started to pull their powers and practice telling them apart and bringing them forward to the tips of the fingers. For the rest of the morning I had them practice holding and manipulating elements like I did with Pixie. While they practiced, I ran off to make them all protein shakes and handed them out without having them pause in their studies. We just didn't have time to slack and it helped that they now have my power reserves, which is to say, they won't feel drained or tired after using their powers and waste time recharging.

After a few hours, they whined about needing a break, I rolled my eyes and slipped out of the room and grabbed a plant from the kitchen.

"We can take a break after you all take turns using your earth magick to make this plant grow. This is tricky because you need to focus your energy into feeling the life of the plant, guiding it to grow without harming or killing the plant. This is also important because learning to manipulate the ground and earth beneath you can be a determining factor in a fight. Can't fight if motherfuckers can't stand." The men chuckled, their deep laughs doing something to my slick heat. I groaned, and Pixie smirked at me.

Bitch. I stuck my tongue out at her. Like she wasn't feeling the same. Ugh, Love, love, love.

I cleared my throat. "So yes, in turns. Vampire, you can go first, I know being under the earth is your thing, you may have practice." I threw him a smirk when he growled at me. Despite that, he focused on the plant, I heard his internal dialogue as he found his earth magick and made the plant grow a few inches. Luca went next and he made the plant go into hibernation. Etienne quirked his head and made the earth move as if the plant was under attack. Dante rolled his eyes and made the plant grow then jumped out of the pot and dance. I laughed so hard. "Dante, mi corazon, this isn't Little Shop of Horrors." He smiled widely at my pet name.

"I know, and I'm not suddenly Seymour, but these fuckers are boring, I bring spice to the party." Pixie rolled her eyes making the plant jump back into the pot and grow a flower. "Party pooper." Dante stuck out his tongue, and Pixie leaned over and sucked it into her mouth, giving him an open-mouthed kiss.

Well, that escalated quickly.

Mind your business, bitch, you got that tongue all last night. Sharing is caring.

If we are going to fight over my tongue, it's only fair if we take this into the bedroom.

I barked a laugh. "Yeah, not going to happen, we can take a break but I gotta check security feeds, the company, and Pixie and I need to order our uniforms for the academy, also you fuckers need to be given several things. So in reality our break is more work. It will be fun!" I said cheerily as I took in my groaning group of five. Pussies.

"Why do we gotta be fuckers all the time?" Etienne grumbled in his sexy French accent. We made our way to the security room.

It's how she deflects her feelings. Don't mind her.

Pixie, STFU, I'm not deflecting, I'm simply trying out different pet names. Fuckers, dickheads, sex gods, they all have the same affection.

I hid my smile as Pixie and I settled around the computers and pulled up our feeds. I ran my hands through my purple strands, while I used my other screens to make sure my company numbers are on track. Yeah, people can have accountants, but accountants eventually ask questions and want to meet. I create different aliases and handle the shit myself. I'm not half a genius. I run at full capacity, thank you very much.

After a few moments of silence, or rather me blocking everyone out, everything checks out and I'm able to breathe a little easier. Council notwithstanding, I care a lot about the people affected by me. All the employees I have, depend on my success, and I don't have the heart to ever fail them. I just cannot fathom the amount of people that would not have holidays or homes to live in. It is part of the reason I make sure all my employees are paid a lot more than minimum wage and are also get checked periodically to make sure they don't mysteriously need an additional bonus to cover expenses.

I felt Dante come up behind me, the smell of his cologne wrapping me up like a security blanket, and pull my lip from my teeth, I didn't even realize I had been biting it while looking over the figures.

They are lucky to have you, Mi Alma, if everyone cared like you do, the world would be a better place.

I threw him a thankful glance.

I appreciate that, however if everyone cared, then life would become a contest. We see it all the time in religions around the world or even community centers, that are literally created to help. I just...want to do more... I don't know...it's confusing...luckily I have had Pixie to ground me and tell me I can't save everyone.

That's because you can't, Luca piped in. I sighed. Logically, I knew that. Still. I shook off the thoughts and instead held Dante's hand and my other hand flew over the keyboard to access our emails. I quickly ordered our uniforms without looking, just putting in the sizes needed.

"Okay so tech time!" I clapped, and Pixie groaned while I stood up excitedly.

"Pix, this is the exciting part. You shut your muggle face."

"I'll show you muggle, bitch."

Etienne stood, and positioned himself between us, shaking his head. I guess he learned that he should just stay shut when it comes to Harry Potter fighting. I threw a smile at him and winked. He smiled. Goodness, why the fuck was he so hot, you realize that Dean Winchester was a walking clit magnet, now I had a more muscle-packed version and I was cashing in on that shit tonight. I wonder if he would be down to cosplay.

"Do I even want to know why you are looking at me with that look?" He calculated. I shrugged.

"Probably not, but we are totally crossing into human territory and cosplaying next year."

Pixie laughed, and the men looked startled.

"Don't be a pussy, cosplaying is so much fun and we can play with the humans!"

I interrupted their protests. "It is happening. Anyways, stay still, I gotta stab you up a little. I need to implant trackers in all of you."

❧ 21 ❧

"A winning effort begins with preparation."- ***Joe Gibbs***
"See? Someone named Joe totally wants me to stab you with a tracker!"- ***Charlie***
"I'll rip his throat out." - ***Dimitri***
"Fucking vampires."- ***Charlie***

P ixie

THE MEN blinked and I had to hold back a laugh. Tech Ellie was scary Ellie. I'm not sure what was worse: the vigilante or the techie. Either way, they were fucked.

"We're gonna let them know, why?" I interrupted her busy hands while they prepped their tracker injectors. I swear this girl has no tact sometimes.

"Oh, okay. I guess. Like they have a choice," she muttered, and I had to hide my smile behind my hand.

"This is just in case that our bond cannot track you, then we will always have access to tech at least in varying degrees so we can track you that way. Ellie invented these, they aren't normal trackers. They are infused by magick so they cannot be destroyed by our practices, but overall they are very reliable and can't be hacked. Only we will have access. You can see, your phones and your new computers and tablets in front of you, will be able to track the ones in Ellie's and mine already. These other trackers will automatically download to your system once installed."

"We didn't realize the computers and tablets were ours, okay, uh, is there ever a case where the bond cannot at least tell a general direction? Do we really need these?" Luca said uncomfortably while looking at Ellie, putting on gloves and practicing her mad scientist laugh.

"Ellie, stop laughing, asshole," I reprimanded her before the guys peed their pants.

She pouted. I rolled my eyes.

"You never know and we don't really dabble in unknown variables when it comes to safety. You are our bonded, we will need to protect each other. This just makes it easier. Just go with it." I cringed while Ellie now tried to make her hair stand on edge. I rubbed my face, and grimaced.

She was scaring the shit out of Luca who didn't look like he liked needles. Etienne was trying to hold back his laughter and failing, Dimitri looked oddly turned on, and Dante was comparing the syringe to his dick through his pants. Completely different personalities, yet, they all melded well. I wasn't kidding yesterday when I said loving them was so easy. They were just all a different version of perfect. When we were together, it worked. Before Dante actually took his dick out, I stood and took the syringe from his hands and nipped his pouted lips, and shook my head. It was a huge syringe but I think Ellie did it because it looked scary.

"I was using that!" he said indignantly. Luca eyed Ellie warily as she walked around with a prepped syringe, laughing maniacally in quiet tones. I rolled my eyes at all of them. My eyes were going to be stuck at the top of my brain at this rate.

"No sweetie, you weren't, shush. Anyways, it doesn't hurt. But it does have a noticeable bump. We hide ours under our tattoos, so we can do yours behind your ears if you want or we can get you guys tatted today. We have a guy with his own shop that works security three days a week, and does all of our work living downstairs. Up to you."

"Oo! I vote tattoos! I would love to get more ink! That sounds like a plan. We can watch movies tonight, and I will call my guys to get us set up to get tattoos as a group before we leave to infiltrate shit. We can heal each other after so they don't hurt." Ellie starts to clap and almost drops the syringe. Dweeb. I love her. I hear the genuine excitement in her voice at the idea of a night-off and just hanging out, getting to know each other more. The men can tell too if the smiles on their faces were any indication. I knew she was freaking out about the love comment but I liked to observe, Etienne and I have that in common, and I knew she felt for them. The bond will tug us together regardless, love may come naturally but the bond will punch us in the heart until we are fully immersed in it. I'm not mad about it though. You try being bonded to a Liam Hemsworth, Dean Winchester and Damon Salvatore look-alikes, and add a freaking Latin novella star, and try to hold back. Half the time, I had to stop myself from calling them by their doppelgänger names.

"I'm thinking we can shower after this and start with a Hunger Games marathon? Maybe watch a few episodes of Supernatural and Vampire Diaries?" Ellie smiled at my suggestion. I could tell she fought between wanting to train and wanting to have fun for the rest of the day.

"Ellie, we can train nonstop in the next few weeks, let's enjoy the time we have, to really hang out."

She sighed. "Fine. Now who's first!" She laughed and jumped onto a chair. I shook my head and turned back to my computer.

Charlie

THE MEN RUBBED their tracker spots as we made our way up the stairs to shower off our training from earlier. Luca and Dante opted for their chest, Etienne preferred his back, and Dimitri wanted his shoulder implanted. Seeing as how they were hiding their excitement about getting tattooed, I'm sure it had to do with their preferred spot to get their ink. I don't know how they helped themselves for this long. Ink was addictive and there were so many possibilities. I was super stoked. I haven't really had a day of just hanging out in a few weeks so the chance to do it with them and have a movie marathon was exciting.

The men all went to their rooms to shower while Pix and I went to our room.

I sent a text to our tattoo-slash-security guard, Louie, to see if he could come up with his equipment in a few weeks. He responded quickly, asking us for details and when I told him it was six of us, he called me instead.

"Ms. Ellie, I can do you one better. I can come by, close up the shop, and bring the entire crew by."

"Oh Louie, you are such a sweetie, that would be amazing. Are you sure you guys are okay with that? I don't want to stop any business."

"Nah, you know we would do anything for you, besides you know, we can always move things around for later, depending on how much work we do," he said sweetly.

"Well, Pix and I will order you all some food, you know the protocols, I'll let you all in when you get to the penthouse. Send me names and account numbers, I'll wire the payments to you all. I'll see you gentlemen then," I said giddily as I disconnected the call and jumped in the shower, overwhelmed with excitement. I told Pixie and she pretty much ran around the room. That girl is quiet but she loves herself some ink.

TRYING to focus on the night in, we took a little extra time to blow-out our hair before we slipped on some regular tight yoga pants, a tee, and some fluffy socks.

It was time for some real bonded time.

We walked out into the living room to set up the television while the guys came out of their rooms. After popping popcorn and grabbing wine, Pixie and I got comfortable under a big blanket, right as the boys swaggered into the living room with gray sweats and nothing else. I resisted the urge to roll my eyes when my inner hussy tried to come out to play.

"This isn't going to work for me!" Dimitri announced, striding over to the couch and picking me up to sit me on his lap.

"Fantastic idea, Vampire man." Dante chuckled, walking over to dump Pixie on this lap. Luca chuckled and sat next to Dante, prying Pixie from his arms and settling her between them, Etienne following suit with Dimitri and I.

I laughed. "Okay, are we all set? What are we watching first? Vampire shit, Hunger Games?"

"I was interested in knowing what this Harry Potting stuff was." Etienne looked intently at us.

Pixie and I immediately stopped smiling. This was no laughing matter. This was now a national emergency.

"Oh, you poor sweet man. Yes, we will have a Harry POTTER Marathon for you." I leaned over and gave him a long kiss. Bless his heart. Sometimes you really have no idea what people are struggling with on the inside, and this? This was one of those times.

We pulled up the movies and when the men complained, Pixie and I each went to sit on Etienne's lap to explain the most important parts, pausing to fill in the blanks the movie missed from the books. This was pure magick, no pun intended.

After the third movie, we took a break, seeking lunch for us, and blood for Dimitri. He seemed a little grumpy.

I laughed as he wrapped his arms around me and bit my neck. "I don't know about you but I'm hungry for something else."

A spike of desire shot through me and I bit back a

moan. Turning around, he gave me a scathing kiss and swatted my ass, winking at me before swaggering over to the fridge.

"Tease," I muttered.

He laughed. "No, I just know that my role as the enforcer would be usurped by you and Pixie if we don't finish this marathon." I laughed. He had a point.

"You know," Dante started, stuffing his face with a sandwich he quickly slapped together. "This is the first time we have really hung out without plotting someone's demise, training, or looking up information in the death chamber."

"You are right, I admit I like it," Etienne added, while he popped a shit ton of popcorn, and finished making sandwiches for the rest of us.

Luca scoffed. "I am a domesticated general. Who would have thought?"

"Aww, green eyes, it looks good on you," Pixie said, getting on her tippy toes and grazing his chin with a kiss. These fuckers were tall.

I leaned my hip on the kitchen island, my eyes tracking how Dimitri's scowl was gone, Etienne didn't have the pensive look on his face and finally looked at ease, Dante was...Dante, and Luca looked comfortable, happy even.

"Eventually we will have to wade through all of the bullshit and find a little bit of peace. Our lives aren't going to get any easier. This gives us a better opportunity to get to know each other too," Pixie added.

"Yeah?" Luca cocked his head, and a beautiful smile lit up his face.

An answering smile lit my face. "She's right. We can get questions in before we start the next movies." I laughed as Etienne strode to the living room before all of us and sat down with his sandwich, popcorn, and beer.

"Okay, before we press play, tell us one thing about you no one else knows," Pixie asked, getting comfortable on the couch.

✹ 22 ✹

"I would rather die on my feet than live on my knees." -
Unknown
"This seems rather ominous. Am I right?"- **Dante**

C harlie

FINALLY, after weeks of training, we were close to the finish line and to celebrate, we were finally going to get our tattoos. We were super giddy.

We took the time to blow-out our hair and put on makeup. If this was going to be a date night, it was going to count. I tossed on a pair of white leggings that accentuated all of my curves and a black see-through tank top with a black push-up bra, and Pixie put on a dark green sleeveless top that showed her midriff and was cut into strips above her breasts, showing off her cleavage, paired with skin tight jean shorts. We finished it off with fluffy socks, and anyone who says that fluffy socks aren't a sexy date outfit, are filthy liars.

The men were sitting in the kitchen, laughing with beers in their hands, dressed in low hung jeans, and those fuckers didn't have shirts on. Pixie and I looked at each other and bit our lips. Picture a fucking cowboy commercial, hell, a firefighter calendar even, their abs underneath, arms rippling every time they flexed just to take a sip of their beers. The deep V had me drooling, especially knowing where that led. *Fuck me.* I must have whispered it out loud because they all turned toward us, and their eyes turned heated.

Etienne

THERE WAS something inherently sexy about confidence. These two women had that in spades. One look at them had me hard as fuck in my suddenly too-tight jeans.

Fuck, does she not realize white leggings are pretty much a man's kryptonite when paired with curves? Luca whispered.

They are killing me, I responded.

Is Pix's ass hanging out of those shorts? Is it appropriate to lick her ass right now? Dimitri's rough voice floated through my head.

I'm going to come in my fucking jeans just looking at them. Do I look casual, guys? I don't know what to do with my hands right now. I rolled my eyes at Dante, although I'm grateful for his comedy right now. I'm very close to saying fuck the movie night and just make one ourselves.

"You ladies look amazing." My voice sounded lower

than normal.

"Absolutely delectable actually, anyone else tired and want to go to bed. Right now?" Dante teased.

Ellie rolled her eyes and smiled at Pixie, they gave each other a high-five. "We won the fucking mate lottery, Pix, holy shit, I don't know where to start first—their abs or the fucking V."

"I don't care as long as I get a taste," she said huskily, and I almost came as she tossed a very provocative image of what she wanted to do to us.

Ellie smiled at her and said, "Louie and the guys will be here in fifteen minutes. Do you think we have time?"

"Fuck yes, I only need five per guy, you take Etienne and Luca, I will take Dante and Dimitri," Pix said as she walked purposefully in our direction. They were just casually discussing this and far be it from me to say no. I didn't even bother to ask who this Louie person was and why he was coming over with more guys. I frowned, slightly, as the thought registered. I felt Ellie press against me, and she whispered, "You won't be frowning for long, sweetie, go sit down on the couch."

They waved us over to the couch, and Ellie settled between Luca and me while Pixie was already pulling the zippers down on Dimitri and Dante's jeans, their eyes focused on her hands. Ellie grabbed a hair tie from her wrist and put her hair up in a ponytail and, I bit back a groan, *the universal signal for best head ever.* She pulled down our zippers at the same time and worked our dicks out of our jeans, we were already hard from just seeing them coming out of the room.

I was hyperaware of her every move as she drew her hand down our chests and gripped our dicks and started to stroke us. Luca hissed and I threw my head back and groaned. Ellie leaned forward and kissed the tip of my dick before throwing me a wink and taking my entire length into her mouth. Fuckk. She worked me over with small licks and deep sucks, hollowing out her cheeks, without skipping a beat while her hand worked Luca over who was looking at her with my dick in her mouth, his eyes hooded. She hummed deep in her throat and my hips jerked while she came up and swirled her tongue on the sensitive head of my dick. While her mouth worked me over, she drew her hand up and down my chest and pinched my nipple.

When I groaned she took my dick out with a pop, switching to her hand, and immediately started to suck on Luca drawing him so deep, I saw his dick pressed into her throat. He threw his head back while she sucked him hard and deep like he liked. Luca tended to like it a little rougher and she had no problem giving it to him. She looked like a fucking sex goddess and she'd slam her head down fast and bring it up slow, driving him crazy.

I looked over to Pixie who was interchanging between Dante and Dimitri in quicker paces, sucking them both almost at the same time within a few seconds of each other. She looked to be keeping them on edge if the way she was setting their jaws on edge was any indication.

Dante closed his eyes on a groan as she took him deep and tightened her mouth and started to hum on his dick while taking him in her throat and he came with a hoarse yell while she swallowed all of him, then when she drew Dimitri into her mouth, he gripped her by her head and he fucked her mouth, thrusting his hips while she moaned at the dominance, and her moans threw him over the edge. She milked him and alternated between cleaning both of their dicks with gentle licks and sucks.

I turned to see Luca grabbing Ellie in a similar fashion thrusting into her mouth and coming into her mouth when Ellie winked at him saucily, and choked him down as deep as he could go. I gripped her head and popped her back on my dick. I liked my dick sucked slowly, I liked to draw it out but fuck if she didn't make me lose control. I pulled her onto all fours and came off the couch and got on my knees and fucked her mouth like I would if it was her pussy. I gripped her by her shoulders and made a few short thrusts before I lost it and came. Holy fuck, her throat was the holy grail. I was so lost with these two, my heart so utterly lost, that I hope I'm never found.

Charlie

Fuck, that so fucking hot. Whoever says that sucking dick was degrading never sucked the right dick. Nothing better than pleasing your significant other or others in this case. It was a different type of sexual high. I loved to be able to put those sleepy, awed looks on their faces. I gave the boys a final lick and suck, and they groaned. I laughed.

"Tuck your dicks away, boys, we have company coming in five minutes."

"How can we wake up when we are dead." Dante groaned.

"Suck it up, buttercup, we just did." I threw him a wink and went to the bathroom with Pix to freshen up and wash our hands because of dick juice. When I came out of the bathroom the boys had their pants done up again, shame really. Luca groaned. "Sugar, you're going to have to stop staring at us like that. There is only so much self-control we can have, even after all of that." I winked at him and turned around as the elevator announced company. I double-checked the men in the elevator and let them in.

"Louie!" I said excitedly as I gave him a huge hug, followed by Pixie, and waved the other men in to get comfortable and set up. The other five men from the shop were all pretty good looking men, lean but muscular, but most importantly, fully tattooed. I'm going to make sure LEDD were just as covered and soon. The shop boys, Tommy, Dean, Jinx, Damien, Cole and Anthony, came to give us all hugs, noticing the men behind us and sizing them up. Louie owned the shop but his boys were loyal and were typically the backup that helped Exousia, remember when I said I have contacts in the castes? These boys pretty much were that, plus a few more scattered around. They may all know me as Ellie but they pretty much took on the big brother type of role with Pix and I once they realized we weren't interested in anything beyond that. LEDD just stood there, shirtless, tall, and gorgeous, not breaking eye contact. I rolled my eyes and smiled.

"Elps! Burns said hi. You two look amazing." He took note of the four men behind us, and added mischievously with a wink, "I know it's been a while since you've seen the boys from the shop, I'm sure they miss your nights with them at the club, I'm sure they appreciate you dressing up for them tonight. They still refuse to find a good girl to settle down, waiting on you and Pix."

LEDD let out a low growl and collectively sent a 'fuck that' down the link. Pixie and I laughed. "Louie, stop causing trouble." Pixie winked and laid her hand on

Anthony's chest. "You know we stopped striping for those boys after that last fist fight broke out. You know how possessive they were getting."

Etienne strode over and snatched Pixie's hand off of Anthony's chest, and gave her a smoldering kiss. "I suggest you stop while you are ahead. I would hate to have to put you over my knee in front of your friends."

"Whatever gets the point across," Dante added with a teasing voice, coupled with a dangerous smile that looked more like a shark smelling blood as he stepped closer to the other men, Dimitri and Luca right next to him.

I rolled my eyes and ushered everyone into the living room while Pixie got everyone beers. As the shop boys started to set up their equipment, inks, and preparing their tablets and special printer for the ink stencils, LEDD just sat on the couch sipping their beers, looking casually dangerous.

"Because of You" by Ne-Yo started playing in the background loudly enough to not even casually ignore it. Louie just observed LEDD, and looked at me and Pixie, who raised an eyebrow. I blushed. Actually blushed. Fuck.

Etienne picked up on it of course, and smiled and nodded to the other guys, who started to actually listen to the song instead of ignoring it. They winked at me and Pix. I growled.

Louie laughed. "I like your friends, Ellie, they fit in well with your volatile ass."

"Break a few jaws and now I'm volatile. I'm a perfect angel, it's not my fault everyone starts it," I muttered as I sipped my beer, rocking back and forth to the beat of the music in the background.

Dimitri stared at me with a smile on his face.

Damien and Cole barked a laugh while Anthony, Jinx, and Tommy hid a smile behind their hands. "One of those jaws was mine, Ellie, I had to go to a healer," Cole said.

"You challenged me at darts and called me a chick. It was your fault." I scoffed. "But I love you now, doesn't that count for something?"

Cole shook his head and chuckled while he wrapped up his machine to minimize the vibrations to his hands while he worked. "Yeah, yeah, I love your crazy ass too, but how was I supposed to know that the purple-haired cute girl was gonna be so damn resistant to my charms, and then punch me."

I pointed at him with my beer. "Louie, that is why they won't settle down. Cole still thinks calling a girl a chick is part of his charm. Maybe I didn't hit him hard enough."

Laughter echoed around the room.

"Oh Ellie, you hit him hard enough, alright, he walked his ass right to my wife to be healed and started to work for me. He wouldn't stop going on about the girl who kicked his ass, his silly story kept people coming back. If you hit him again, we may double our weekly appointments. So have at it." Louie chuckled.

I laughed. "I'll think about it. Boys, come to think of it, Dimitri challenged me to a game of darts when he first met me and even called me princess."

The boys started to laugh. "Man, and you're still alive to tell the tale?" Anthony piped in, shaking his head. "That has to be a fucking miracle, she's punched people in the nuts before even finishing that word."

"I don't even know why calling a female princess is derogatory these days," Dante threw in.

"Are you kidding me? Have you seen Disney movies? I mean other than Moana and Elsa, everyone is a damsel in fucking distress, totally not me." I scoffed.

"Okay, that's fair. But Rapunzel was pretty badass too." He smirked.

"Sure, keep talking and you're going to be seeing the same lights she was seeing," Pixie added, and the boys barked out a laugh.

Dimitri got up and sauntered to me, and wrapped his arms around me, drawing my hair to the side and kissing my neck. "No Letting Go" by Wayne Wonder started to play on the system, and I groaned while Dimitri smirked against my neck.

The shop boys stared slack-jawed. "I got lucky I guess, now she is stuck."

"Yeah, yeah. Shut it. I still have a reputation to uphold." I laughed while he started to rock to the beat with me to the song and spun me around in a circle, then kissed me. God, these lips.

I'm glad you love my lips, they will need to be all over you soon, we need some alone time, just us.

Deal, vampire, I'll be the Anita Blake to your Jean. His laughed echoed in my head.

Louie cleared his throat. I blushed.

"Right so, sorry, I'm rude. Anthony, Cole, Damien, Jinx, Tommy, Louie, let me formally introduce you to Dimitri, Luca, Etienne, and Dante," I said as I pointed everyone out. "You all know Pix and I have been bonded for years, we were lucky enough to meet these four and our magick sparked. Turns out they are our mates as well."

"Wow, that's...wow." Jinx blinked in surprise and the guys looked at us slack-jawed. "Little sisters, we are so happy for you, people are lucky to find one mate and you ladies have each other and four more. That's incredible," Jinx said, sounding suspiciously emotional.

"If you fucking cry, Jinx, I will nut-punch you, you will find your mate too." He laughed and smiled sadly but gave me and Pixie a hug and went to shake the hands of the guys, the rest following suit.

Louie clapped his hands. "Well, any mate of Elps is family here. Let's get you all comfortable and we can start on your ink. All my boys are unmatched in talent except by each other, well, only difference is that Tommy also does the piercings in the shop," he boasted. He loved his team and it was evident on his face. He got those boys out of the castes and helped them become talented artists and gave them something to hold on to when everything always seemed so bleak. Louie was a good man. "Grab a chair and they will work on your designs," he continued, "so we all know what we are getting or are we keeping it a surprise for when we are done?"

"Surprise," LEDD said at the same time. Fuckers.

Pix and I shook our heads. "I have an idea but I guess since it's a secret"—I rolled my eyes—"we can all do that. I'll open a link with you and your artist and you guys can discuss in privately."

"You can do that?" Damien said incredulously. I laughed.

"You have no idea of all the things I can do." I winked at him, and he blushed and turned around.

"Too much information, little sister," Louie muttered.

We settled into our chairs once the secret stencils were created and the men got to work. It was cathartic. I was sending healing magick to everyone in the room to avoid them getting tired. We had a Hunger Games marathon playing in the background, and Luca kept muttering that someone stole his face and we were teasing him the entire time. After sitting for a few hours, we all took a break and ate Chinese takeout before settling back down and watching a few episodes of Supernatural while the machines kicked back up.

"I do not look like him, he looks like a skinny version of me." Etienne scoffed.

"He is not skinny, he's lean and sexy. You just look like you eat muscles for breakfast, at least he solves paranormal crimes. Let me know the last time you fought off a demon." No one is allowed to insult Dean Winchester on my watch. He scoffed and ignored the TV.

"If you're going to be ungrateful about meeting your twin, then I'll just put on Vampire Diaries." The men groaned as I switched it on.

"Holy shit, he totally looks Like Dimitri. He even has the scowl and evil look down. Fuck. That's creepy," Dante exclaimed, and Pix and I snickered. Dimitri glowered at the TV.

"I'm better looking," he muttered darkly. I couldn't hold back my laugh. Thank God, we got an early start and I had healing magick because our sessions took a long time. The boys finished before Pixie and I, and they all went to the workout room to talk man shit while Anthony and Louie finished up on Pix and I.

"I take it you two are head over heels?" Louie whispered.

"What makes you say that?" Pixie asked with a smirk.

"Well, I know your tattoos are secret." He rolled his eyes. "But if what Ellie is getting is any indication, then you must be getting something similar. You two always were more in tune with each other than most people I knew that were fortunate enough to be bonded. I also see the way you two look at those men, it's more than a bond. You two are falling hard if you're not already there."

I sighed. "You are a perceptive old man," I said affectionately. "It is confusing, Louie, can someone really fall in love this quickly. With Pix, we were young, we started as best friends, and then it exploded when we got older. But this time, there is no wait for puberty, it's like we fell into this and I keep expecting to hit the ground. I don't say this often, I'll deny it if you ever repeat it, but I'm scared."

Anthony and Louie looked at me and smiled.

"Little sis, the great Ellie, is scared? That is certainly a first," he said with a small smile. "People wait for their whole life to have the chance to find their bonded, you and Pix are fortunate to have five, each. That's incredible. If the way they look at you two is any indication, then they fell right along with you. The ground never comes when you're in love, Ellie. You'll fall forever, that's the magick of it all." He gave Pixie a hug then walked up to me and held my chin and gave me a kiss on my forehead.

"Sis, this is real, don't be afraid to embrace it, we heard you'll be going to the academy, we know who they are. If we thought they were shit, we would have kicked their asses when we walked in. If the castes cannot be there with you, knowing they will be, will make things easier for us here. You and Pixie are two of the strongest women we know, love only makes you stronger, at this point you'll be invincible."

I choked back a sob and wiped my eyes. Fuck this emotional moment.

"Emotions suck Anthony. Stop it." I laughed. "But point taken, don't fight it." I winked at Pixie. "We got this, well I do. Pixie doesn't fight shit, she's stronger than me there."

"I'll miss you boys, but we are going to change shit, and having a strong family here and a family there will certainly make us invincible. We love you, Ant."

"Hey, what about us?!" Cole walked out with the boys behind him. I laughed.

"Yeah we love you fuckers, too," Pixie joked, and I blew them all kisses.

He's right, you know. Etienne's voice sounded in my mind.

"About what?" I asked Etienne suspiciously, just how much did they hear.

We fell too, Luca's voice responded. My eyes snapped to him and swallowed at the look in their eyes and turned away.

I cleared my throat. "So are we ready to show off now? Who is going first?"

After we finished, it was well past 9 o'clock. I was excited but a little nervous to show the boys my work, we all separated and sat on different sides of the room, so no one could peek, the anticipation was killing me!

Dante went first, he took off the large cover on his chest and we gasped. Fuck, it was beautiful. His entire chest now had two huge motorcycles with two pin up girls on them. The girls were exact replicas of Pixie and I, down to hair color and style. He had me on my demon bike and Pixie on her purple and black bike. The details were incredible, the curves perfect. He even had me in the outfit he first met me in; leather pants with my combat boots and black crop top. Pixie was dressed in the outfit she wore when we went to patrol. Beyond the bikes was what looked like purple streaks coming from the bikes' exhaust pipes. It was intense and beautiful and he even caught my asshole smirk, and Pixie's soft smile. Pixie looked a little shocked while I was in awe.

"Holy fuck, Dante! Tommy, this incredible. It is perfect, how the hell did you get every single detail of my bike down like that? That's just insane."

Tommy scoffed. "I'm an artist, sis, we have seen you on your bikes all the time, it was a piece of cake down to the looks on your faces. If you look closely, Pixie's eyebrow is raised and your fists are white, knuckling your bike." I laughed at him, Pixie and I took turns to give Dante a kiss.

"It's beautiful, papi chulo, thank you. You're really stuck now," I joked.

"I was never going anywhere, I'm not stuck, mi amor, estoy bandito," he whispered to us. He just told me he was blessed. Fuck me.

Etienne stepped up. "Me next." He turned around, and shit. He had a dark angel with her wings down back-to-back, with a fairy, also with her wings down. The fairy was done in all colors and the dark angel was done in shades of gray but the feet were wrapped in a thin purple streak and the hands of the fairy and angel reached for each other, setting off the same purple spikes. Both of the girls had their faces facing up with serene expressions. Underneath the figures were words reading, 'Mon Eternite.'

Pixie and I traced the words. "What does this mean Etienne," she whispered.

"My forever," he whispered. My breath caught. This was getting very emotional. He reached and gave Pixie a kiss, then caught my lips with the same intensity.

"Fuck."

Dimitri took off his cover from his arm and shoulder and the scene depicted made me laugh at first, then I got a closer look. He chose to have a half sleeve done, trailing from his collar bone to his elbow. It was a vampire, holding a female close with purple hair about to bite into her neck and his arm wrapped around a brunette, hands splayed across her stomach. The tattoo was mostly in shades of gray, black, and white. The back of the tattoo was beautiful architecture that looked like a castle throne room. He really went into the full details of the vampire theme. I had to laugh. Like Dante and Etienne, he also wove in streaks of purple around his hands and fangs. Within the tattoo were the words 'Usque ad consummationem saeculi.' Until the end of time, in Latin. Goodness gracious. They were going to kill Pix and I at this rate; all these emotions.

"I thought you hated to be called a vampire," I teased but it was strained by the emotion in my voice.

"For you I'm anything you want me to be, anyone else calls me a vampire, I'll kill them." He quirked a lip at that.

"Guess that means I'm next." Luca slowly stripped his bandages off and exposed his piece. It wrapped from his left peck all the way down to his elbow. He took a different approach to his tattoo, he had thick green and black vines wrapped up his arm leading to his chest. The vines were set on fire but instead of regular flames they were tinged in black and purple with accents of red and yellows. The tattoo had a three dimensional effect, which helped the background of the tattoo stand out more. Under the tattoo were four distinct male silhouettes with a curvaceous female silhouette on either side. It appeared as if the flames around the tattoo touched everything but them, which were settled right over his heart. His tattoo in particular didn't have any words on it that I could see but the full wrap around his muscular arm was phenomenal. It was as if the vines were moving every time he flexed. It was impressive work.

"Cole, this is incredible. It looks like it's going to jump off his skin! I love the shadows over his heart too. LEDD you went all out, I'm...wow." I looked at Pixie, and she was suspiciously blinking a little too much. I am rarely made speechless but the emotion in the room was over-whelming but comforting at the same time.

Dante

WE MADE OUR GIRLS SPEECHLESS. I knew they would be happy once they saw our new ink, we had another trick up our sleeve to show them later too.

"Okay Elps, it's your turn! Pixie, do you want to go first, mi amor, you look a little pink over there," I teased at the blush, creeping up her face.

God she is beautiful, she just glows.

Yeah, she is something else. Dimitri said in response, and a chorus of agreements followed shortly after.

"Yeah, okay I'll go next." Pixie took off her cover, and holy fuck. No wonder she took an extra couple of hours. She had an entire sleeve done, I have no idea how Anthony was able to work that fast or if he had some type of speed power but goodness, it was ridiculously detailed. From her forearm, she had a sugar skull female with the full face of color turned to the side so you could only see the profile. Around the female's profile, seemingly caressing her face was a skeletal hand that led to a skull with similar sugar skull designs without the actual human look. The eyes were sunken in but still seemed hyper focused on his live bride. Around the duo that took up her entire forearm were purple roses and dark shadows. The shadows continued but started to turn into smoke that went down her forearm and started to take on a three-dimensional effect.

Beyond the smoke was a solitary female, her wind-swept hair taking on a life of its own. The female was looking out into a forest of darkness, the moon and stars overhead, knees drawn up to her chest. The lower piece wrapped around her entire forearm as you had to look around it to get the entire picture but on the female's back, carved and dripping blood, the only color in this portion of the piece, were the words: 'In the darkness, my soul will always call out to yours' written by the smoke that was causing the effect of the picture seemingly coming to life. The shades of gray were startling, except for the blood dripping from the female, still the entire piece flowed. He packed in so many little details that the entire piece looked like a work of art, not just a tattoo. The fine lines of the hair being swept away mimicked by the way the trees swayed as well, the way the words were viciously carved on the back of the female facing the lake. It was as if you can almost touch her and she would come to life. I blew out a breath, this was incredible work.

"This is gorgeous, mi amor, the detail is incredible." She beamed and gave me a kiss.

"Thanks! I am in love with the details. Anthony really kicked ass on this piece. Did you notice anything else?" She turned and winked at Anthony. The boys came closer to inspect the tattoo, trying to figure out what she was referring to, and after a few minutes, Etienne smirked.

Inside of the arm directly where the girl is sitting, the blood is dripping to the ground instead of stopping, it runs in five different streaks. Each streak is one of our names in script. It looks like it's part of the blood running, very subtle, just like her.

Fuck, I am beyond turned on right now.

You are always turned on and whipped as fuck. Dimitri rolled his eyes.

We ALL are around them. Besides Dracula, you're the one with Hotel Transylvania tattooed on his arm, so who is calling who whipped? Dante laughed out-loud.

Ellie broke the silence before we did. "Baby, that is beautiful." She grabbed her ass and brought her in for a kiss. The shop boys laughed but looked elsewhere and we were just stuck looking at them, watching while Ellie drew her hands up Pixie's back and gave her a hair tug before drifting down to her neck and leaving a lingering kiss.

Pixie stepped back, breathless. "Okay stop trying to distract us, it's your turn."

Ellie rolled her eyes, then winked. "Ruining all my fun."

Louie stood to the side, seeming very excited, proud, and emotional. I wonder what it is that she had done. She took a deep breath and uncovered her arm.

Starting down from her shoulder was a woman with her face pointing down, covered in a black hood. What was visible of her face was half skull and the other half had a smile with red lipstick. The woman was curvaceous and was draped in a cloak that parted to reveal abs and tight black pants, she was holding two flaming swords, crossed one in front of the other, that were dripping in blood. Upon a closer look, the swords said, 'I promise death.' The scene wrapped around her arms, and behind the female was a blood red moon, and a dark road littered in skulls and corpses. The cloak was dragging behind the female in the blood that seemed to run in a river beneath her feet, which was covered in cuts and bruises. In the clouds, the words: 'Power is earned not given, or else it's taken by Force' were written.

If that wasn't intense enough, the darkness flowed into her forearm but drifted away and the scene was completely different. The intensity kicked up a notch, however, in a very different way. In the center of her forearm, were two females, back to back holding hands similar to Etienne but without the fairy and angel wings. This is visible when she turned with her palms facing up; clever. The females were nude, the profiles hidden as they looked down toward what was hanging from their hands.

I gaped. The women were very perfectly tattooed, showing every curve of the female body from the shape of the thighs to the perfect bend of the knees and arch of their feet. No details were spared as the nipples even had a dusky pink color and the curve of the neck was amazing as it led from a very detailed collar bone. Pure magick, it was like Louie wrapped his soul into the details. Between their hands was a very detailed pocket watch about two inches, set with a time. The watch was a shiny silver and brass, the numbers in Roman numerals, and the time was set to 11:53.

Behind the females, were the simple, yet very pronounced, outlines of four men. Even those outlines captured muscle structure and tone. From those outlines exploded a watercolor landscape that wrapped around her forearm. The water colors depicted a city of color and a dark road, where the women stood in the center. When the watercolors met on the ulnar side of her forearm, words started to form from the tendrils: 'Con Nuestro Amor, El Tiempo Paro, y Nuestro Corazones Latido.'

I was stuck, I felt like I couldn't breathe. There was absolutely no way we could have ever been so lucky. I had to tear my eyes away from the newly drawn ink and grabbed her chin, moving past the guys, so she could look at me. "I Swear" by All-4-One started to play from the suspiciously quiet sound system these past few minutes. I rolled my eyes, but I pressed a gentle kiss to her mouth before pulling her close and looking down at her perfect face. "Mi corazon no latido hasta que yo te conoci a ti y a Pixie. Yo te adoro mi alma. Por siempre. Te lo juro."

She looked up at me with tears in her eyes and I kissed each closed eyelid. "No, honey, this is pure magick, no need for tears." I wrapped her in my arms.

"So anyone going to tell me what the tattoo actually says or should I just pretend she is saying that she loves how long my...fangs...are," Dimitri teased. It was like the twilight zone, seeing that sullen motherfucker actually joke and laugh. Creepy as fuck, gave me fucking shivers.

Pixie smiled and shook her head. "It says, 'With our love, time stopped and our hearts beat' or rather our hearts started to beat is the gist of it. Dante then told her that his heart didn't beat until he met us." Her voice caught but she continued, "And promises that he loves her, his soul, forever." I grabbed her hand and brought her in for a kiss, tugging her hair to run my tongue across her tongue rings and stroke her tongue with mine.

"He isn't wrong," Luca spoke up with the other two murmuring their agreements.

Louie cleared his throat, I forgot they were all here for a few. "Well, the boys and I are going to head out, I have a feeling the next thing you want to show them, we shouldn't all be here for." He barked a laugh, and Jinx, Anthony, Damien, Cole, and Tommy groaned, murmuring about little sisters. The men walked around saying their goodbyes and admiring each other's work, pausing briefly to look at the designs when looking at Ellie's hooded tattoo, before packing up.

The boys and I helped them downstairs to Louie's apartment.

When we dropped off the equipment and were about to leave, Louie stopped us outside his door. "Take care of them, boys, we have known them for a long time. They think they are invincible, and I'm not going to lie, sometimes it seems like they can be. You think we don't know who you are and what your goal was when you all hit the streets?" He scoffed. "Shit, you think we don't know who Ellie truly is and what she does for this city? We love them, they are family even if we aren't blood. Our community, this town, thrives because of them." He sighed and shook his head. "We all feel change coming, you would have to be dead to not feel the charge in the air, but we would like to let you know we are here and you can all depend on us when shit hits the fan." Louie slapped us on our shoulders and closed the door.

We rubbed our hands down our faces and looked at each other, smiles tugging our faces. We felt the twinge of the fresh ink, pulled the healing magick on the way back to the private elevator, and healed the tattooed area. Magick is helpful sometimes. No need for three-four weeks of healing. I grinned and whistled, knowing I was going back to our women and that we had a little extra in store for them.

23

"There's a bit of magic in everything, and some loss to even things out." **Lou Reed**
"In a world full of Magick, the most amazing thing, to me, is the magick of the bond." - **Dante**

D ante

WHEN WE GOT BACK to the apartment, the girls had already taken a quick shower and were in pajamas on the couch. We smiled at the image, they looked so comfortable and it was surreal just walking here and feeling like we were coming home. Knowing we were due to leave soon was going to be an interesting experience in itself. Having to deal with compromises and fake engagements when the only women we wanted and needed were right in front of us.

"We are going to take a quick shower, you ladies wanna settle here or do we want to hang out in the rooms instead?"

"Rooms, I think. I'm a little tired to be honest," Pixie said with a yawn. She got up and pulled Ellie from the couch, who was staring at the news.

"You guys go lay down, I need to finish watching the news, there's some interesting shit going down in another town, I wonder what's going on," Ellie murmured. Pixie gave her a kiss and she looked at us and shook her head, I took that as our cue that she wouldn't be getting up for a while.

We headed to the room for a shower and we laid down on the bed, exhaustion claiming us all.

Charlie

NOTHING BOTHERED me more than an unsolved mystery. The news was highlighting a few more disappearances, but they were vague. Something sat wrong with that and I couldn't put my finger on it. There had to be more ties to it.

There was something going on beyond our town. I know I had to focus on our community first but when the time came, I may have to look into making a few alliances beyond the magickal side of our town. Not only were there other communities with their own Councils, there were hundreds of other otherworldly creatures out there and it's time to realize that our weakness is our seclusion. I put it in the back of my mind, but I was going to put out feelers in the meantime. If there was one thing that hacking had taught me, it was that no information that's digital, can be hidden from me, even within wards. Magick is great, but it cannot stop all technology.

I took advantage of everyone sleeping and headed into my office and started pulling up various towns and their Councils, their magickal universities and their instructors.

While our town had an academy for the Shadows, which were officers of a sort, there were other towns that had academies for students to practice and hone their magick for the good of their communities beyond being lap dogs. Those were the places we needed to work with, if it was just to learn how to effectively run a town. When we disbanded this Council we were going to need a shit ton of help. I leaned back in my chair and took note of a few places, one being Delorean University, a school for high Council children. I scoffed, pretentious I am sure, but I had the system pull up all information about the school anyway. I wanted to be thorough. I had a suspicion that the best way to the Councils were by learning about their family histories. My systems were going to be working overtime, but I needed shit done right. I sighed and rubbed my head. Something told me that the problems in our town were just the tip of the iceberg and I'm not sure if that excited me or put me on edge, but it was the only way to find out what our Council was up to. As it was, there was nothing coming up about communications with the other towns, other than that of regular open communications and events.

I ran an encryption program I developed to pick up coded messages, and started to make sure that was focused between the various communities as well. Call it a hunch, but when my gut told me to search, I searched.

HOURS LATER, I let the searches run, completed some notes and trudged up the stairs and crawled into bed. Dimitri immediately reached for me and cuddled me closely, and I fell asleep with a smile on my face. Pixie and I were used to my late night wanderings but it felt good to know she was up here being taken care of while I let my mind relax and catch up to itself.

Pixie

THE NEXT FEW days flew by and before we knew it, the boys were gone, and Ellie and I were locking everything down, and making sure the security had everything they needed, our numbers and emergency backup numbers. They also had access to our trackers if anything happened.

We made sure our people were well fed and had extra funds just in case. All cameras were working and word got around that Exousia was leaving for a bit but things were monitored and handled. Everyone seemed to be on high alert. We had confidence that they would come together but it felt good to know they could reach us as well.

Despite it being four in the morning, I smiled at Ellie as she triple-checked her devices and packed before jumping on her bike. We needed essentials only as the uniform sets were delivered to the rooms. We had the boys take our computers just in case we were checked before entering so that we were set, but Ellie insisted on keeping her phones. I pity whoever tried to take those.

"Ready?" I teased. She laughed and shook her freshly dyed purple hair.

"Yeah, sorry. Let's go. Everything is set and locked down. Let's enjoy the ride." She smiled and we cranked our bikes and pulled out of the garage and headed into enemy territory. Shit was about to get real for the Council, they literally had no idea what was coming to their front door. I smiled in anticipation. I was going to love bringing them down several notches.

We drove up to the Capitol city, pulling in a lot of attention on our bikes, and I laughed under my black-out helmet. I always hated this damn city. All the pretty lights and clean streets that didn't smell of desperation, and people trying to make ends meet. Of course, the further you drove away from our city the better the towns became, however, the city was just overly opulent. I scoffed, as we traversed the smooth streets and passed the main citadel government building and the two large buildings on the side, which were their libraries and convention center; where they mostly held large events and huge parties that showed off wealth. Except, libraries didn't require round-the-clock surveillance and guard duties. The buildings themselves were amazing, pure white and downright glimmered in the sunlight. They were surrounded by beautiful well-kept gardens and small pathways that forced anyone walking to do so, in a single file line in either direction in order to accommodate two-way traffic. They wanted people to slow down and take it all in, the power, the beauty, the money.

You could argue that I was jaded, but the truth was I knew how they worked, I knew their blueprint plans; I damn near studied them as much as I practiced my magickal skills. If there was one thing you should know, it was your enemy and your own skill set. Anything less than that was sure death and then what was the point of living for your purpose if your purpose has no direction? No. Ellie and I were more than prepared and although realistically, shit can go all the way to west bumble-fuck, we shouldn't have to go into this situation blindly because of all maybes. Learn what you can, thrive, and prepare mentally and physically for the worst. We sped past the buildings deeper into the capital, the academy itself was about half a mile past the main city, nestled in the woods. It made sense really, training the warriors and then when they came out of the woodworks, it was like "wow magick." I rolled my eyes.

Pix, reign in the negative thoughts. We know what we are getting into. Let's take it one step at a time, we already have a plan of action and several backup plans. We got this.

I wasn't projecting my thoughts.

You didn't have to. I pick up on the emotions. Let's get this shit handled. Yeah?

Yeah. I sighed. *Let's fuck shit up.*

Charlie

I KNEW SHE WAS ANNOYED, angry, and overall underwhelmed by this stupid city and all it represents. I felt the same, I cannot pretend otherwise but what kept me going was the thought that soon I will be closer to what I needed, and boy, was I going to fucking get it.

We pulled up to the gate of the academy, you wouldn't even know it was an academy really. It was in the middle of the forest with big black gates for fuck's sake, it could have been the house of some creepy vampire for all we knew. There were guards stationed at the sides of the gates, you wouldn't see them at first, but I guess you can't be a shadow if you couldn't blend in. We pulled up and sat on the bikes, making them approach us, their look of obvious disbelief when we took off our helmets was comical.

"You sure you are in the right place, ladies?" the guard asked, not unkindly, one point to him. We said nothing as we gave him our identification and our passes. Their eyes bugged out a little when they saw our passes.

Another guard cleared this throat. "Well, uh, I guess you are. We do have to search your bags, it's protocol." He looked at us like a teenager who wanted to look at panties.

"Actually it's protocol to check our person if warranted, which admittedly probably makes you more excited, but I highly doubt it warranted," I said smoothly, leaning forward, my legs on either side of my bike, my forearms on the handle bars. "So what's the excuse? It's too early for this shit and we still gotta go get dressed and meet at the training grounds in forty-five minutes so make shit quick or get the fuck out of our way."

"Who the fuck do you—"

"I'm Ellie, and if you finish that sentence, I will make you fucking regret it." I narrowed my eyes, disrespect will never be acceptable and prejudice even less with me.

"Benson, cut that shit out, it's too early for this bullshit," the other guard said, rubbing his head.

"Ladies you are clear, looks like you were vouched for by the top Elite team, that's admirable. I look forward to getting to know you. My name is Julian, I will be one of your instructors along with Dimitri, Luca, Etienne, and Dante." He smiled genuinely, one of those infectious smiles that had Pix and I smiling back. He raised his hands and the gates opened.

"I will see you soon. I hear from the instructors that" —he winked—"the first day is the hardest." I laughed.

"I'm looking forward to it," I replied, putting my helmet back on, revving in my bike and moving forward, sticking my middle finger out at Benson as we drove by. The sound of Julian's laughter followed.

We followed the path we memorized and pulled in front of our buildings, parked our bikes, putting a protection spell on them, while we took our backpacks toward the accommodations. We had already manipulated them so we would be closer to the exits and the boys, so we quickly found our shared room and used our special keys that Luca gave us the day before to get in.

For a room in a warrior academy, it was nicer than I thought. I'm not sure why I pictured a dark and dank room with a couple of cots. Two beds, an en-suite shower, a couple of desks, plush carpeting. Honestly, it was unremarkable, just a lot more than I expected. I closed the door behind us and started the settle in.

"This is nicer than I thought it would be," Pixie echoed my thoughts as she threw her bag on a bed, and I grinned.

"Yeah, I was thinking the same." I went to the bathroom to wash my face and noticed all our extra things were already in the room.

"Looks like the guys are already here." I pointed at our equipment. "We have thirty minutes, let's set up the security cameras before we get dressed and head out."

We worked quickly before we turned to our dressers and went to grab our uniforms.

"You gotta be fucking kidding me."

"This is a joke, right?" growled Pixie. I shook my head, taking in the tight Lycra material and long sleeved crop top, I looked in the closet and at least there were combat boots.

"I guess with the other women being here they wanted to show them off to their future husbands, although to be perfectly honest, this is a sexual harassment issue waiting to happen."

I pulled on the uniform, and I meant that literally, I was curvy, damnit. I choked as I looked at Pixie in her outfit. We wear leather and crop tops on the regular, we train in shorts and sports bra, but these outfits were literally like being butt ass naked and someone painting us with black ink. I ordered our sizes but a size or two up might have stopped our breast from looking like a fucking meal.

"Yeah, if you look like that, I don't even want to know what the fuck I look like in this shit. At least it covers our new ink." I sighed, bending over to pull on my boots, when I felt Pixie come up behind me and smack my ass. She giggled and I rolled my eyes as I turned over.

"You look hot as fuck, bright side is the boys will probably die of a heart attack." She laughed and wrapped her arms around me and brought me in for a kiss. I leaned my forehead against hers after, and sighed.

"Ready?" I asked, looking at the time. We had ten minutes to get to the training grounds.

"Yup, we got this, Ellie, one step at a time. We get in, infiltrate the school, then the Elite teams, and then get closer to the Council. We got this." I laughed.

"Well, when you put it like that, I guess we are almost done." She stuck out her tongue in response and we walked out of the room.

The halls were empty, I'm sure the other members were already there, eager beavers. We walked quickly, taking a quick right straight onto the grounds. Another benefit, the training grounds are behind the instructor quarters. A brief three-minute walk later, we stood outside a huge black domed building.

"Well, shit, they take the Shadow name a little too seriously, huh?" I muttered.

"Well, I guess we wouldn't live up to the name if the building wasn't at least black, I voted for all black dorms and buildings, but got shot down for the fifth time. I'm starting to think they don't value my opinion," said a familiar voice behind us. We turned around and looked up, *goodness gracious, did Thor realize he was missing? Because something told me he didn't realize he was.*

I smiled at the pleasant surprise. "I guess it would be pretty morbid in that case. I mean we don't train demons," I quipped.

"Don't we though?" he responded and frowned, turning his head.

10 Months Ago

"Baby which club are we going to again?" I heard Pixie ask from the bathroom, while I tugged on a black dress to go with my purple spiked heels.

"Mirage! It's on the edge of the border, it's supposed to be a new club where all shifters, magick users and others are on neutral ground." I turned around to find her behind

me, full makeup on with no towel. I groaned and bit my lip avoiding the clear distraction and walked around her, leaving her to laugh at my reaction, to finish my own makeup.

"Sounds like trouble waiting to happen," she joked after a few moments, walking into the bathroom with tight black leather pants, red heels, and a halter top begging to be tugged off so I could wrap my lips around her nipples. Judging by the spark in the eye, she knew where my train of thought went as well.

"You're going to be the death of me," I muttered wrapping my arms around her and leaning on the door frame of the bathroom.

"Possibly, but damn, it would be a good way to go." She winked, pressing her lips against mine. We let our hands roam, our kissing becoming more feverish before we broke apart, catching our breaths.

"Damn, I love you." I ran my hand across her face.

"Right back at you babe, now let's go."

We made our way out of the penthouse and headed to the garage, nodding at our security guard. Foregoing our usual rides, our amazing bikes, we jumped into a sleek black beauty we called midnight and peeled out of garage, making our way to the Club.

About thirty minutes into our ride, ten minutes of those in complete darkness other than our headlights, we drove up to a club made completely of black glass with a line around the block. There were waitresses outside, taking drink orders, and even everyone outside looked like they were having a good time.

I let out a long whistle. "Well, that's smart, make money from the wait," I said as we admired the building.

"Who owns this club anyway?" Pixie asked.

"Remember I mentioned that a client I have been working with for a while, has several businesses and recently starting getting into the nightclub scene and asked me to do all the security measures for the club?" I paused as she nodded.

"Well, she asked me to come by when we had a chance and here we are." I informed her, bringing my car to valet and getting out of Midnight. I walked around the car to meet Pixie who was helped out by a Vampire. I smiled, grabbed her hand, and made our way to the front of the line.

"This is beautiful," Pixie murmured.

"Thank you, this really has been quite a success and I owe it all to Charlie," a deep, melodic, sultry voice spoke, and despite the noise, it reached us effortlessly.

"Alessandra, it's a pleasure to see you again." I gave her a hug, admiring her lush curves in her all-black leather attire, her hair swept up to show her neck and a beautiful red amulet, she once told me it was a family heirloom.

"This is my bonded, Pixie." I smiled, and Pixie reached out to give her a hug as well, a show of trust among vampires.

"Ah yes, I have heard a lot about you. Come, come, let's head inside. I have a VIP area for my most trusted guests." Alessandra smiled warmly leading us inside.

I whistled low, the club was at top of the line in all aspects. Leather booths, multiple floors with what looked like bars that spanned wall-to-wall on three sides of the room, and incredible aerial performers dancing to their own sensual beat.

"Shit, can I move in here?" Pixie joked and Alessandra responded with a deep chuckle, her hips swaying as she led us to a VIP room with its own bar and servers.

"This is just the bare minimum, I will have to give you the full tour later. Here we are." She gestured to a red velvet booth with a ridiculously handsome guy seated at the end, looking at his phone. "I'll be back shortly, I like to do my rounds but this seated here is Drew, he is one of my... most trusted advisors," She trailed off and winked, taking her leave.

"Ahh, two beautiful females to keep me and my friends company." His deep timbre smoothly enraptured us.

"Holy wow, you're like Thor's doppelgänger," Pixie whispered, and he chuckled in response.

"I have to agree with that." I moved into the booth, my hand on Pixie's back as she sat down next to me. We signaled the waitress for a drink and settled into the booth, making small talk.

"Trainer for the Elite Shadow Guard, huh?" I exchanged a small smile with Pixie. "Impressive." I sipped my drink.

"Yup, you can say that." He looked a bit uncomfortable.

"I always wondered about the all-black," I joked. "Demon trainers or protectors of the people?"

"I stopped telling the difference a long time ago," he murmured under his breath. Exchanging another look, Pixie and I stood up.

Seems like a genuinely nice guy, nothing nefarious coming from him. Time to dance the night away? I asked Pixie via our shared mind-link.

Yes, please! she responded with gusto, and I contained a chuckle.

"Well, Drew, it was a pleasure to meet you. It's unfortunate we couldn't meet your friends. Maybe later?"

He stood up with us and smiled warmly. "Yes, later,

they should have been here by now. Shame. I think you would have hit it off with those four good men." As we walked to the dance floor, we heard his voice ring out: "Luca, Etienne, Dimitri, Dante, took you lot long enough!"

We didn't look back and we tore up the club with smiles on our faces.

P IXIE and I mimicked his facial expression, the way we did months ago when we first met Drew. Another Elite Shadow Hunter, during one of our rare but enlightening nights out, in fact it was meeting Drew that set the cogs of my brain whirling. *It looks like he still doesn't like the way things are being run.*

"Hmm." Pixie looked at me. "I think we will decline to answer that question. I'm Pixie, this is Ellie. What's your name?" Oh, right, pretenses. It's why she was my better half.

"Nice to meet you ladies, no seriously, very nice to meet you." He winked at us exaggeratingly and looked us up and down slowly before he reached his hand out to shake our hands. "I'm Drew, one of the instructors." We shook his hand, and nodded.

"Well then"—I pointed at the door—"ladies first," I said. He barked out a laugh and shook his head.

"Yeah, I like you already, Ellie. This should be fun." He smiled mischievously as he walked in and we followed behind him. He went to stand at what we assumed was the front of the class, as all the instructors were there and all the students looked like ducks out of water.

Ready for our grand entrance? I asked Pixie.

Baby, I'm always ready. Let's do this. She smiled.

※ 24 ※

"Your attitude may hurt me, but mine can kill you." -
Unknown
"It's like you know our women."- **Luca**

L uca

ALL EYES SNAPPED to Ellie and Pixie as they strutted into the room and walked right to the front of the room. There was no confusion on their faces, no worry, just cool indifference and confidence.

We had decided on no mental communication with them, in order to keep our faces schooled and our attention focused, but holy fuck, if it wasn't for the other four women who walked in ten minutes ago, we would not believe what they were wearing for uniforms. Clearly, no one ever intended for Pix and Ellie to look like they walked out of Sir-Mix-a-Lot's video set.

They stood with their legs apart, arms behind their back, hands clasped, very clearly at attention; and Benson and Drew smiled appreciatively as everyone else got the hint and mimicked their stance. Well, at least they knew how to command a room.

There was no need for us to raise our voices as the room was already quiet. We all had our little quirks that gave us the ability to lead, to be instructors. Other than being great fighters, Etienne's ability to pick up on lies could easily toss out the weak links, and Dante's ability to seamlessly blend into someone's thoughts came in handy for anyone who wasn't one hundred percent in the game.

I cleared my throat. "All right, baby shadows, looks like the council decided to surprise us this year. We have six female recruits this year. Two of them were personally invited by one of the top tier teams, and I look forward to seeing how they work with the group. Now to introduce ourselves, I am Luca, an Elite team leader, and I specialize in tracking and a couple of elements. So if any of you bitch out, I will find you." A few nervous chuckles came from the group. I wasn't joking.

"I am Dimitri, I will be your worst fucking nightmare. Let's get that clear right now. I have speed as my advantage so I suggest if you don't want to break a few bones, you learn how to shield effectively because I will make it my personal mission to sort of the weak links." Dimitri's low growl echoed throughout the room. I smiled internally, taking in the nerves in the room ramping up.

"Bonjour, petite Shadows. Je m'appelle, Etienne. I

can pick up on all your lies and truth, for those who do not have that skill, that is fine. I will also be training in air manipulation. However, keep in mind we will all be training in combat in weaponry so there will be ample time for us to get well acquainted." Etienne nodded his head, quiet and reserved.

Good job scaring them, big guy, I'm sure they will all want to butter your croissants after that smooth French introduction. Ellie's voice trickled through the link, and we had to school our faces to stop from laughing.

"I'm Dante, and tsk tsk, baby shadows, I can read your minds, and I promise you none of your pick-up lines will work on the ladies in this room, do better, I'm ashamed already." He shook his head as the room burst out in laughter. "I also have a few tricks up my sleeve you will all pick up on during combat, but I won't spoil the surprise." He winked and went back to observing the room.

"Hello recruits, I am Drew. Also an elite team leader like Luca. I will be leading the hunt for deserters. We take this training seriously. We have cities to protect and we do not have to coddle insecurities. You are all here for a reason. This year, every person here was brought on by personal invitation from a shadow, which can either help or hinder you depending on the quality of shadow who recommended you." He paused and smiled widely as a few recruits nervously shuffled their feet. "Oh no, don't look nervous. I just suggest you all rise to the occasion and be the better version of yourselves. Or don't"—he shrugged—"I haven't had a good recruit tracker hunt in years." He smirked.

"My name is Julian. I will be working with the water and fire elementals. I won't bother getting to truly know you for at least a couple of weeks, unless you truly

impress me. I do not have time nor patience for slackers."
He nodded curtly.

You didn't have to be able to read emotions to pick up
on the combination in the room of excitement, cockiness
and the fear coming from the cadets. It was invigorating. I
loved to scout, but this is what I thrived for. Teaching,
breaking my soldiers down, and removing bad habits
piece by piece, and then building them back up into Elite
soldiers.

Charlie

"ALRIGHT, we are going to start training with a little
random demonstration." Luca jumped off the platform
and walked to the front of the crowd, and other instructors followed. Fuck, he was gorgeous.

"What do you think, gentlemen? One of us against
one of them before we start to pair them off to determine
skill sets?" Luca looked at the other men and smirked.
Drew's eyes lit up with excitement.

"A way for them to have a taste of what to expect? I
like that. Are we holding back?" Drew asked rhetorically.
Dante, Etienne, Dimitri, Luca, and Julian smiled
viciously. I smiled internally, trying to keep my game face
on but fuck it was hard.

"Everyone, circle formation now," Dimitri barked,
cracking his neck, looking every inch a murderer. I tried, I
really did, but I couldn't help myself.

*I swear the moment we are free from here, I'm
climbing you all like a spider monkey.* I turned to hide my
face and went to get into the circle the class was forming.

I rolled my eyes. What made these recruits so special? No seriously, the girls followed direction easily enough but the men were distracted. You would think having women around was a weakness and it was making me itch to teach them a thing or two. I glanced at Pixie.

I wonder if when they said no holding back, they knew that these guys were going to hold punches when coming to combat with us? I asked her.

Seems like it. I think it's their way of making it known to not hold back on the females. But I have a doubt they will use the council daughters as a demonstration just yet. I think he's aiming for physical strength. She theorized. I had to agree. Our musings were answered a few moments later when Drew came walking around the circle and pointed at me.

"You, the smart-ass, come forward," he said with a smile. The boys frowned, and my vampire growled in my head. They didn't know about the exchange we had outside so I had to laugh.

"You think it's funny?" Drew asked, one eyebrow raised.

I smiled, walking into the center of the circle shaking out my shoulders. "Oh, I think it's hilarious...sir..."

"And what is that, baby shadow?" he inquired, walking his fine as Thor ass backward to the center.

I shrugged." Nothing much sir, I simply appreciate the compliment to go first. I like to show everyone how it's done." I winked and he burst out laughing. He turned back to the guys, and grinned.

"I admit, Luca, when I heard about these two, I had my doubts, but I can see the appeal now. I hope she can back it up." Drew smiled good-naturedly.

Luca shrugged. "Good luck is all I can say." He

chuckled and faced the class. "Okay class, Instructor Drew is going to demonstrate a... physical confrontation." Everyone in the circle, except for Pixie, looked around nervously.

"Excuse me, sir?" One of the guys spoke up. "Are we to hold our punches?" He sounded genuine. At least I didn't have to chalk him up as an asshole, just a misguided guy. I was itching to get going.

"Non," Etienne spoke up this time. "We go full force in the field, we go full force here. I don't give a fuck if there are females in this class. Everyone can take a hit, lets' see if you have what it takes." The guy nodded and faced forward, looking a little conflicted.

"Let's begin," Drew said sharply, clearly as eager as I was.

I turned all my focus on him, still my senses open and watched him as he circled around me. Keeping my arms loose, I let him walk around me and attack me from behind. I internally started playing "You Ain't Ready" by Skillet in my head as I sidestepped the attack, and kicked to the side, catching him in his kidneys as he moved quickly. *It's fucking on.*

I attacked ruthlessly, turning to my left and approaching him directly, using his height against him, I punched him in the throat. He grabbed my arm after I made impact and went to turn it but I went with the movement and flipped to the left, the direction he was turning my arm, surprising him as it jarred my arm loose and I used the momentum to roll to the floor into a push up position, putting all my weight on my arms as I swept my lower legs and made him crash onto the floor on his back.

Grappling with a man his size is never ideal but I took

my chances as he turned quickly to pin me underneath him, both arms to my chest. He left my legs pinned to his chest, and rained a flurry a blows to my face. I felt my left eye close up and I smirked, turning my face to spit the blood pooling into my mouth onto the floor. He laughed when I blew him a bloody kiss and jerked my right knee to the side, bringing my arms with his own force, turning to the side, effectively catching him on the side and rolling out of the pin hold. Still on my back, I used my upper body to flip back up to my feet and bounced on the soles of my feet as he turned around to face me again.

He growled as he approached me head-on, punching out, and I ducked his hit. Side stepping and punching him on the side with a combination that left him gasping. Feeling like I was in a Star Wars movie, no seriously, I felt a disturbance in the force, I flipped backward, simultaneously throwing a punch outwards. I looked forward, as much as I could with one eye in full working order, to see that Julian had jumped into the battle. *Two on one, awesome. Like sex, but with like four less people.*

They attacked at the same time. Julian moved to get me from behind he pinned my arms behind my back as Drew punched me in the gut and in the face in a combination that would have left me breathless if I wasn't totally invested in wiping the floor with these motherfuckers. I kicked back hard on Julian's shin, making him lose balance as I kicked out with both of my legs and knocked Drew back just enough for me to use my momentum to flip Julian forward onto the floor in front of me. I stepped forward, kicking him in the stomach before he was able to grab my legs. No way was I grappling with two large men, always a better advantage on my feet.

I threw an elbow up and out, catching Thor in the

chin, before I turned my body and followed up with a punch to the head.

"Combine! Now!" shouted Dante, and I was immediately surrounded by water and being suffocated with air at the same time. I closed my eyes and focused all my fire elemental power to evaporate the water while arcing toward Drew to stop, what I'm sure, was his air attack. As predicted, he turned his air to curtail the fire and fanned my flames higher, burning the water away faster. I pulled all my concentration to earth to knock them down and pin them to the floor with vines.

I held them down effortlessly as I stood up and straightened myself, slicking my sweat-soaked hair back.

"Holy shit," Drew and Julian breathed at the same time. I smiled brightly at them and winked.

I walked back to the circle with the gazes of the class now sizing me up. I gave Pixie a fist bump and faced forward.

"Uh, aren't you forgetting something?" Luca laughed, pointing at Drew and Julian.

"Not that I can remember," I said as I sat on the floor to stretch my muscles before they tightened up after all of that.

"Ouch, my manhood, are you telling me I wasn't memorable?" Laughed Drew. I winked at him and let my vines go, letting them up from the floor, not answering. He knew he was good as fuck. Although I wondered why Julian didn't go all out.

He wanted to let the cadets see that sometimes two defensive attacks aren't always the best option. Pixie's voice sounded in my head.

I held back a laugh at her jumping through his thoughts.

That's fair, but I would love to see him going at full power. Come to think of it, have any of them gone at full power yet?

Nope, but then again neither have we. No reason to yet.

I nodded at her assessment, wondering when that time will come.

The rest of the class progressed pretty rapidly, everyone taking turns sparring and the guys giving out corrections. Before we knew it, it was time for supper and everyone started to file out of the dome. I hung back with Pixie.

"Good training, instructors." I grinned mischievously, Drew and Julian looking at me with joking scowls on their faces.

"Yeah, yeah. You kicked our asses, we know." Drew rolled his eyes.

I laughed. "You got a few good hits in. I have to remember I'm fighting beyond my caliber right now. I won't be making the mistake again. Hopefully."

I continued jokingly, "And well, honestly you shouldn't walk around looking like Thor *and* getting your ass beat. It's just sad." I pointed out. I danced away as he went to fake-grab me and smiled, when Luca actually grabbed me and held me close, scowling at the gentlemen. Their eyebrows shot up and I groaned internally. *Smooth guys, real smooth.*

I was about to say something when I felt the doors and magick filled the air. Turning around, my eyes fell on a group of people, if you could even call them that. With white hair and pointed ears.

"Hey, little sis," the one in the center spoke, and I

turned and looked into the eyes of someone who could pass as my twin. *Holy shit batman. Disney is really real.*

TO BE CONTINUED in Verdant Kiss, Concealed in Myths Book 2 and Insurrection, Concealed in Shadows Book 2

"Fuck no! When you said I could choose my college, I wasn't under the impression I would be disowned by doing so." I'm furious, beyond, actually. X, my cat, snarled next to me. She always got upset when I did. I honestly think she would've eaten dear old dad had I given her the chance. Okay, cat was a loose term, she was actually an all-white mountain lion. She had followed me home one day from the zoo, and well, Dad had to pay a lot of money to keep the zookeeper quiet. A lot of magic users had familiars, but, well, my baby is more like a super one.

This is a cluster fuck of epic proportions. College is supposed to be my time to finally be out from my father's thumb. The perfect, magical family with two and a half kids and a white picket fence. You know, the American dream.

I look around my father's perfectly maintained study. Custom desk, custom chair, and I'm sure the fucking air is customized for his highness. I scoff. American dream, yeah right. I'm sure the American dream doesn't involve magical families living within their sweet bubble of normality. And I'm pretty damn sure it doesn't involve one of those kids from some random magical family being adopted and thrust into our family, then suddenly moving in to maintain the perfect image for dear ol' Magic Chancellor Jacobs. Or a mountain lion, now that I think about it, yet X is a fairly new development, and no one, except anyone on the estate that is, knew about her.

Everyone thinks my dad is charming, and I suppose he used to be before he suddenly wasn't. My stepbrother moved in when I was ten and he was fifteen, apparently to show the American Council that my father cares about our magical youth. Suddenly, it's Zane this and Zane that. My personal favorite, 'oh Zane is excelling well with his magic, Hudson, you can learn a thing or two from Zane'.

Well, you fucking think? He's five years older than me.

He snarls. "You'll go where I tell you to go, things have changed. I donate way too much to that university for you to go to some random non-magic, human school in New York. I think not. You'll be going to school with our people. You have a duty to this family. You're a child of the council!" he sneered.

I roll my eyes. "Silly me, I thought I had the unfortunate honor of being your child. This is ridiculous, I've spent enough years under your tutelage. I'm the strongest user of any child of the council," I punctuate that with air quotes and heavy sarcasm.

I mean seriously, after that fucktwat Zane left, things were finally a little easier around here. The prodigal son had left, and I was free at last. And by easy, I mean I'm literally able to walk around without the creepy fuck staring at me and laughing uproariously, with his own personal council, or band of dicks as I liked to call them. They were always with him, whenever Dad would comment on my magic. Council kids stick together, except me. I can't stand the pretentious attitudes, the snark, and expectations that I'm supposed to be prim and proper underneath all of that. No. What you see is what you get. Sarcasm, top of her class in all magical classes and human relations. Another thing I took to piss my father off. He thinks humans are useless, I disagree. They have guns and we certainly aren't bulletproof, so we need to get off our damn pedestal.

"You're trying my patience, Hudson. You'll not only be going to the university, but you'll be expected to be at the top of your classes and extracurriculars that I have chosen as well." He hands me my new schedule.

DeLorean University of Magic. My heart stops. This is Zane's school, but he should've graduated by now. I release a heavy breath. I never asked what he did after university. I assumed he left and died in a ditch, you know, naturally. Well, that was my dream anyway, until he showed up for the holidays and shit for like five years. Dream deferred, but a girl could hope. At least, I haven't seen him in two years, not since I was eighteen. The last day I saw him, changed me in more ways than one. If I saw him again, I would probably nut punch him, or lick him. I haven't decided which.

I shook my head and took a closer look at the schedule and my eyes flew open. "Father, this is an accelerated schedule. You want me to jam pack four years of study into two years? When am I supposed to be able to enjoy college? And how in the world can I possibly take all these classes?" I continued to read through the schedule and rule book as he ignored my complaints and screamed. "Dad, okay, seriously? This is insane. A UNIFORM," I shrieked, "It's supposed to be university and I have to wear, what is this? A red pleated skirt, black blazer, a black button-down, and a freaking red cravat? Why couldn't they just tie? And oh, this is rich, black kitten heels, that's a major no. If I'm going to this forced Hell, I'm wearing my combat boots. How is anyone supposed to kick ass in heels, Father?"

He smiles, for a moment it looks like the father I remember in passing memories, then as quickly as it appeared, it disappears. Welp, there goes that possible sitcom moment. "Hudson, you're leaving tomorrow to prepare for your schedule. You're not there to have fun. You're there to succeed and work for the Council, in whatever capacity we need you. Period. If it'll shut you up, I'll allow the combat boots, but not the ratty ones you insist on wearing. I'll order several pairs and they'll be in your apartment when you arrive on campus."

He lifts his hand before I object. "Yes, you'll be living

in an apartment instead of a dorm." He shudders. "No, I had this apartment built on the outskirts of the university for easy access but still hidden from prying eyes."

I growl, and X growls with me as we both stood up, ready to just fucking leave this stupid ass customized box. He rubs his nose, which pretty much means I'm getting on his nerves and am about to be dismissed anyway. "You won't be alone. Some of the other Council children will be there, but you're the only one on the accelerated path. I expect only the highest marks and I'll be checking in often with the school board and your instructors." He smirks. "Your extracurriculars will be focused on combat, both magical and physical. You've been excelling in those for years here, I expect nothing less. I even cleared it for your cat to be there with you."

"You know, if you keep repeating the same damn words over and over again, it's just going to cause your intellect to remain stagnant, Father." I grin and walk out of his office, slamming the door before he can respond. If I'm being forced the fuck out, I'm going to make his life hell.

Chaos and cats are coming DeLorean, buckle the fuck up.

ACKNOWLEDGMENTS

This book hurt. Even though Veiled was technically the first book I published, Infiltrated was the first book I wrote. I was so nervous about this book and I guess I still am. BUT, I still made it through.

For several fucking years, I have dreamed of writing a book. For all those years I read instead, and I grew inspired. I have survived suicide attempts, bullies, assholes on I-95 and motherhood (Okay, I am barely surviving that.)

Point is, I was pushed to write and then I was tossed over the cliff by my best friends, Anna and Marjolein. I found my confidence and I waded through some interesting waters until I found an amazing team of people who helped me grow as a writer and as a person.

Anna and Marjolein, thank you for simply being everything you are. I can't wait to move to the UK and take it by storm with you two bad bitches by my side.

To Bibi and Ash, you both understood that same vision and gave me some of the best advice. (Even when Bibi would message me and start with "So feel free to tell me to fuck off but..." or "lube up, shit is about to get real..." I knew she did it with the best of intentions.)

Zainib, you are by far the most supportive and incredible editor anyone could ever ask for. I am truly grateful to you.

To my amazing beta team, thank you for everything you have done. This book wouldn't be here without you all either.

Shannon, whenever I need you, you are there. You are so freaking incredible.

Finally, to my four little girls, this is just the beginning of my journey. I waited long enough, and I'll always be the mom that encourages you to push until you embark on your dream. Nothing is out of your reach because your dad and I will always be there to lift you up to reach them. I love you. (Eventually, you'll be old enough to read this book, but until you're ninety-six years, just know I mentioned you here.)

ABOUT THE AUTHOR

It's funny, really. For years I have been this super avid reader. The kid in the corner with a book who grew up to the woman in the corner of the club with her Kindle app. (HAHA) I joined a group of readers/authors/bloggers, a lot like me, who were raunchy, fun and used the word 'fuck' a lot. These ladies taught me something about myself; if I wanted to truly be a version of myself that made me proud, I just had to go for it. About a day later I started writing my first book.

I curse a bit too much, I mom a bit too hard, I get tattoos like they're going out of style, and I love a bit too strongly. All in all, I have never been able to do anything in my life without it being TOO MUCH. I'm okay with that. Those qualities are deeply ingrained into the heroines I write. The badass females who won't take no, who won't stop fighting and who cater to no one, but still love, care, and cherish relationships and connections. Heroines who accept their sexuality and their desires and accept all others for theirs as well. My heroines inspire you to take it all without being apologetic, and that is who I strive to be every day and who I hope my kids aspire to become.

So, if you found me, don't hide, enter my World of Smoke and Shadows and find your forbidden desires. (AND some super forbidden ones as well, hey who the fuck am I to judge 😉)

Join Me!

Follow me on Instagram @RubySmokeAuthor

Visit me at www.RubySmokeAuthor.com

Join my Facebook group- www.facebook.com/groups/rubysmokereadergroup/

Made in the USA
Columbia, SC
20 May 2021